When war comes to London in 1939, Ronnie Smith is
scared and excited: scared of the bombs that fall at night,
but excited to race his friends to collect the best bits
of shrapnel every morning.

But for Ronnie, the battles aren't just in the sky and on
the streets. They're at school and at home too. His little
brother is up to no good with a secret job and dangerous
new friends, and Ronnie's worried he's getting himself
into big trouble.

Ronnie's desperate to help his little brother. But he isn't
expecting to uncover secrets that could change the fate of
the whole war...

*"A compelling journey through the mess and fragility and love of
what it means to be a human. Jenny Pearson must be the best
children's author writing at the moment." Katya Balen,
Carnegie Medal-winning author of* October, October

9781805312963 | £7.99 | 9+

UNCORRECTED PROOF COPY

This is an uncorrected proof copy and is not for sale. It should not
be quoted without comparison to the finally revised text. It does not
reflect the quality, page size or thickness of the finished book.

All specifications are provisional.

Paperback 8th May 2025

ISBN: 9781805312963   £7.99   368pp

*With thanks to the Imperial War Museum for reviewing the
historical accuracy of this book.*

First published in the UK in 2024 by Usborne Publishing Limited, Usborne House,
83-85 Saffron Hill, London EC1N 8RT, England, usborne.com.

Usborne Verlag, Usborne Publishing Limited, Prüfeninger Str. 20,
93049 Regensburg, Deutschland VK Nr. 17560

Text copyright © Jenny Pearson, 2024.

The right of Jenny Pearson to be identified as the author of this work has been asserted by
her in accordance with the Copyright, Designs and Patents Act, 1988.

Cover illustration by Tom Cole © Usborne Publishing Limited, 2024.

The name Usborne and the Balloon logo are Trade Marks of Usborne Publishing Limited.

All rights reserved. No part of this publication may be reproduced, stored in a retrieval
system or transmitted in any form or by any means, without the prior permission
of the publisher.

This is a work of fiction. The characters, incidents, and dialogues are products of the
author's imagination and are not to be construed as real.

A CIP catalogue record for this book is available from the British Library.

ISBN 9781805312963

Printed and bound using 100% renewable energy at CPI Group (UK) Ltd,
Croydon, CR0 4YY.

MIX
Paper | Supporting
responsible forestry
FSC® C171272

JENNY PEARSON

SHRAPNEL BOYS

USBORNE

CHAPTER 1

It was the first Friday in September when Arthur Davey, Graham Talbot and Harry Scott, or *The Wreckers* as we'd later come to know them, were shipped off to the countryside with all the others, leaving me, Micky and Lugs nothing short of delighted. There'd been talk for a while of evacuating kids out of London to where they'd be safe if Hitler ever sent his bombs. Still, when the day came and we watched our rival gang, along with well over half our school, troop off down the road to the station, it was hard to believe they were actually going. War hadn't even been declared yet. I suppose this was just more preparation – like the gas masks we always had to carry and air-raid practices and the posters encouraging men to sign up.

They filed out of school, singing *The Lambeth Walk*, like they were off on holiday. A pack of mums chased after them waving and wailing and shouting that they'd be coming back home soon and to mind their manners whilst they were gone.

We weren't so emotional in our goodbyes, and while a tiny part of me wondered if we were missing out, I was glad to be staying behind, and I reckon Micky and Lugs were too. And to show that, we'd given Arthur and his lot the three bare-bum salute as they were marched out the school gates. Arthur presented us with one of his fingers – one that caught a clip round the ear off Mr Hedley, the older years' schoolmaster, which was an added bonus.

We watched as the crocodile of kids disappeared round the corner, off to their new lives with not much on them but a change of clothes, a gas mask and the hope of an adventure. But I knew the adventure weren't about to happen where they were headed. They could bang on all they wanted about seeing green fields and real live cows, but the truth was that if war did come, they were going to miss it and seeing a few blades of grass and some sets of udders weren't ever going to make up for that.

Mum wasn't ever going to send me and Micky. She said that she couldn't bring herself to do it, that maybe it was selfish, but she'd miss us too much. Besides, I was twelve and Micky not far off – we weren't exactly babies. If she ever tried to pack us off to some folks we'd never met, I'd made it clear that I would march straight back to Deptford. She needed looking after, and since she'd finally kicked Dad out two years earlier, as the oldest, that was down to me.

As the last of the evacuees turned the corner, I jumped down off the wall I was sitting on. "Come on," I said, slinging my arms over Micky and Lugs's shoulders, "with those three gone, we're going to run this place."

"Ronnie and Michael Smith! Billy Missell! Here! Now!'

Billy is Lugs's real name, but we call him Lugs on account of the size of his ears. Reckon he could take flight if the wind picked up enough. Lugs might not sound all that flattering, but it's affectionate like. You can't go round giving a lad a nickname that's nice. I mean, he's covered in freckles, but he'd never live it down if we named him after those.

"I said, here, NOW!"

We all swung round to face the source of the booming voice. Mr Etherington, our headmaster, was storming towards us. He was wearing the black suit and tie he always wore, and his white moustache was twitching with fury. He walked with a slight limp, which he'd have people believe was the result of a bomb blast from the Great War, but the rumour is he actually fell on a rake in his allotment when he was digging up spuds. I asked him about the rake once. Been gunning for me ever since.

"Yes, sir?" I said, as innocently as I could. "What can I do for you on this fine September morning?"

"Less of your cheek, Smith!" he spat.

"Which one, sir? Me left or me right?" I grinned and stared him square in the eyes.

Look, I know nothing good comes from winding up the headteacher, but sometimes I just couldn't help myself. He's the sort that gets off on making you feel like nothing. Like you're worthless. You have to stand up to bullies. Learned that from my dad – when he was around.

"Both!" he blasted and came to a stop right close to me.

He was a tall, broad man and full of fury. "You like to expose your backsides do you, boys? Think it's funny, do you?"

Micky gulped and shook his head.

"Only on special occasions, sir," I said, which made Lugs snigger, but did not amuse old Etherington that much.

He bent down and moved his face closer to mine. I kept my eyes on him and the smile on my face, even though inside all I wanted was to turn and scarper.

"Here's a special occasion for you!" he said, his breath hot and angry. "Miss Grimshaw, fetch the cane, quick about it!"

I didn't react. I wasn't particularly thrilled about copping a caning, but I knew there were nothing I could do about it now.

Miss Grimshaw, the younger years teacher, trotted off eager to do Etherington's bidding. The headmaster straightened up, turned to the rest of the kids who were milling about the playground and barked. "Line up! Roll call!"

The kids rushed to their usual spaces, shuffling to fill in the gaps that our classmates had left, all the while snatching glances at us.

"Blinkin' hell, Ronnie," Lugs whispered. "You've gone and done it now."

Micky shook his head and scowled at me. "You and your bleedin' mouth."

Miss Grimshaw came back into the playground and handed the cane over with a smile. If you're thinking that 'cos she teaches the younger years she'd be all kind and sweet, think again. She's a Doberman in a cardigan. Mum reckons if you

8

sent an army made solely of Miss Grimshaws we'd have the war done and dusted in a week.

Etherington held the cane aloft. It was pale in colour and had a slight curve to it – probably from all the backsides it'd whacked. "Turn round, bend over. You first, Mr Missell."

Three thwacks Lugs got, right across his buttocks. The whole school, or what was left of it, winced in unison each time the cane came down with a snap.

Lugs didn't make much of a sound, but his eyes were streaming when he straightened up and he was fighting to stop his chin from wobbling.

Etherington pushed back the limp strand of hair that had fallen in front of his eyes. "Michael Smith, you're next."

Micky didn't do so well, he yelped with each strike. Our Micky's always been a bit soft. He is the youngest though, and scrawny with it. He were born just over nine months after me, 'cos he was in a rush to get here – according to Mum. But I dunno why anyone would be rushing to get to ours. Our next-door neighbour, Vera Green, calls him a surprise miracle. I would have thought all miracles were surprises though, ain't that kind of the point? I told her that, but she weren't having none of it. Insisted on giving Micky a rub on his head for luck whenever he wasn't quick enough to duck out her way.

When he stood up, our Micky was trembling, and tears were flowing down his face. The look he gave me, well, that was hard to take. "It will be alright, Mick," I whispered. "Don't let him see you cry. Never let them see you cry."

"Oh, shut up, Ronnie," he snapped back, rubbing his eyes furiously with his cuffs.

I put my gas mask on the ground and got into position with my hands on my knees before Mr Etherington asked. Dunno, felt better to do it than follow an order from him. I waited and braced myself for the sting of birch on me bum. I reckoned I was down for more than the other two, on account of my lip. Six of the best, most likely. I took a breath and clenched my jaw to bite away the anger and humiliation that were boiling inside of me. I'd been caned before – I knew how much it would hurt, how that strip of wood seemed to cut right into you.

But nothing happened. Instead, I heard the sound of Mr Etherington's footsteps heading across the playground.

I swung round and saw the looks on Micky's and Lugs's faces. Annoyance and anger on our Micky's, confusion on Lugs's.

"Sir! Sir? You forgot about me!" I called after him.

"Back to class! All of you!" he ordered, not even turning round to look.

"Mr Etherington. Sir?"

If he could hear me, he didn't acknowledge it.

A rage flew up inside me. That weren't fair. That weren't right. It was my fault. I should be caned too.

"Sir!" I shouted. "You need to come back here and cane me like the others!"

The kids who had started to walk back to their classrooms all stopped where they were. No one spoke to Etherington the way I was. No one told him what to do.

"Oi! SIR!" I bellowed.

Etherington stopped. Then turned round slowly.

"You need to punish me," I said. "I need to be punished."

Whispers rippled through the playground. Kids were looking at me like I'd lost the plot. Maybe I had, but the sense of injustice was burning in me so hot, I couldn't stop myself. I needed to feel the same pain that our Micky and Lugs had.

"Who says I'm not punishing you?" Etherington said icily.

"I...I don't understand."

"You're not a very bright boy are you, Smith?"

"I dunno, sir. Me mum says I have my moments."

"This cane won't ever touch your skin again, Smith. You step out of line, and one of your friends will pay the price." His eyebrows raised in this superior kind of way, and I thought about knocking them right off his face.

"I have my moments too, it would seem," he said, like he was right pleased with himself.

"You can't do that!" I said.

"But I can. You'll learn, Smith. I shall teach you that, for boys like you, enemies are easy to make, but friends will be much harder to keep. Now back to class! All of you!"

And with that he marched off into the school building.

I didn't know what to do with myself for a moment. My head was whirling, trying to make sense of what had happened. I just stood there, looking at the door Etherington had disappeared through. Don't think I would have moved if it hadn't had been for Lugs giving me a nudge.

"Don't listen to him – what's Etherington know about friends?"

I nodded, but something about my headmaster's words had knocked me. I followed Lugs to the back of the line of kids and stood behind our Micky, who shot me another dark glare.

"You okay?" I whispered, trying to show I was concerned – that I was sorry.

Micky didn't turn round, just said, "What do you think?"

Miss Grimshaw blew her whistle, spraying spit everywhere, and cleared her throat. "With so many children evacuated, those of you who remain will be taught together. By me."

Lugs groaned behind me. "Today just keeps getting better and better."

On the way home from school, Micky skulked along behind me, kicking a stone down the pavement, refusing to talk. It's about a mile walk between the terraced houses to our place on Heston Street. I tried to hang back with him to try and cheer him up, to help me feel less guilty as much as anything else, but he wasn't having any of it.

"Don't worry, Mick," I said. "I promise I'll stay out of trouble and keep that backside of yours safe."

"Yeah right," he said and stormed off ahead.

When we got back to ours, Vera, our next-door neighbour, was standing at her garden gate, smoking a cigarette. Vera's always smoking a cigarette. She was wearing a headscarf, tied in a knot at the front, and an apron that was covered in flour. The sleeves of her blouse were rolled up, showing her impressive forearms.

"What's happened to you, Micky?" she said, frowning. "You're walking like you've had an accident."

Micky glared at me. "Ask Ronnie."

She raised her eyebrows. "What you gone and done now, Ronnie Smith?"

"It was Mr Etherington," I said.

"You ought to keep your noses clean round him," Vera said, momentarily disappearing into a cloud of cigarette smoke as she exhaled.

Micky jabbed his finger at me. "It was all his fault."

She tutted, then coughed. Vera's cough is really loud and sounds real phlegmy. "You should be looking out for him," she said after she was done coughing, "you're the eldest."

"I can look out for myself," Micky said and stropped off indoors. But that weren't true then and it's not true now.

I slung my bag and gas mask over the banister and went to see if there was anything to eat in the kitchen. It was one of Mum's days off from working as a nurse at Lewisham Hospital, which meant there was a good chance she might have baked something. I stopped before going inside though, because I heard voices. Mum was sitting at the table in the front room with Mary from a few doors down. Mary looked in a right old state.

"I just don't know if I've done the right thing," she was saying.

I guessed she was talking about sending her Susan off to the countryside with all the others. I think she probably had done the right thing in Susan's case. She's a right prissy madam. She weren't the type to make the most of the excitement what was coming if war was declared.

"You just did what you thought was best." Mum rubbed her hand. "They'll be back by Christmas. That's what everyone's saying. Now, more tea?"

Mary crumpled into a sobbing mess and Mum turned to me and said, "Don't just stand there! Put the kettle on, Ronnie."

I opened my mouth to protest – I wasn't some ruddy charwoman, but Mum said, "Do not make me ask twice, Ronnie Smith."

I decided that one run-in was enough for the day and clattered off to the kitchen and set about making a pot of tea.

"Who knows…" Mum said, as I unceremoniously plonked the tea tray in front of them a few minutes later. "There might not even be a war."

CHAPTER 2

I didn't think Mum would be right about there not being a war. Britain had been preparing for ages. Gas masks had been issued and air-raid shelters had been built. The government had even said that no one could show lights after dusk, so Mum had got me and Micky to cover all our windows with cardboard. Besides, I'd heard Vera talking to the postie a couple of weeks back. Postman Stan had said what with the Russians saying they wouldn't fight Germany, war was inevitable. And, sure enough, two days later on a hot Sunday morning, around eleven o'clock, the Prime Minister, Neville Chamberlain, came on the wireless and said war was happening.

Micky, and the welts on his backside, weren't quite as angry and he was just about speaking to me again. We were kicking a ball about in the road with Lugs when Mum shouted at us to come in.

"The Prime Minister is making a statement!" she hollered from the front door.

I picked up the football. "What *another* one?" The Prime Minister was always banging on about something.

"Don't you disrespect Mr Chamberlain! Just get inside and listen."

We trundled into the sitting room and stood in front of the wireless, Vera from next door tagging along too. Mum turned the volume up and we all waited and listened as Mr Chamberlain's voice rang through our house.

As I listened to what he was saying, I felt a surge of dreadful excitement billow through me.

War.

We were at war with Germany.

Mum sort of crumpled down onto the sofa with a right grim look on her face. I don't think she was experiencing quite the same sense of exhilaration as I was. Back then, I didn't know what war meant, not really. But I knew it meant something. I knew it meant that things were going to change. And, I guess, that was all that mattered to me. I wanted things to change.

"Flippin' heck! It's happening then?" Lugs was the first to break the silence after Mr Chamberlain cleared off to crack on with his plans to take down Hitler.

"They said never again. The Great War was supposed to be the last one," Mum muttered, her eyes all glassy.

Vera took a very long inhale on her cigarette then said, "Got that wrong, didn't they?"

Lugs said, "Dad says never trust politicians any more than a fart when you've got a dicky stomach."

Mum blinked and Vera said, "Don't much care for the image but your father has a point."

As messages about cinemas and dance halls closing burbled away on the wireless, Mum just sat there, staring at the wall, not saying anything.

"It'll be alright," I said, giving her shoulder a squeeze. "You've got me and Micky here. We'll look after you."

Mum looked from Micky to me and forced a smile. Before I could offer any more words of reassurance that I was ready to take on the role of man of the house, a wailing noise started up outside.

"The air-raid warning!" Mum said, leaping to her feet.

"Hells bells!" Lugs yelled. "They're quick off the bat!"

Mum headed to the hallway. "Quick. Under the stairs. Everyone. Move it!"

We all crammed into the cupboard under the stairs whilst the air-raid siren continued to blare. Apparently, the government had said that under the stairs is the safest place to be, but I bet you wouldn't find that lot squashed in a cupboard when the bombs rained down.

"Gerroff my foot!" Micky shouted as I bustled into him.

Lugs piled into me, followed by Mum then Vera who had to have a good few goes at getting the door shut.

"There's not enough room!" Micky said as were plunged into darkness. We all jostled about, and I got an elbow in the face and a knee in the back.

"Lugs, you'll have to head home," Micky said, letting out a frustrated sigh.

"Cheers for that, Mick!" Lugs said.

"We can't send Mrs Green out," Micky said. "She's old and infirm."

"How's this for infirm?" Vera said, giving him a clip round the ear.

"If everyone would just stand still, we'd be fine!" Mum said.

"We'd be finer if Lugs went round his!" Micky said.

"We've been at war with Germany for all of twelve minutes and you're turfing me out into a war zone! How's that for loyalty?"

"There's no war zone out there," Vera said. "Not yet anyway. And there's plenty of room. Just stand tall and straight."

"What are we all doing under the stairs if there's no war?" Micky asked.

"Precaution, I suspect," Vera said, "better safe than sorry."

"Mrs Green, your cigarette!" Mum said. "I'm not going to be the family who burned themselves to death on the first day of the war! We'd never live it down!"

"Right you are, Cathy." Vera took two more puffs before she put it out.

"You should get yourselves an Anderson bomb shelter," Lugs said. "We've got one in the garden."

"Why don't you take off there then?" Micky said. "Go and get bombed with your own parents!"

"Micky!" Mum said, then for some reason she swiped *me* round the head.

"Ow! What did you do that for?"

"Sorry, love, I thought you were your brother."

"I'll pass it on," I said and turned and clouted Micky.

He didn't take kindly to that, and we ended up in a bit of a tussle, which resulted in more elbowing and shoving and stepping on feet.

"For the love of all things holy!" Vera shouted. "Will you two pack it in or I'll tan your backsides, so I will. Your mother has it hard enough without you two carrying on!"

She was right. We needed to be better, for Mum. But Micky couldn't resist giving me a final elbow in the ribs. So I had to turn round and give him a quick jab in the guts.

"I can't spend the war like this," Mum said, I think mainly to herself.

We settled down then and stood quietly, listening. Waiting for the bombs to drop, or for the all-clear siren to sound to say it was safe to come out. We'd done practices before, but this was different. We weren't at war before.

It wasn't a bomb that dropped though.

"Sheesh, what's that smell?" Micky said.

"Ah sorry about that," Lugs said.

"Crikey, Lugs!" I choked. "That's a right air-bender."

"You scared or something?" Micky asked.

"No! Had turnips for my tea yesterday."

"Good Lord, Billy!" Vera said. "When they warned us about being gassed, I didn't think they meant like this!"

"Sorry, Mrs Green. I tried my best to hold it in for you all."

"We appreciate that you tried, Billy," Mum said, which seemed a bit forgiving under the circumstances. "Oh heavens, that reminds me, the gas masks! We haven't got them! Should I go and get them?"

"Just wait, I'm sure it will all be fine," Vera said. "I'm sure it's only another practice. I'll rub young Micky's head for luck – just in case."

"Do you have to?" Micky groaned.

"I think we all should," I said.

Mum said, "Ronnie, stop antagonizing your brother and just be quiet and wait."

After what seemed like ages, but was probably not that long at all, the all-clear sounded and we all stumbled out of the cupboard.

"Thank goodness," Mum said. "Another test."

"It was certainly that," Vera replied. "You need to see about an Anderson shelter, Cathy. You know on your nurse's income you won't have to pay. My Bob's got a friend. Johnny's his name. Think he lives north of the river, but he comes this way a lot, I reckon he'd put one in for you."

Bob was Vera's son. Him and his missus used to live next door with her, but they disappeared one day. Vera reckoned he'd got a good job working the docks up in Newcastle. Talk was that he'd got himself in over his head with the wrong sort.

"We can do it," I said.

Mum cupped my cheek. "My good boy." Then she turned to Vera. "Please do ask this Johnny. I'd be really appreciative. Do you want some tea, Mrs Green?"

"I just said we'd do it!" I said but Mum and Vera were already heading to the kitchen.

"Saves me getting one. I can just duck in with you. Don't fancy sitting the war out on my own," Vera said as they disappeared through the door.

I wonder now whether it would all have been different if Johnny hadn't had turned up the next day, with his shovel and swagger. I sometimes think Johnny Simmons did more damage to me and Micky than anything Adolf did.

CHAPTER 3

You know how you can take against some people instantly? Well as soon as I clapped eyes on Johnny Simmons, I knew he was one of those people. There was just something about him I didn't trust. Something shifty in the way he held himself. How his smile never met his eyes. Not that Mum or Micky seemed to notice. They thought he was wonderful. Even Vera was charmed, and I once heard her tell Mum all men apart from her son Bob were useless.

It was Monday, and Micky and I had just got home from a fairly uneventful day at school. When I say uneventful, it wasn't exactly without event. But it had been nothing major. There'd been talk about the war announcement – discussions about when the Nazis might show up – but mainly Lugs, Micky and I were enjoying being the biggest kids at school what with Arthur Davey gone. We walked a little bit taller. At playtime, without Arthur, Billy and Harry around, we won Jimmy Jimmy Knacker, which established us as the new kings of the playground. But Miss Grimshaw seemed to be keeping an extra-close eye on me, no doubt at Mr Etherington's request. She'd taken my English work and held it up against one of the younger kids' writing, and said, "Ronnie Smith, pray do tell me, how is it an eight-year-old produces neater work than you?"

I said, "Would we say it isn't as neat?"

"Yes, we most definitely would." She laughed coldly then jabbed her finger at my slate. "Look here, what does this word even say? How am I supposed to read this?"

I said, "What word, miss?"

"*Metaphor*," she said. "How can anyone read that?"

I said, "Seems like you can read it just fine to me."

That hadn't gone down too well. She started spluttering, her pinched face becoming extra pinched as she tried to think of a response. Micky and Lugs flashed me concerned looks and I remembered it was their backsides on the line and not mine.

Before she could explode, I said, "I'm sorry, miss. You're right. I'll do it again."

So, I had to do it again but at least it meant no one got a caning and Micky wasn't in a mood with me when we got back to ours.

Vera was leaning on our fence, not hers, when we reached home. She was smiling and making a sound which I think was giggling. I'd never heard Vera giggle before. Didn't think she was capable. She had more of a deep belly laugh that usually turned into a coughing fit.

"Alright, Mrs Green?" I said.

Vera didn't answer, she was too busy watching someone.

That someone was Johnny Simmons.

He was digging up our garden, shovelling dirt onto a pile for the Anderson shelter. He'd pegged out a rectangular shape with string and was about halfway done. Johnny was wearing a white vest which showed off his muscles. He was glistening with sweat and, I think, arrogance. Mum came out of the house holding a glass of water. She'd pinned up her hair and had her nice frock on. She'd had an early shift at the hospital so she must have come home and changed specially.

"Here, Johnny, I've brought you a drink," she said.

He stopped shovelling, leaned on his spade and said, "You're an angel, Cathy."

Mum handed the glass over and I saw them lock eyes and I didn't like it. I didn't like it one bit.

"I'm just so grateful to you for doing this," Mum said.

"We could have done it," I said, "couldn't we, Micky?"

Micky shrugged. "Dunno, he seems to be doing an okay job of it."

I kicked at the pile of dirt. "Yeah, but I'm saying we could have done it."

"Ronnie, don't be rude!" Mum said. "We're very lucky to have Mr Simmons's help."

"Please, call me Johnny. And if you want to help, Ron, there's a spade over there."

"My name's Ronnie," I said, a bit snappish.

"Ronald James Smith! Mind your manners!" Mum turned to Johnny. "I'm sorry, I don't know what's got into him."

Johnny downed his water in two gulps, wiped his mouth on the back of his arm and gave mum the glass.

"Come on, son. Show me what you're made of." He picked up a spare spade and chucked it at me. "Get digging."

For a moment, I considered walloping him over the head with it. I wasn't his son. But when Micky said, "Give it here, I'll help," I was spurred into action. I'd show this Johnny Simmons what I was made of – if that's what he wanted.

"Suit yourself," Micky said when he saw me grab the spade. "If I'm not needed, I'm going round Lugs's."

I began digging. Furiously. Johnny watched me with this smirk on his lips. Every shovel I brought up and emptied onto my pile, he matched with a bigger one. I dug faster. He dug faster too, all the time shaking his head, almost laughing at me.

Mum and Vera left us to it. Vera headed in to ours saying, "See, Cathy, didn't I tell you? He's a good sort that Johnny."

I kept digging. Throwing earth onto my pile, watching as Johnny outpaced me. After half an hour, I was hot, sweaty and exhausted.

"Take a break, if you need one," Johnny said.

"I'm fine."

"I'm taking a break – you can carry on if you want."

I didn't want, but I needed to prove I could carry on longer than him, so I kept digging while Johnny sprawled out on the grass, watching me. "You've got spirit, I'll give you that."

I ignored him.

"Could do with someone like you."

I stopped for a second to look at him. "What do you mean?"

"A hard worker. Someone with guts. Have you got guts, Ronnie?"

"Yeah, I got guts."

"Thought so. You remind me of myself when I was your age."

I carried on digging, pretending I wasn't interested. "What is it you do?" I said, trying not to sound like I cared.

"Question should be what *don't* I do."

"What's that supposed to mean?"

"I do all sorts, Ronnie. There are lots of ways to make money. If there's a pie, you can bet I've got a finger in it."

"Right," I said. It didn't take a genius to work out he probably wasn't the honest type. I bet he was into all sorts of dodgy dealings, but I wasn't going to ask any more. He looked like he was enjoying himself too much. That was Johnny's way. Never actually answering a question. Not honestly, at least.

He got to his feet. "You like money, Ronnie?" I looked up and he caught my eye. He nodded. "Yeah, thought so. Who doesn't? Maybe one day you can come work for me."

"You're alright," I said. "Think I'd prefer to work for myself."

He grinned, then said, "We'll see." He picked up his spade and started neatening up the edges.

"Wouldn't be any need for this," he said as he plunged his spade down into the grass.

"Need for what?"

"Shelters and the like. I reckon Mosley has it right, Britain should mind its business. This is a foreign war. A Jew's quarrel."

I stuck my spade into the ground. "Who's Mosley?"

"You walk around with your head in a bucket? How can you not know who Oswald Mosley is?"

I shrugged, embarrassed that I didn't. "Might have heard the name."

Johnny rolled his eyes like he didn't believe a word of it. "Oswald Mosley is the leader of the BUF."

"What's that then?" I said, trying to sound casual.

"A political party who put the people of Britain first." Johnny stopped digging and leaned on his spade. He looked at me, his eyes glinting strangely. "Mosley knows what this war is really about."

"And what's that then?"

"It's the Jews, see. They've got a vendetta against Germany – this is all about protecting their interests. They don't like the fact that Hitler's stopped 'em doing what they want."

I frowned. That didn't sound right to me. "I thought it was because Germany invaded Poland – that Hitler wants to expand his Empire."

"That's just Jewish propaganda, trust me."

Trust him? No bleedin' chance.

He started on the edges again and I picked up my spade and began to shovel more dirt, thankful the conversation was over.

A few moments later, he looked up and nodded over to the kitchen window where Mum and Vera were watching us.

"Your mum seems nice."

27

I didn't know what he wanted me to say to that and I didn't want him talking about Mum, so I didn't answer.

"What happened to your old man?"

"He went off."

"It happens." He shrugged, like he might know something about Dad's leaving himself. "You think he'll be back?"

"Doubt it."

"Sorry to hear that," he said, sounding more pleased than sorry.

I chucked some more soil onto my pile. "Glad to see the back of him."

"Like that, is it?"

I stuck my spade into the ground really hard. "Yeah, it's like that."

Johnny nodded. "Must be hard on your mum."

"She's fine. She's got me and Micky."

"I'm sure she is." Johnny looked back at the window and gave Mum a wave.

Annoyed, I stopped digging. "Don't you reckon we've dug enough?"

"Yeah, that's got to be about four feet deep," he said. "Grab those tees and channel sections and we'll put in the ground framework." He pointed at the pile of metal. "Those long bits."

I picked them up and he watched me move them over to the hole. It would have been easier with both of us, but I wasn't about to ask him for help. We placed them at the sides of the hole. Then we moved on to the back arch – two corrugated sheets of steel. Once they were bolted in place, we put in the front arch, then the middle section.

"That'll do for today," Johnny said, standing back to inspect our work. "Not a bad job that."

"I can finish the rest myself tomorrow," I said. "It's just the insides to finish and putting the dirt on top."

"Don't worry, I'll be back." He winked at me. It wasn't a good wink. Not like I'd get off Lugs. It was a wink which told me that he'd be back, whether I liked it or not.

Mum came out with Vera to inspect our work. "Haven't you boys done well!" she beamed. "Johnny, you must stay for tea. I've made corned-beef hash."

Johnny looked at his watch. "Believe me when I say that I'd love to, but maybe tomorrow?"

Mum and Vera both looked disappointed. I wasn't.

"Are you sure you can't stay?" Vera asked. "Cathy makes a lovely hash."

"I've got some business to attend to tonight, but I'll be back bright-eyed and bushy-tailed in the morning to finish off."

"Who does business at night?" I asked.

"Every hour is a working hour for me, kid."

"Okay, tomorrow then," Mum said.

"I shall look forward to it." Johnny flung his shirt over his shoulder and sauntered off down the road, whistling as he went.

"He was nice. Wasn't he nice, Ronnie?" Mum said, watching him as he disappeared round the corner.

29

I shrugged. "Seemed a bit full of himself to me."

Mum crossed her arms and glared. "Ronald Smith, Mr Simmons is building us the shelter to keep us safe. And he's doing it for nothing – just out of the goodness of his heart. I will not have you speak of him like that. When he's round here, you treat him with respect, you hear me?"

I nodded.

"Good, now go and fetch your brother. It's getting dark and tea's ready."

Mum's right about a lot of things. She's usually right when our Micky is fibbing. She was right when she finally told Dad to leave. But she wasn't right about Johnny Simmons. That man doesn't do anything for nothing. And from what I've seen, there's no real evidence that he has a heart. Not one that goodness comes out of at any rate.

Some people try to gain power by dropping bombs and sending in their armies to flatten everything. Others, they're a little quieter about it. Johnny Simmons, well, he was one of those quieter ones.

CHAPTER 4

The next morning, I woke up with sore arms from the digging and an itch in my brain about Johnny Simmons.

When I mentioned it to Micky, he pulled on his school trousers and said, "Seemed alright to me. You've got a problem with everyone."

I chucked my pillow at him. "I don't." Then I said, "You heard of Oswald Mosley?"

"Nope, you got a problem with him an' all?"

"Hurry up! You're going to be late!" Mum bellowed up the stairs. "You boys washed your faces?"

"Yeah!" Micky shouted back, even though we hadn't.

I sat on the end of the bed and put on my socks, my only pair without holes in. "I wish Adolf would hurry up and get on with this war. Then maybe we wouldn't have to go to school."

Micky looked out our bedroom window as he buttoned up his shirt. "Wonder what's taking him so long. Doesn't feel like we're at war. Thought there'd be more fighting – planes dropping bombs from the sky – that sort of thing."

"Me too. Bit disappointing really."

The door flew open, and Mum stomped into the room, her hair rolled up in pipe cleaners. "What's taking you so long? Ronnie! You said you'd washed. You're filthy!"

"Strictly speaking, it was Micky who said that we'd washed."

"He looks clean! You're the one with a face that looks like you've spent the night snuffling about in the dirt! Get in that bathroom and sort yourself out. I won't have people thinking I'm bringing up a street urchin."

"How about I don't go to school today and I finish the Anderson shelter?" I suggested.

"How about you get in that bathroom before I hose you down in the garden?" Mum said.

"But Mum—"

"Don't you *but Mum* me. Get yourself clean and get yourself to school."

By the time I'd washed my face, grabbed some bread and butter to eat on the way to school and found Micky's shoes, there was no way we were going to be on time. We ran all the way, our gas masks bouncing about on our backs, but everyone was already in class by the time we'd got to the school gates. Mr Etherington was standing on the steps, chin stuck out, arms behind his back and a satisfied expression on his face.

"Here we go," I said as we approached him.

"Don't wind him up," Micky muttered.

"Good morning, sir," I said cheerfully. "Beautiful day, isn't it?"

"You are late." He almost looked pleased about it.

Without missing a beat Micky said, "We had to stop and help an old gentleman who had taken a stumble in the road, sir."

He said it so convincingly, I very nearly believed him.

Mr Etherington glanced down at me from up on his step. "Is that so?"

"He was in a terrible way, sir. We had to help him," Micky continued.

"And where is this gentleman now?"

"Sitting at home with his leg up, having a nice cup of tea which we made him. Ain't that right, Ronnie?"

"Err...yeah?"

"He was awful grateful, sir. Asked us what school we went to and when I told him here, he said he weren't surprised we were such good citizens, what with having you as the headmaster."

I thought he'd pushed it a bit far with that, but Mr Etherington, well, he lapped it up.

His chest puffed up a little. "On this occasion, I will overlook your tardiness. But I am watching you. Off you go, join your class."

We hurried past him and down the corridor to the classroom.

"Can't believe he bought that, Micky," I said. "You're lucky he didn't figure out you were lying."

"That's the difference between us. I talk us out of trouble, you talk us into it."

It was hard to argue with that at the time, but the thing about lying is that you can't do it for ever. At some point, someone's going to find out.

I'd asked Lugs back to ours after school saying I wanted his help with the Anderson shelter. What I actually wanted was him there, so I didn't have to talk to Johnny Simmons alone. I thought Lugs would see there was something shifty about him, even if Micky didn't. When we got back to ours though, Johnny was just patting down the last of the soil on the shelter roof while Mum and Vera clapped.

"It's finished," I said flatly.

"Isn't it wonderful?" Mum said. The pipe cleaners were out of her hair, and she'd pinned it in quite a fancy do for a Tuesday.

Vera nodded. "Best one on the street in my opinion."

"Have a look, lads," Johnny said, "see what you think."

Micky ran straight inside. "This is way better than hiding out under the stairs!"

"I'll put some things in – curtains, pillows – make it all comfy," Mum said.

"I'll take a bottom bunk," Vera said. "Don't think I'll get myself up into a top one, what with my knees."

"Of course," Mum said. "You're the reason we have one in the first place. You and Johnny," Mum said, smiling at him. "You don't mind do you boys?"

"Nah!" Micky shouted from the shelter.

It was fine with me too. I didn't fancy Vera rolling out and flattening me in the night. That would not be a heroic way to go.

"I'm gonna take a look," Lugs said, pushing past me. "Nice! Think it's bigger than ours."

"They're all the same size," I called after him.

"You don't want to look, Ronnie?" Johnny asked.

"My eyeballs work fine from here," I said.

Mum rolled her eyes. "For heaven's sake, Ronnie. Take a look!"

I poked my head in. "Yeah, looks like a shelter." It was bare except for a couple of wooden bunks that did not look comfortable. To me, it looked a bit like the inside of a tin can.

Mum scowled, "I'm sorry about him, Johnny. Come inside for a cuppa, I'll put a pot on. Boys, you've got an hour or so before tea."

Johnny smiled at me then went inside, but Mum hung back to give me a rollicking. "You'd better sort that attitude of yours out, Ronald Smith. Just remember who cooks your meals."

Vera went back to hers and started taking her washing in and I stood and watched as Lugs and Micky messed about in the shelter, pretending to shoot Nazis with invisible guns.

"Try and be good, Ronnie," Vera said folding a pair of underpants that were large enough to act as a ship's sail. "It's nice for your mum to have some company. It's been a while since your dad left."

My jaw clenched like it always did when I thought about Dad – about his temper that had all of us treading on eggshells.

35

Number 16 Heston Street had been a battlefield when he'd been around. I was glad he was out of the picture and didn't much like the thought of someone taking his place.

"Heard he's joined the forces. Signed up back in March," she continued.

"Who?"

"Who do you think? Your dad. Mr Stanley saw him down the Prince Regent the other week."

Mr Stanley, or Postie Stan as I called him, was known for delivering gossip as much as letters. "So? Why should I care?" I said. To be honest, I was a little surprised. Mum had said it was the Great War that had changed my dad. Turned him into a different person. I dunno, maybe he thought fighting in a second one might change him back.

Vera pulled another pair of ginormous pants off the washing line and flapped them up and down. They caught the air and inflated like a parachute. "You're right, you shouldn't. The less said about him the better. Terrible business that. Your mother deserves some happiness."

"It's alright. Micky and I have that covered."

She picked up the washing basket and hoisted it onto her hip. "You know what I mean. She needs adult company."

"Don't see why. She's got us. She's got you. She's fine."

Vera shook her head and looked skywards. "Just be good, Ronnie Smith. Now, off you go, play with your pals. I'm going to take my smalls inside."

"Smalls?!" I said, before I could stop myself.

Her face puckered like a week-old flan. "I'd scarper if I were you."

I gave her a big grin. "Lovely chatting with you, Mrs Green."

I found Lugs and Micky crouching down at the back of the shelter. They'd smeared mud on their cheeks and were hiding from an invisible enemy.

"Nazi!" Lugs shouted when I walked in.

They then pretended to pepper me with invisible bullets from their imaginary guns. I fell to my knees, rolled onto my back and gave a proper good performance of a dying soldier.

Micky stood over me and gave me a little kick with his foot, "Is he dead, Private?"

I opened one eye. "Not completely!" Then I leaped up and started to pretend fire back at them. They both jumped on me and bundled me to the ground. We wrestled around for a bit, until they pinned me down and sat on my back.

"Do you surrender, Nazi scum?" Micky asked.

"*Nein!*" I shouted.

"I've got something that'll make him!" Lugs said, then shouted, "Turnip power!" and bent over and farted on my face.

"Stone the crows! Alright, alright! I surrender!" I shouted as I thrashed about under Lugs who was killing himself laughing.

Eventually, I scrambled free and laid down on the grass. Lugs and Micky dropped down either side of me.

"So, nice chat with your girlfriend?" Lugs said.

"What?"

"Mrs Green. You seemed to be taking a special interest in her underwear."

I gave him a thump. "You did not just say that."

Micky laughed.

"And you can shut up."

"I didn't say anything!" he protested.

"What were you talking to her about anyway?" Lugs asked.

"Not much. She told me Dad's joined up. While ago apparently."

Micky bolted up right. "Did she? Has she seen him? Spoken to him?"

I propped myself up on my elbow.

"Go on, what did she say?" Micky's eyes were lit up with excitement. Despite everything, he missed our dad. And that annoyed me. I wished he could just forget him. Like I was trying to.

"Postie Stan saw him drinking down the Prince Regent."

"So, he's here? In Deptford?"

"I dunno, do I? Probably been sent off to fight already. Everyone his age will be gone soon, I reckon."

"My dad won't be going," Lugs said.

"Why not?" I asked. "Aren't you Jewish?"

Lugs gave me quite a look. "What's that got to do with anything?"

"I dunno," I said, suddenly not sure. "Johnny said the war's a Jew's quarrel."

Lugs sat up. "What? Is he a fascist, or something?"

38

The way Lugs spat out the word *fascist* made me think it were something bad. "Maybe. What's a fascist?"

"The Nazis are fascists."

"How can Johnny be a fascist then?" Micky asked. "We're at war with the Nazis."

"Fascists aren't just in Germany." Lugs looked down at the grass. "We've got home-grown ones too."

"Like that...Oswald someone?" I said, trying to remember the name Johnny had mentioned.

"Mosley. Yup, he's one. My dad says that fascists are just people who think their nation is superior to others and that the nation is more important than the individual."

"That wrong, is it?" Micky asked.

"It is if you don't agree with whoever is in power. Take Hitler. He's a dictator, right? Then what he says goes. And Hitler, he happens to think that some people are lesser. He reckons Jewish people are a common enemy. Calls us a problem." Lugs picked up a stick and rammed it in the grass and started wiggling it about.

"That's just daft. You're not lesser," I said, then because he looked so glum I added, "Specially not in the ears department."

"Thanks, Ronnie." Lugs sort of smiled, but it looked heavy at the edges. I suppose I didn't really understand, *couldn't* really understand what he was talking about.

I still wasn't completely certain I knew what a fascist was, but Johnny definitely had the air of someone who thought he was better than everybody else, so maybe he was one.

"So how come your dad won't fight, Lugs?" Micky asked. "Don't he want to stick one up Hitler?"

"He won't. Says he's a pacifist."

"You what?" Micky gasped. "Why?"

Lugs shrugged. "He don't believe in fighting. Doesn't think it's the answer."

"But it's a man's duty to go," I said. "To serve king and country, least that's what I've heard."

Lugs looked down at the floor. "He don't see it like that."

"Sheesh. Sorry about that, Lugs," I said. I reckoned a pacifist was just about the worst thing you could have for your old man. After mine, that is.

Chamberlain had made it law for all able men between the ages of eighteen and forty-one to join up. But the way people saw it back then it was a man's duty to go. The brave and right thing to do – and if you didn't go you were a coward. If I'd been old enough, I wouldn't have thought twice about enlisting.

"Yeah, sorry, Lugs," Micky said. "If anyone asks, we'll just tell them he's got something wrong with him."

"Like what?" Lugs asked.

Micky scrunched up his nose. "Dunno. Flat feet? Hear that'll stop someone from going."

"Flat feet? That's not going to keep 'em from sending him," I said.

"Maybe he's missing a liver then," Micky said.

I laughed. "That would stop him. You've only got one liver, Mick."

"I meant kidney! Say he's only got one of them, Lugs. We'll back you up. You don't want people finding out he's a coward."

"Thanks, Mick," Lugs said, solemnly. "I appreciate it."

We sat quietly for a moment. I thought both Micky and I were feeling bad for Lugs, but then Micky said, "Do you reckon Dad will come by before he goes? You know – to say goodbye?"

"Doubt it. Hope not."

Micky's shoulders dropped a little. "He might go and not come back, Ronnie. Don't that bother you?"

I took a moment to answer. "No, Micky, it don't. You remember what it was like when he was around."

"He weren't all bad," Micky said quietly.

That's the thing with our Micky, the person he tells the most lies to is himself. Our dad was a drunk and a bully and we were better off without him.

"I wish that were true, Micky, really I do, and I know it's hard, but the best thing you can do is put him out of your mind."

Micky did a big gulp, then a sniff, then cleared his throat and I knew he were trying to stop himself from crying.

"Aw, Mick, I didn't—"

"Don't *aw Mick* me. I'm fine."

"Good. Course you are. You don't need him. You've got me—"

"And me," Lugs said.

"Yeah see, and Lugs." I slung my arms around both their shoulders. "Best mates, hey? We don't need anybody else when we have each other."

"Best mates," Lugs said.

"Best mates," Micky said.

"Spit on it?" I said and spat on my hand and held it out.

"Yeah, spit on it," Mick said and spat on his hand and pressed it into mine.

Then Lugs hoiked up a massive blob of phlegm which dangled from his lips, before finally flopping into his palm, which he held up and said, "Yeah, spit on it!"

"Urgh, Lugs! Afraid you're on your own there!"

"Fair enough." He wiped his hand on the grass. "Now?"

Micky pulled a face like he still weren't keen, but I nodded at him, and in turn we clasped each other's hands.

"No matter what happens," I said. "We're bonded now."

"Don't mean you can get in trouble with old Etherington and think we'll be okay with it, though," Micky said. "I'm not taking another caning because of you."

"I know," I said. "You won't have to. Here, do you reckon Etherington is a fascist? He behaves like a dictator, don't you think?"

"Nah," Lugs said. "He's just a bully."

We lay back down on the grass – the sun was starting to set.

"Hey," I said. "Do you reckon Johnny Simmons will sign up to fight?"

"Probably," Micky said.

That was a good thought. Maybe Johnny would disappear as quickly as he arrived.

CHAPTER 5

That evening, after Johnny had finished the shelter, he joined us for tea. He sat at the head of the table, where Dad used to sit. Mum fussed around him, giving him more spuds when he said he'd had enough and all the extra gravy. He talked non-stop about himself, without ever saying that much about what he actually did. He made it clear that he wasn't short of a bob or two though. He told jokes that made Micky and Mum laugh. He said that it was the best meal he'd had in months. Mum blushed. I glared.

"It's nothing special," she said.

She was right about that. "It was spam, spuds, cabbage and gravy," I pointed out.

"It was a culinary triumph, Cathy!" Johnny said.

"I'm glad someone appreciates my cooking," she said, raising her eyebrows at me.

"When are you joining up, Johnny?" I asked. It probably sounded like it came out of nowhere, but all I'd been thinking about since he sat down at the table was when he'd be going.

And the further away – the better.

Johnny sighed and put his knife and fork down on his plate. "Nothing I want more than to be able to go and do my bit."

"So why aren't you then?" I stuck my fork into some overcooked cabbage. "Is it because you're a fascist?"

Mum gasped and almost dropped the water jug. "Ronnie! Whatever are you saying?" She was looking at me with these huge, horrified eyes, and I realized I wasn't actually sure. I hadn't much thought about it before it came out of my mouth.

"I'm sorry, Johnny, he doesn't know what he's talking about! Ronnie, you simply cannot go around calling people fascists!"

"It's okay, Cathy," Johnny said calmly. "The boy's clearly confused. We had a chat about the war when we were building the shelter. He's got the wrong end of the stick, that's all."

I didn't think I had, but even if I was wrong, it didn't change the fact that he wasn't doing his duty and fighting. "So, why aren't you fighting then?" I asked.

"Ronnie, enough!" Mum cried. Then she said more quietly, "He might not want to talk about it."

Johnny shook his head and smiled. "It's alright, Cathy. I don't mind."

"Not missing a liver, are you?" I said and Micky almost choked on his last bit of spam.

Mum covered her face with her hands. "I am so sorry, Johnny."

"Not my liver, no," Johnny said, straight faced. "It's the old ticker, see. I might look as strong as an ox, but it could go at any time."

"Oh, Johnny," Mum said. "That's terrible."

"Yeah, terrible," Micky said, sounding like he actually meant it. You'd have thought he'd be able to spot a liar what with all his practice.

"Seemed alright out there when you were building the shelter," I said.

"And that's what I told them at the conscription office. I said, *Look at me! Have you ever seen a better specimen?* Did fifty press-ups right there in front of them."

"You didn't!" Micky said.

"I did," Johnny said. "Like this!"

Then he got he got down on the floor and started doing press ups. "One, two, three—"

Mum laughed and covered her mouth with her hands. "Johnny, stop!" she giggled. "You've just eaten!"

"Five, six, seven—"

"Johnny!" she said, her mouth breaking into a huge smile. "Stop!"

"Okay, okay! If you insist!" He sat back down at the table, grinning, and Mum whacked him gently with a tea towel. "Honestly!"

I looked at them smiling at each other and I didn't like it one bit.

"So," he continued, "when that didn't work, I tried to bribe them to ignore my medical records. I said, when I go, I'd rather go on a battlefield and I was willing to pay to see that happen, but they weren't having any of it. Forced a medical exemption certificate in my hands and booted me out the door."

I gave Micky a look which said *Are you listening to this rubbish?* but he didn't notice. It looked like he was almost under some kind of spell.

"You shouldn't feel bad," Mum said.

"That's the thing," Johnny said. "Truth be told, I feel dreadful about it." He paused for effect. Then he gulped and stared out the window with this fake sad look on his face. "I should be out there, fighting."

"Where?" I said. "In our garden? And what fighting? I heard all them fellas who've signed up are only training in the countryside. I'm sure your heart could cope with that."

If he heard me, he chose to ignore me, because he put his head in his hands and let out a sob. A grown man, fake crying at the dinner table! I couldn't ruddy believe it!

I was proper astonished. I looked from Mum to Micky thinking, *You seriously can't be buying this!*

Mum scowled at me, got to her feet and put her hands on his shoulders. "Johnny this is not your fault! You tried! I'm sure there will be plenty of ways you can help the war effort here, and I for one, am glad you're not going."

Johnny looked up, all serious like, and put his hand on hers. "Thank you, Cathy. Hearing you say that don't half make me feel better. Like you've fixed a part of me that was a little bit broken."

"Oh, Johnny," Mum said.

I was barely able to hold back my laugh and ended up spluttering into my water. I was incredulous. I learned that word from Mr Etherington. He used it about me when I fell asleep in class when he was reading *The Golden Fleece* for the billionth time.

Think my spluttering reminded Mum that me and Micky were still in the room. She got a bit flustered and almost knocked a glass over. "Right, I'll clear the plates. Jam roly-poly for pudding."

When she was out in the kitchen, Johnny put his hand on my shoulder and squeezed real tight. "You got a bike, Ronnie?"

"What?" I said, which seemed like a reasonable response because the bike thing had come out of nowhere.

"Not a difficult question. I asked if you have a bike." He was smiling at me, but I dunno, it felt menacing.

"No."

"How's about I see to getting you one?" He squeezed a bit harder.

Now, obviously, I wanted a bike. But not from him. I knew if he wanted to give me a bike there'd be a reason behind it. "Nah, you're alright."

"I don't have a bike!" Micky said. "I'll take one."

Johnny turned to look at Micky. "You?"

"I'd love a bike!"

"He don't need a bike," I said quickly. I didn't want our Micky owing him something.

"Shut up, Ronnie, yeah I do."

Johnny let go of my shoulder and rubbed his chin. "Yeah, yeah. Maybe that'll work."

I said, "What'll work—"

But before he could answer, Mum walked back in from the kitchen carrying a plate. "Hey presto! Roly-poly!"

I usually love jam roly-poly, but I'd lost my appetite. I couldn't sit at that table any longer. Johnny's presence was filling up our whole house. I felt smaller – squashed almost. Just like I used to when Dad was around.

"I'm going outside," I announced, my chair screeching across the floor as I got up.

"But Ronnie, love, it's jam roly-poly!" Mum said.

"Don't fancy it," I said and stormed out the room.

Micky said, "I'll have his share." Then, as I closed the front door behind me, he added, "Mum! Johnny's going to get me a bike!"

Outside, I took a deep lungful of the cool September air. I stood looking up at the stars, imagining fighter planes streaking across the sky overhead.

I laid down on the grass and let out a sigh. Johnny might have built our shelter, and he might have offered to get me a bike and he might have made Mum smile more than I'd seen her smile in years, but I knew. I knew deep down in my bones he were no good. Being around my dad had taught me about men like him. Smiles and swagger when things go their way. Fists and anger when they don't.

I was still there, on the grass, trying to push memories back down inside me, when Johnny left. I jumped up when the front door opened and the light from inside momentarily spilled out across the garden.

"See ya, Ronnie," he said as he walked by me.

I didn't answer – didn't want to.

He stopped and turned round. "I said, *See ya, Ronnie.*"

I grunted in response. He wasn't going to get a cheery farewell from me. Not unless I could be sure he wasn't coming back.

He covered the ground between us in two strides. "That weren't very polite now, was it?"

Before I knew what was happening his hands were at my collar and my feet were off the ground. He lifted me up, so I was eye to eye with him. "You'd better get used to me, Ronnie," he snarled. "I'm going to be around here a lot. A whole lot."

I stared back, trying to catch my breath. It wasn't the first time I'd been held up by the collar, but I'd always seen it coming before. I admit it, I was scared.

"I am not a man to get on the wrong side of. You understand?"

I nodded and managed to catch my breath and say, "I understand."

He stared at me until I looked away. Johnny smiled. Set me back on my feet, smoothed down my shirt. Then he ruffled my hair and said, "There, that's better. Now I think you oughta apologize for how you've been with me tonight."

49

"Sorry," I muttered, hating the feel of the words on my lips.

He put his hand to his ear. "You say something? Didn't quite catch that."

I spoke a little louder. "I said, I'm sorry."

"Glad to hear it." He looked back towards the house. "She's a good one, that mother of yours."

I didn't respond. I was hot with rage and humiliation, and I didn't want to let it out.

"Well, is she a good one, Ronnie? Can't you say anything nice about your own mother?"

I didn't want to talk to him about Mum, but I forced myself to say, "Yeah, she's a good one."

"Needs a man in her life, don't you think?"

My jaw clenched. "That's up to her."

"That it is." He checked his watch. "I'm off now. See ya, Ron.

He looked at me, expectant.

"See ya, Johnny."

"There's a good lad." He tapped my cheek a couple of times. His hand felt big and rough. It felt like Dad's. Then he turned and left.

Like an unexploded bomb, the anger built inside me as I watched him jump over our gate and strut off down the road whistling. Without turning round, he held his hand up and waved goodbye. He'd won. And we both knew it.

The front door opened behind me. "'Ere, Ronnie!" Micky said, bounding up to me. "Johnny's promised he's going to get me a bike! Isn't he great!"

CHAPTER 6

That night, while Micky and I lay in bed, listening to Mum singing as she tidied up downstairs and got ready for her night shift, I couldn't get my run-in with Johnny Simmons out of my head. Whether he was a fascist or not, it was pretty clear he was trouble, and it was also clear that he had designs on Mum. I thought about telling her and Micky what had happened in the garden, but I couldn't. I guess I felt ashamed. That it was my fault somehow. Micky was so excited about that damn bike and Mum, well she seemed all giddy and happy, and I didn't want to be the one to take that away.

She came in dressed in her uniform. "I'm off to work now boys," she whispered, even though we were both wide awake. "If you need anything—"

"We know, Mrs Green is next door," I said.

"We never need anything, Mum," Micky said through a yawn.

She went over and kissed him on the forehead and then did the same to me. "I know. My two brilliant boys. Where would

I be without you? Now, I must go, or I'll miss the bus, and my gentlemen will be wondering where I've got to."

Mum's gentlemen were the old boys she looked after on her ward. I reckon she was a good nurse. She always talked about her patients with fondness. She once told me that half of nursing is just showing somebody that you care.

"You know where your gas masks are and what to do if you hear a siren?"

"Yes," we both said, a little wearily.

"You know I hate to leave you."

"We'll be fine, Mum," I said. "You don't have to worry."

"Okay, sleep well and dream the best dreams," she said and turned out the light.

After we'd heard the front door close, I said, "Micky, don't get your hopes up about this bike."

"Johnny promised."

"And you believe him?"

"Why would he say it otherwise?"

"Dunno, to get Mum on side."

"Think he already did that building the shelter."

"You didn't believe all that about him having a dodgy heart, did you?"

"Seemed genuine to me. He don't strike me as a coward."

"Just be careful, alright?"

I heard him roll over. "Whatever, Ronnie."

"Night, Micky."

"Night."

Mum wasn't back from the hospital when we got up for school. Sometimes that would happen. She wouldn't want to leave a patient who needed her. Micky and I decided to have the rest of the jam roly-poly for breakfast and ate it as we walked to school.

"Dunno why we can't have this all the time," he said, spraying crumbs everywhere. "Beats porridge any day of the week."

"I don't think you can have a bad day if it starts with jam roly-poly," I said.

We collected Lugs on the way. He was covered in scratches but seemed dead excited about something.

"What's happened to you?" I asked.

"We've got rats!" he announced happily.

"Congratulations?" I said, unsure why he seemed so pleased about it.

"Rats did that to you?" Micky frowned. "How big were they?"

"Mum reckons they're the biggest she's ever seen," Lugs said.

"And the scratches?"

"Oh, they're from Tiger."

"Tiger?" I said.

"Our new cat. Dad got him because he thinks he'll get rid of the rats."

"Has it worked?"

"Not yet, but he's still learning. He's a stray and a bit set in

53

his ways. He's only got one eye. Think he must have lost the other in a scrap. Don't really like to be petted. But he'll come round. Animals love me."

"Do they? What about the time you were bitten on your bum by your neighbours' dog?" I said.

"He was just overexcited. It was a friendly bite."

"Or when you were attacked by that duck down by the river?" Micky added.

"That was a misunderstanding."

"And there was the time you got knocked out by that police horse."

"I sort of ran into it, can't really blame the horse. I've had a few unlucky incidents, that's all. But honest, animals love me, and Tiger will too."

"Right you are, Lugs," I said, grinning at Micky.

School started off okay that day. We had arithmetic in the morning with Miss Grimshaw, which I'm not too bad at. Then we had another air-raid practice, which was alright because it meant it took up some lesson time. The school shelter was below ground and ran under the playground. It's a bit miserable down there to be honest. It's dark and cramped and we have to sit on these benches that make your bum go numb. Miss Grimshaw made us recite our times tables, but because we had our gas masks on, there's no way she could make out what we were saying. Lugs and I just shouted out random numbers and she was none the wiser. At break we played tag in the playground. But in the afternoon, Mr Etherington showed up.

He read out another passage from *The Golden Fleece*. He loved that blasted book. He has a right droney voice and what with me not sleeping well the night before, because I'd been thinking about Johnny, I was finding it really hard to keep my eyes open. And then the inevitable happened.

I was woken by the whacking sound of Mr Etherington's cane on my desk.

"Answer the question, Smith!" he demanded.

I looked at him blankly.

"Go on, then, answer. Or were you not paying attention?" He was pretty much frothing at the mouth.

"So," I began, hoping desperately for divine inspiration. Micky and Lugs were watching me, with these big, worried eyes. "Jason and them argonauts went and stole that golden fleece."

"That was NOT the question!" Mr Etherington blared.

"Perhaps...sir, maybe you could remind me of the question again...please?"

"The question," Mr Etherington said as he started to pace through the rows of desks, "was what was the significance of the golden fleece?"

Now, I hadn't a clue, but I had to chance a guess. "Did it have special powers, sir? Like did the wool keep 'em extra warm? They didn't have many clothes in those days, did they? It was all loin cloths and sandals, weren't it?"

55

Some of the girls sniggered and Micky put his head in his heads, which suggested to me that I was a little wide from the mark.

"Authority and kingship! The fleece is a symbol of authority and kingship and anyone with half a brain would have known that, *if* they had been listening."

"That would have been my second guess, sir," I said.

"Does it not seem interesting to you, Smith, that you would not recognize a symbol of authority, because it does to me!"

"I shouldn't read anything into it, sir."

"Michael Smith, Billy Missell, come to the front."

I felt a surge of panic. Micky shot me a dark look and Lugs let out an audible groan as they got to their feet and made their way to the front of the class.

"Yes, I imagine it is tiresome to be friends with young Ronald here," Mr Etherington said. "Perhaps you will think more carefully about the company you keep in future."

"No, sir, please," I said. "Don't punish them. It was me who messed up the answer. I bet they both knew. You can give me double what they get, just don't punish them."

"Palms up," Etherington said, and Micky and Lugs turned their hands upwards.

"But sir—"

"Authority..." Etherington began as he brought down the cane onto Lugs's hand, "must..." another whack for Lugs, "be..." and another, "respected."

Etherington paused and wiped the sweat from his top lip. "Now you say it, Smith."

"But sir—"

"SAY IT!"

I closed my eyes. "Authority." I winced at the cracking sound of the strike on Micky, "Must..." another strike, "be..." and again, "respected." And a final, harder hit.

I opened my eyes again – the cane was still trembling in Mr Etherington's grip. In fact, he was trembling too. He took a breath, composed himself, then placed the cane down on the teacher's desk. "Now you two, be seated."

Micky and Lugs sat back down, both cradling their left hand in their right.

Micky wouldn't look at me, but when Lugs did, I mouthed, "I'm sorry."

On the way home, I tried to apologize properly. "I'm sorry, I just fell asleep, that's all."

Lugs was blowing on his palm. "God knows how you could fall asleep with Etherington in the room. It's like being in the presence of that ever-watchful dragon from that Golden Fleece story."

"I dunno how I did. I am sorry. It won't happen again."

"At least it wasn't our arses this time," Lugs said.

"Micky," I said. "Are you okay?"

Micky sighed. "Yeah, it's like Lugs said, at least it wasn't our arses."

"Mr Etherington hasn't made you want to stop keeping company with me, has he?" I asked.

"Not like I've got any choice, is it?" Micky said. "I live with you."

"Lugs?"

"Yeah, we're bonded the three of us, nothing that Etherington can do that can break that."

"Good, I'm really glad to hear it," I said.

But it wasn't Etherington who was going to test the bonds of our friendship. That was somebody else.

CHAPTER 7

There was a knock at the door on the Wednesday morning of the following week. It was early, before we'd even left for school. I was just coming down the stairs, pulling my jumper over my head, when Mum shouted from the bathroom, "Who's knocking at this time of the morning? Will someone get that?" She'd not been in long as she'd had another night shift.

I unbolted the latch and opened the door, and there standing on the front step, in a blue Royal Air Force uniform, was my dad. Well, a version of my dad at least. He was clean shaven, and his eyes were bright. On his feet, in place of his usually scuffed work boots, was a pair of shiny shoes and his hair looked tidy under his cap. On the left breast of his jacket was a badge – a winged brevet. It was hard to match up the man standing on the doorstep to the image I had of him in my head – stained vest, red in the face, fury in his eyes, bottle in his hand.

"Hello, Ron," he said. "Blimey, you've grown."

I didn't say anything. Couldn't say anything.

Dad shifted from foot to foot. Almost like he was unsure

of himself, nervous even. "Aren't you going to invite your old man in?"

Micky came thundering down the stairs. "Who is—" He stopped on the bottom step, his eyes wide. "*Dad?*"

"Alright, Micky lad?" Dad said.

Micky nodded, his mouth hanging open.

"What are you doing here?" I asked.

Dad looked me square in the eyes. "Got some things I need to say."

"What happens if we don't want to hear them?"

"That's your choice, Ron."

Mum came down the stairs, bleary eyed. "Who is it?" She stopped midway when she saw him and steadied herself on the banister. "*George?*"

Dad took off his cap when he saw her. "Hello, Cathy," he said. "You look well."

"George? You look...you look..."

"Different? I am. I've changed. I told you I would." There was an urgency to his voice that I'd never heard before.

Mum didn't move, her knuckles turning white from holding the banister so tightly.

"Can I come in? I'd rather not say what I've come to say here on the doorstep."

"I...I don't know," Mum said.

"Please, Cathy. I'll go as soon as I've finished. I promise."

I gave her a little shake of my head, but Micky looked at her and nodded eagerly.

Mum looked at us both, then closed her eyes and nodded too. "Okay, you can come in. Boys, off you go to school."

"No chance!" Micky said. "I'm not going anywhere."

"And I'm not leaving you alone with him," I said.

I thought Dad would lose it when I said that, but he didn't. Instead, he said, "They should stay. They need to hear this too."

Mum didn't look sure. "I don't think—"

"We're staying," I said.

Mum let go of the banister and pulled her dressing gown tighter round her. "Fine, I'll make some tea."

Dad took a step inside. "It's okay, I'll do it."

Mum looked rightly taken aback. I don't think Dad ever made a cuppa in all the years he was at home. Pour himself some whisky, that he could do, but not make a pot of tea. He walked past me and into the kitchen, leaving me to close the door behind him.

Mum came down the last few steps and said to me and Micky, "We'll just hear him out and then he goes, okay?"

We sat down at the table, a weird tension filling the room, not saying anything just listening to Dad clattering about, opening and shutting cupboards. Eventually, he brought Mum a cup of tea that was so strong it almost looked like tar.

Mum picked it up and took a sip. "Lovely," she said, although her face said otherwise.

Dad pulled up a chair and sat down. He did a couple of big sighs and opened his mouth like he was about to speak, but no words actually came out.

"You're in the RAF?" I said to break the silence. "Mrs Green didn't mention that."

Dad gave half a smile. "And here's me thinking Mrs Green knows everything."

"She's been good to us," Mum said, sounding a little irritated. Then she sat forward in her chair and said, "George, why are you here? It's been two years."

"After I left—" Dad's voice came out a bit crackly, so he cleared his throat and started again. "After I left—"

"After we threw you out, you mean," I interrupted.

"Yeah, well after that, I wasn't in a good way."

"Shame," I said.

"Shut up, Ronnie," Micky said. "Just let him speak."

Dad continued. "See, I got to thinking about the kind of man I was and the kind of man I wanted to be, and I realized the distance between those two men was as wide as the sky."

"And the rest." I placed my elbow on the table and put my chin on my hand, like I wasn't interested. But I was. I was listening to every single word he was saying.

"I wanted to mend my ways. Be a better man. Be able to look myself in the mirror. So, a month or two after I left, I went down to the RAF recruitment office and joined up," Dad said. "Thought at thirty-eight it was about time I mended my ways."

"But George," Mum said. "The last time – the war," she paused, searching for the words. "It was the war that changed you."

"I was young. Too young. Not much older than the boys are now, and I didn't make a good account of myself."

"What do you mean?" I asked.

"Some people find courage on the battlefield. I was not one of those people. It's haunted me for years, and I have to make amends." He paused. "I have to make amends for a lot of things."

I didn't know much about what Dad did in the Great War. He wouldn't talk about it. He was only seventeen when he'd gone out with the last lot of British troops in 1918 to fight in the second battle of the Somme. He and Mum had been sweethearts when he'd left. When he'd first come back, she said he'd seemed alright. I guess over the years though, what he'd seen started to affect him.

"So, what are you? A pilot?" Micky asked, his eyes full of admiration.

Dad allowed himself a small smile. "Yeah, Micky, I am."

"An actual pilot, who flies planes?"

"An actual pilot who flies planes. It wasn't easy. I was a lot older than a lot of the other lads, but I completed my initial officer training course back in May, in Cardington. Then I went to Hatfield for Elementary Flying Training School and learned on Tiger Moths. I thought if I was going back to war, I'd rather see it from the air this time."

"Tiger Moths?" Micky said, his voice more breath than sound.

I could see from the look in Micky's eyes, he'd been swept up by Dad's talk of making amends and change. Maybe I felt something start to shift in me too. But he'd tried and failed to sort himself out before, and I couldn't let myself believe this time would be any different.

"I don't care what you are, or what you've flown," I said. "You're not coming back."

"No, I know I'm not. That's not why I'm here."

"Then why are you here, George?" Mum asked.

"To apologize. To ask for forgiveness, I suppose. I wasn't a good husband, and I wasn't a good father."

"You can say that again," I said.

"I understand you're angry," Dad said. But how could he understand? If he did, he would never think that turning up after so long with nothing but words and a fancy uniform would make up for what he'd done. I felt my insides trembling with anger.

"It's just, there's a war on—" he said.

"Is there?" I said. "Someone should have said something."

He ignored me and spoke to Mum instead. "Who knows what's going to happen. I wanted to make sure I'd told you I was sorry, in case, well in case there's a time that I can't."

I'd heard enough. He was here to ease his own conscience. He wanted us to rid him of his guilt.

"I'm going to school," I said.

"Ronnie!" Micky said, grabbing my arm as I walked past him. "Didn't you hear what Dad said? He's sorry."

"I heard and now I'm going."

"Let him go, if he wants," Dad said.

I pulled my arm free from Micky's grip. "I do want."

I grabbed my gas mask from the coat hooks and stormed

outside, slamming the front door behind me. Then I kicked the watering can across the grass.

"You alright?" Vera was leaning on the fence having her morning cigarette.

Her voice and face were full of concern and before I could stop myself, I burst into tears. I hadn't even known they were coming, but they flowed hot and free down my cheeks.

I tried to make a run for it out the gate, but Vera blocked my path and next thing I knew, she'd pulled me into her massive bosom and hugged me.

"There, there, lad. It's okay, let it out."

I tried to resist for a moment, but in the end, I gave in.

"Forgive him? How can he even ask that?" I blubbed.

"Who you talkin' about, love?" Vera said.

I pulled away, I didn't want to be spotted cuddling anyone in the middle of the street, let alone Mrs Green. "Dad," I said, wiping my nose on my sleeve. "He's in there right now, acting like a few words will make up for what he done."

"Oh," she said, looking anxiously towards our house, "I see."

"And Micky and Mum are just about to lap it all up. After everything he did to us. It's still him, under that fancy uniform. People don't change, do they, Mrs Green?"

"Oh, I don't know about that," she said. "But one thing I do know for certain, is that the world does. It changes so much I'm surprised any of us can keep up with it. We get far too few chances in life, Ronnie. Be sure before you choose to let one pass you by."

CHAPTER 8

Despite Mrs Green's words about the world changing, life in London didn't change much in those first few months following Chamberlain's announcement that we were at war. War, it seemed, had forgotten to show up. It was something that happened elsewhere. We heard reports of what was going on in Poland and Belgium and British ships being sunk out at sea. Men went off to France in the event of an invasion there, but to me, it felt like Adolf had forgotten all about Britain. People were calling it the phoney war and that seemed about right. Sandbags slouched in front of buildings, like they were bored of waiting. At school, we practised for air raids and gas attacks, but it all seemed a bit pointless.

Dad was stationed not far from us, down in Biggin Hill, flying Hurricanes or so he said. He wrote the occasional letter, that Mum and Micky would read together, and I would read secretly on my own. It annoyed me that his words still managed to find a way into our house. It annoyed me more that I wanted to read them. Mum said she was pleased for him – that he'd sorted himself out – but she weren't going to take him back, not in a month of Sundays.

I still had a suspicion that Johnny was a fascist, even though I weren't that straight in my head about what one actually was. I wanted to find out more, but I weren't sure who to ask. S'pose Mr Etherington was the obvious choice, what with him being a teacher and all, but I weren't about to strike up a conversation with him voluntarily. All Mum would say was that they were hateful people, and she was glad that their popularity was on the decline.

Johnny Simmons's popularity, however, was very much on the rise with Mum and Micky. He was round ours most weeks. He liked to turn up at ours with gifts. Flowers and chocolates for Mum, comics for me and Mick. I read them, but I always felt a bit annoyed at myself for enjoying something he'd given me. When we were done, we'd pass them on to Lugs.

Johnny would do the odd job here and there and Mum would give him dinner and bang on about how wonderful he was. Guess you could say they were a couple. I stayed out of his way as much as I could. He was always as nice as pie, but I kept expecting his mask to slip. For the guy who'd held me up by the collar to come out, but he was on best behaviour. Biding his time, I guess.

Johnny had been getting closer to Micky too. I suppose when one dad takes off, there's a space that needs filling. Micky had taken to idolizing him. Especially since Johnny had made good on his word and bought him a bike. They seemed to have formed this bond, and they'd go off for walks together.

I asked Micky one night over tea, "What do you and Johnny talk about when you go on these walks of yours?"

Micky swallowed his mouthful of mash. "All sorts of stuff. Johnny's real clever. He sees things differently. Doesn't think that the war should have happened. That Chamberlain should have talked to Hitler."

Vera, who'd joined us that evening, almost choked on her cabbage. "Speak to Hitler? He must be away with the fairies."

Mum put her cutlery down on her plate. "I think what Mrs Green is trying to say, is that it would have been wonderful if a peaceful solution could have been found, but I don't think Hitler would have listened to anyone."

"Guess it depends on what they were saying," Micky said.

I didn't know what Micky was talking about at the time, but I got an idea the week before Christmas.

Mum had left for work early and Lugs, Micky and I were on our way to school. Lugs was still covered in scratches – Tiger hadn't come round to being cuddled, or caught a rat as far as I knew, but Lugs wouldn't give up on him.

"Reckon he had a hard life. It'll take time for him to trust again. But he will," Lugs said. I wasn't so sure about that.

It was cold that December morning and as we walked down New Cross Road, Micky and I blew dragon's breath in the air. When we turned the corner onto Childeric Road, Micky pulled out a copy of *The Dandy* he had stuck in his gas-mask box. He'd got it from Johnny.

"Almost forgot, I brought you this. Haven't even read it yet, thought I'd give you first dibs."

Micky handed the comic over to Lugs, who grinned with delight. "Cheers, Mick! Let's see what Desperate Dan's been up to this week."

He turned the page and his face paled. "This some kind of joke?"

"It's *The Dandy*, so probably," I said, not really paying attention.

Lugs came to a stop on the pavement, looking at Micky like he was searching for an explanation.

"What's up?" I asked and looked at the comic. Inside was a newspaper. The word ACTION was emblazoned on the top with a lightning bolt through the O.

Micky snatched it off him. "It's nothing."

"It's not nothing," Lugs said, his eyes fixed on Micky.

I didn't know what was going on, but I knew it was something. "Micky, what's *Action*?"

"I dunno," he said, putting the paper under his arm. He sounded casual but he had a shifty look in his eyes.

"It's a newspaper promoting the British Union of Fascists, I heard my dad talking about it," Lugs said, his voice wobbling a little. "Telling people how bad Jews are and how great Hitler is."

"Hells bleedin' bells, Mick! What you doing with something like that?" I said.

Micky let out an exasperated sigh, like we were making a fuss over nothing. "I dunno where it came from. It probably got in there by mistake."

"Oh, come on! Johnny gave it to you, didn't he?" I pressed.

"No," he said, annoyance flashing in his eyes, "maybe the person he got the comic from put it in there."

"Pull the other one," I said, annoyed too. "Johnny told me the first time we met that the war was a Jew's quarrel."

"He ain't got nothing against Jews, not really. He just thinks that the war shouldn't be happening. He thinks that Britain should just stay out of it, you know, look after itself. And I agree, I don't see why Dad should have to go and fight some foreign war."

I grabbed the paper out from Micky's armpit and bopped him on the head with it. "Would you listen to yourself? You think it's alright to stand by and let Hitler stomp into any country he wants to build his empire?"

"No, I'm not saying that." He lunged for the paper, but I pulled it away.

I kicked at the ground, angry that Micky was defending Johnny. "I knew he was one of them fascists."

"Johnny's not a fascist, he just doesn't think we should be fighting, you know, like Lugs's dad."

With his voice shaking with rage, Lugs said, "My dad isn't anything like Johnny." Then he stepped forward and shoved Micky.

Micky stumbled backwards and held up his hands. I could tell he was surprised. I was too.

"I'm sorry. I didn't mean to upset you." Micky snatched the newspaper out of my hand, leaving me holding onto the front and back page, and crumpled it up. "Look, it's rubbish. All rubbish. I don't believe any of that stuff about Jewish people." He drop kicked the newspaper ball and booted it down the street. "I just thought that the not going to war bit sounded alright, you know?"

Lugs looked at him for a long minute. He was about to say something when we heard a shout from the end of the road.

"Oi!"

We looked up to see three familiar faces. Arthur Davey, Graham Talbot and Harry Scott were at the end of the road by the school gates.

"Would you look who it is!" Arthur shouted.

"Flamin' hell, what are that lot doing back? I hoped they'd been evacuated for good," Micky said, although I think he was pleased of the interruption.

Lugs rolled up *The Dandy* and stuck it in his back pocket and I folded up what was left of the paper and stuck it in mine. I was going to have a proper look and decide what to do about it later.

"What a morning this is turning out to be," Lugs said. "Don't suppose they'll leave us alone!"

"You never know," I said. "Let's hope the countryside has mellowed them a bit."

As soon as we got to the school gates, I knew no mellowing had taken place. Arthur had always had a mean look about him, his face usually fixed in a sneer, but I could tell that something was different. His eyes were harder. His face sharper. Harry, who was pretty tall when he left, now looked even more lumbering. He had to be pushing six foot. And Graham Talbot, well, he looked exactly the same – blond, blue-eyed and arrogant.

"How was the countryside?" I grinned. "Squeeze many udders?"

Arthur had me up against the wall in less than three seconds, his arm against my neck, Graham and Harry pinning me either side. "Don't talk about things you know nothing about."

We'd had a few scuffles before, but the rage that was coming off Arthur was new, and it took me by surprise. I wasn't going to show him that though. "Not a fan of the cattle after all then?" I choked out.

I caught a sharp punch in the ribs for that. Just before they dropped me to the floor, I noticed the look in Arthur's eyes. It was unnerving. There was something behind the anger – fear, sadness, I wasn't quite sure. I stayed kneeling, trying to get my breath back. Lugs rushed over to me, but Micky, he took a step back. He's not usually one for wading in to trouble.

"Crikey, Arthur, what you go and do that for?" Lugs asked.

"Just saying hello, weren't we?" Arthur said.

Harry, who might be massive but is about as sharp as a marble said, "I thought we were roughing him up."

Arthur turned to him and said, "Harry, will you do me a favour?"

"Sure."

"Just keep your mouth shut."

"You here for long?" I asked, all casual like, as Lugs helped me to my feet. "Or just passing through."

"Oh, we're back for good," Graham said, folding his arms. "No sense staying down in the countryside while there's naff all going on in London."

"I ain't ever going back to that house," Arthur said, and I believed him.

"That's wonderful news. We've missed you," I said.

Harry's eyebrows shot up his forehead. "Have you?"

Arthur scowled at him. "You ironed your brain or something?"

"I just didn't think they'd be pleased to see us back, that's all. What with us being enemies and all."

"He was being sarcastic," Arthur said.

Harry thought about it for a moment. Then he actually growled at me. "You being sarcastic, Smith? You better not be." Then he turned back to Arthur and said, "Hang on? What does sarcastic mean again?"

Lugs said, "We could tell you, but it would be hard to explain without actually being sarcastic."

"Do you want to take one in the stomach too, Missell?" Graham asked.

Lugs held up his hands, causing his coat to hitch up. "Nah, thanks for the offer, but I'll pass."

Arthur's eyes fell on the copy of *The Dandy* that was sticking out of Lug's pocket "What's this?" he said as he grabbed it.

"It's a trombone, what do you think it is?" I said. "Now give it back."

"This week's copy too." Arthur flicked through it, then rolled the comic back up and put it in his waistband. "Thank you, you shouldn't have."

"We didn't," I said and shoved him, hard into the wall.

"Leave it, Ronnie. It's not worth it," Micky said, pulling me back.

He was probably right. Last thing I needed was to get caught scrapping by Etherington. It would be Micky and Lugs who would cop it then.

Arthur laughed as we walked away. "Sure is good to be back."

My fists balled up tight in my pockets and I wished for Arthur Davey to be whisked back to whatever farm he'd been staying on.

CHAPTER 9

When I got home after school, my thoughts had turned from Arthur and the others to what I was going to do about Johnny. I needed to see what he'd been filling Micky's head with. I charged straight in through the front door and spread what I had of the newspaper out on my bed. The headline read *For Britain, Peace and People. No War for Jewish Finance.* It was weird to see what Johnny had said – blaming the Jews for the war – in print. Like it gave his words some credibility. It weren't true though. He could have it tattooed on his backside, but it wouldn't change the fact that we were at war because Hitler was invading other countries.

I flipped the page over. On the other side, it detailed Oswald Moseley's plan for the BUF – that's the British Union of Fascists. It mentioned patriotism – putting the country first and carrying out the will of the people - which didn't seem like bad things, but what I read next properly shocked me. Mosley said that, if he came to power, he would immediately deprive all British Jews of citizenship and deport all those he considered "undesirable". He thought they were a threat to the British way of life and said that he'd maybe ship them off to Madagascar. I'd never even heard of Madagascar! There was no way I was going to let Lugs get sent there.

With the newspaper as evidence, and knowing what Mum thought of fascists, I thought I had all I needed to prove to her that Johnny was a wrong'un and get him out of our lives for good.

When she came in from work, I told her that I wanted to talk to her privately. So, when Micky went out on his bike, we sat down at the kitchen table. I was halfway through explaining when Johnny showed up.

"Johnny," Mum said, all serious. "Could you sit down a moment? Ronnie has been telling me some troubling things."

Johnny looked at me, his face full of fake concern. He closed the kitchen door, then put his hand on my shoulder and gripped it tight. "Everything okay, lad? Anything I can do?"

"Yeah, you can get out of my house, you bleedin' fascist!" I said.

"Ronnie!" Mum said. Her voice was even, but I could tell she meant business. She stared at Johnny, with this challenging look in her eyes. "Give Johnny a chance to speak."

Johnny looked from me to Mum, like he was confused. "What's the boy talking about?"

Mum cleared her throat and placed her hands in her lap and got straight to the point. "Ronnie says you gave Micky a copy of *Action*. Is that true?"

Johnny laugh-spluttered. "What? No, why would I do that?"

"He had it hidden in the copy of *The Dandy* you gave him," I said.

"Well, that explains it!" Johnny said triumphantly. "It must have got in there by mistake. I'll admit, it's not easy to get you boys those comics. I don't always know where my guy gets them from. But I won't be using him again, I can tell you that."

Mum clutched her hand to her chest and exhaled. "Oh, I see. That makes sense."

Johnny ruffled my hair and smiled at Mum. "So, are we done here?"

"No, we're not *done*," I said. "I don't believe it was an accident and it don't explain why Micky thinks there shouldn't be a war. He's been reading that rubbish and believing it!"

"Lots of people don't think there should be a war," Johnny said. "And I'll admit, I'm one of them."

"Yeah, but some people think there shouldn't be a war because they don't like the fighting and others don't think there should be a war because they think that Hitler's doing the right thing and should be left to it."

Johnny held his hands up. "Woah! When have I ever said that Hitler's doing the right thing? Me believing in peace and a newspaper accidentally finding its way into your possession does not make me a fascist. You need to be careful what you're saying, lad."

"Johnny's right," Mum said. "You can't go round accusing people of being fascists."

Johnny moved behind her and put his hand on her shoulder. "It's okay, Cathy. I can see how he got there. It doesn't help that this damn heart of mine stops me from signing up and proving myself. These are confusing times, especially for children. He did the right thing coming to you if he was concerned. I'll have a word with young Micky – set him straight."

Mum reached up and touched Johnny's hand. "Thank you for understanding. I had to ask."

"Of course you did."

Mum smiled and clapped her hands together. "I'm so glad we cleared this up. Do you feel better now, Ronnie?"

I looked up at Johnny, standing behind Mum, his hand on her shoulder and a smirk on his face.

"I really hope you do," he said. "I want things to be right between us."

I nodded. "Yeah, things will be right between us." He'd won again. But I wouldn't let him win next time. I'd make it right. I swore then that I'd prove to Mum the kind of man he was.

I didn't have to wait long, because I got a sniff that Johnny was involved in something crooked on Christmas Day.

CHAPTER 10

I f I'd realized that the Christmas of 1939 was going to be our last Christmas before rationing, I may have made more of it. As it was, I spent the day in a bit of a sulk because we had to share it with Johnny Simmons. Micky was happy he was there though. After the newspaper confrontation, Johnny had taken Mick out for one of their walks, to have a chat like he told Mum he would. When Micky came back, I asked him what Johnny had said. He told me that he'd set him right on a few things. I'd asked him straight out, brother to brother, if he thought fascism was wrong and he'd said, "Course, Ron." But I weren't convinced he meant it.

Vera came round ours too. She would've been on her own what with her Bob being up in Newcastle. Vera said that her daughter-in-law's Christmas dinner weren't worth the train journey and so Mum had invited her to join us.

All Christmas Eve, Micky kept peeking through the gap where the blackout paper had peeled away from the front window.

"Father Christmas won't come if he knows you're watching," Mum said, but I knew the father he was looking out for wore a blue uniform, not a red one.

He didn't come, Dad that is. I reckon that was a good thing – it would have got mighty awkward with both Johnny and him in the house. Father Christmas did show up. I got a card game called Blackout. On the packet it said, *The Amusing Topical Card Game. The Game to Cheer You Up. Everybody's Playing it!*

It would take more than a pack of cards to cheer me up with Johnny Simmons around, but Mum said it would be fun to play. Mrs Green fell asleep midway through the first game. I think her polishing off most of Mum's port had something to do with that. Our Micky won, but he would, he cheated all the way through. He thought no one had noticed but I reckon everyone else was feeling too festive to point it out and I wasn't bothered about losing because I was already in a mood, so I didn't mention it either.

Micky got a *Beano* annual off Mum and we both got penknives from Johnny.

"Genuine British Army issue clasp knife that," Johnny said when Micky flicked out the blade.

Mum looked a bit worried about her sons being given stabbing implements. "That's very kind of you, Johnny," she said, "but they're not to leave the house, understand boys?"

Johnny gave Mum this fancy butterfly brooch. It looked dead expensive – came in a velvet box. Mum snapped the lid shut as soon as she saw it and tried to hand it back. "No,

Johnny, this is too much!" she said. "I couldn't possibly accept it."

"Yes, you could," Johnny said. "Now put it on or you'll ruin my Christmas."

Vera said, "Don't be daft, Cathy. Put it on!"

Mum pinned it to her cardy and looked in the mirror. "This is far too special for the likes of me."

"Nonsense," Vera said. "It suits you perfectly."

We had an enormous turkey that year. One of Mum's gentlemen, who clearly wasn't short of a bob or two, had one delivered to ours to say thank you for the care she'd given him. It was so big it wouldn't fit in the oven, so Mum had to pull the legs off and cook them separate. Micky and I both prefer brown meat, but as Johnny and Mrs Green were guests, they got the legs. Micky got the sixpence in his Christmas pud.

"See, told you he's lucky, didn't I!" Vera said and rubbed his head. "And as cute as a bug's ear with it."

Micky scowled. "Think it's time you leave off the port now, Mrs Green."

Johnny left when it was dark. Mrs Green was snoring away on the sofa when he said he had to go out to work.

"On Christmas Day?" Mum said. "Surely not!"

"What kind of work?" I asked.

Johnny ignored me. "Thank you so much, Cathy. It's been a wonderful day. Then he gave her a kiss on the cheek.

It was two hours later, I was helping Mum with the dishes, Micky was reading his *Beano* on the floor in the front room and

Mrs Green was still snoring away, when there was a heavy knock on the door. It made Mrs Green leap from her slumber and shout, "Ay, Caramba!" which made everyone jump, then laugh.

The laughter stopped though when Mum opened the door. Outside, was a hulk of man, with a jaw like a table. He was smartly dressed in a pinstriped suit, with a gold signet ring on his little finger. He smiled and spoke politely when he saw Mum, but there was something about him that seemed hard.

"I'm sorry to trouble you," he said, in an East-End accent, "but I've been led to believe that Johnny Simmons might be here."

I went over and stood next to Mum. "Are you the police?"

I was hopeful that he was, that he might be there to tell us Johnny was a criminal, but my question seemed to amuse him. He laughed a deep, deep laugh. "Nah, kid. Just a friend of Johnny's that's all. You seen him?"

Mum said, "I'm afraid he left about two hours ago for work."

"Is that so? Now, that is a shame. Was hoping to catch him and wish him a Merry Christmas. He's a good fella, our Johnny."

I think he was trying to sound friendly, but his gravelly voice made him sound a bit menacing to me. Not that Mum seemed to notice.

She smiled and said, "I can let him know you dropped by next time he's round, Mister...?"

"Dimes. The name's Dimes. Tell him that I have a little proposition that I think he'll be interested in." He took off his hat and gave Mum a nod. "Please accept my sincerest apologies for disturbing you on this fine Christmas evening. You folks have a lovely time."

"And you too, Mr Dimes," Mum said. "Have a very merry Christmas."

Mr Dimes put his hat back on his head and stuck a cigarette between his lips. Before he lit it, he said, "That's a lovely brooch you have there. Gift from Johnny?"

Mum touched the butterfly and blushed. "Yes, however did you know?"

"Call it a hunch," he said, then he lit his cigarette and disappeared off down the street in a billow of smoke.

I stood in the doorway watching him, until he turned the corner out of view. Mum clearly didn't think Mr Dimes was suspicious but, to me, something about him didn't feel right. It didn't feel right at all.

Before I could think about what I was doing, I bolted out of the front door and raced after him. I heard Mum shout my name, but I ignored her. I wanted to find out who this Mr Dimes was, and what connection he had to Johnny.

I caught up with Dimes on Tanner's Hill. He was just closing the door of his car – it was a Rolls Royce Phantom III. Don't often see cars that fancy round Deptford, and it almost made me lose my nerve. But I knocked on the window and he rolled it down.

Dimes looked me up and down, all curious like. "Yes?"

I was panting from running but managed to gasp out,

"Was just wondering, sir, if you had a message for Johnny? Thought you might be more comfortable talking away from me mum. Seems a shame to come all the way out here and not deliver a message if you have one."

He studied my face, and I tried my best not to look nervous, don't know how good a job I did of that, but I must have done alright because eventually he nodded and grinned.

"So, Johnny's got himself a new recruit. Always good to have new blood on board."

I wanted to ask *on board with what?* Whether it was something to do with being a fascist, but I didn't think that was the sort of thing to blurt out to a guy his size in case I was wrong. He might not take too kindly to it. And if I *was* wrong, he'd realize I had no idea what he was talking about, so I just said, "Yeah."

"Tell Johnny to tread carefully at the moment. He needs to keep his nose clean. I'm working on something big, and I'd very much like him to be part of it."

"Tread carefully?"

I must have looked confused because Dimes said, "Yeah, tell him not to do anything stupid like get himself nicked, I'm going to need him around."

Dimes then rolled up the window and headed off down the street, headlights off because of the blackout order.

I watched as the car turned the corner. I realized I was breathing really quickly, and my hands were shaking. I was onto something. I didn't know what it was, but I was definitely onto something.

We didn't see Johnny for a week or so after Christmas. Johnny had a habit of disappearing for a few days at a time, but I think Mum had begun to worry. I had started to hope that he wouldn't be back or that he'd maybe got himself nicked. But then, in the second week of January, he showed up and I was ready to ask him some questions about Mr Dimes. I knew I'd have to be careful about it though. I'd been expecting some sort of payback after I'd challenged him over the newspaper, but it never came. That made me more nervous, if anything. Maybe he knew that. I also hadn't forgotten the run-in we'd had in the garden.

Mum hadn't long left for work and Mrs Green had come round to heat up our tea, when Johnny showed up. Vera was grumbling on about the fact that bacon, butter and sugar had just been rationed.

"How am I supposed to start the day right without a bacon sarnie and a couple of sugars in my tea?" she said. "Uncivilized is what it is."

"Suppose being at war is a bit uncivilized," I said.

"Yes, I suppose it is." She laughed and set a plate of egg and chips in front of each of us. "Make the most of it, boys. It won't be long before they'll be rationing everything."

Johnny appeared in the kitchen. He'd stopped knocking at the front door and started treating the place like his own a while back.

"Johnny!" Micky said, right happy to see him.

"Alright, son," Johnny said and rubbed Micky's head. "Your Mum not in?"

Micky shovelled a forkful of chips into his mouth. "At work. She's on lates this week."

"I'll see if I can drop by in the day tomorrow then." I thought that meant he'd be off, but he sat down at the table. "Any spare for me, Mrs Green?"

"Of course!" She cracked another egg in the frying pan, then grabbed a fistful of chips off mine and Micky's plates.

"Hey!" we both shouted.

"Behave," she said, "you've more than enough."

Johnny started shovelling our dinner down his neck while I angrily stabbed my chips with my fork.

"Where've you been?" Micky asked. "It's been ages since you came round."

"It's not been that long," Johnny said. "You know me. Busy grafting, that's all."

"A man came here looking for you after you left on Christmas day," I said.

"A Mr Dimes," Vera said. "Handsome fella he was, if I remember rightly."

I watched Johnny closely, trying to gauge his reaction.

"He'll be delighted when I tell him that," Johnny said, not looking at all concerned.

Vera hit him with a tea towel. "Don't you dare!"

"So, you're not in any trouble then?" I asked.

Johnny jabbed a chip into his egg yolk. "No, why would

you think that?"

"He told me to tell you to tread carefully – to try and not get yourself nicked."

An embarrassed smile seemed to freeze on Vera's face, like she didn't quite know how to react, and Micky gave me a look, like he was wondering what I was playing at. I kept my eyes fixed on Johnny. He finished off his mouthful, then shook his head and laughed. "That's Albert, always the joker. We go way back. Ran into him the other day actually."

Vera's face relaxed, then found its way into a frown for me. "Let the man eat in peace, Ronnie."

I ignored her. "He said he was planning something big."

"He's always planning something big. One of the best businessmen I know. Thrown a lot of work my way over the years." Johnny mopped up the last of the yolk with another chip then slapped his hands on his thighs. "Talking of work, I'd best be going. 'Ere Micky, walk us out, would you?"

Micky gulped down the last of his milk and said, "Course, Johnny," like some kind of lackey.

As they left, Mrs Green wittered on to me about life without bacon again, but I shushed her and put my ear to the door.

"What the heck are you up to, Ronnie Smith?" she said.

I turned round and hissed, "Trying to listen but it's a bit difficult with you harking on!"

She blustered on about my cheek and describing the various things she had a good mind to do to me, which meant that I could hear naff all of the conversation going on in the hall.

When Micky came back into the kitchen he had this strange air about him – like he was walking a little bit taller.

"What was all that about?" I asked.

"Nothing much, just chatting."

"Didn't sound like nothing."

Micky stared right at me and said, "Then there must be something wrong with your ears."

Later that night when Micky and I were in bed, I tried asking him what Johnny had said again.

"Told you, he didn't say nothing. Just asking how Mum is, that's all."

"Nothing to do with this big plan that Dimes bloke was on about?"

"No, what plan?"

I guessed he was lying, but there wasn't much I could do about it. If Micky wasn't going to tell the truth, I hadn't yet figured out a way to make him.

"Micky," I said. "If ever you get into any trouble, you have to promise to tell me about it."

"Why would I get into trouble?"

"I don't trust Johnny."

"You don't say. You've given him a hard time since he got here and all he's done is try and help us."

"He tried to turn you into a fascist."

"Sheesh, Ronnie. Give it a rest! He didn't! I can't believe

you're still going on about that."

"Look, if anything happens you need to tell me. I'm always here. Understand?"

"Blimey, Ronnie, what's with the deep and meaningfuls? You're not Dad."

"I know I'm not. But Dad's not around so I'm just saying remember that I am."

"You worry too much," he said, switching off his bedside light. "Everything's fine."

CHAPTER 11

I woke up the next morning to find that I was the only one in the house. Mum wasn't back from her shift at the hospital which wasn't unusual, and Micky wasn't in his bed, which was.

It's not like him to wake up before me. On the mornings Mum's not there to drag us out from under the covers, it's usually me that has to pull him out by the ankles. Still a bit sleepy, I padded down the stairs, you never know, a small miracle might have happened, and he could have been making breakfast for us.

He wasn't in the kitchen though. Our house isn't that big, so it didn't take me long to figure out that he wasn't at home. I started to worry immediately. Micky's not the sort to go off on his own. I didn't bother to change out of my pyjamas, just ran straight next door in my bare feet to see if he'd gone to Vera's.

She opened the door in her nightie and a cloud of cigarette smoke.

"What you banging on my door for at this ungodly hour?"

"You got our Micky in there?" I asked, peering round her and hopping from foot to foot on the cold paving slabs.

"Not with me, love. Why would you think that?"

"He's not at home," I said, the worry building up in me. "Don't know where he's got to. It's not like him to disappear without saying anything."

She grabbed her coat off the banister and stuffed her feet in her shoes. "Don't worry lad, I'm sure we'll find him."

We'd only got to the gate when Micky screeched to a halt on his bike in the road.

"Where the bleedin' heck have you been?" I shouted.

Micky shrugged, like nothing was wrong. "Fancied a ride on my bike."

"You what?" I said.

"You heard. Went out for a pedal, that's all."

"Went out for a pedal? Went out for a pedal?!" I couldn't believe my lugholes. "At this time?"

"It's no big deal. I'm back now."

"Did Johnny put you up to this?" I asked.

"Yeah, Johnny said, *Hey Micky I want you to go for a bike ride tomorrow morning.* Of course he didn't put me up to this. Couldn't sleep that's all... I was thinking about Dad."

The way he mentioned Dad, tacked on at the end like that, suggested to me that he'd come up with that excuse that second.

It worked on Vera though. "Oh, love. It ain't easy, is it? But you should have told someone you were going out. Ronnie was worried."

"He had no reason to be." Micky wheeled his bike past us, dropped it down on the front lawn and marched into the house.

I looked at Vera open-mouthed, but she just shrugged and said, "Mystery solved, now get back inside before you catch your death."

On the way to school, I tried to question Micky about his early morning bike ride some more, but he wasn't having any of it. He was clearly lying, and I knew it had something to do with the secret conversation he'd had in the hallway with Johnny.

When we got there, we stood in line in the playground while Mr Etherington addressed the school. There were fewer kids again. Most of those who'd come back for Christmas had returned to the countryside. But Arthur Davey and the others were true to their word and had stayed in Deptford. Apparently, Arthur's mum had tried to send him back a couple of times, but each time he'd done a runner back home from the train station. In the end, I think she gave up trying.

"It's just a weird thing to do – cycling that early. I know you're lying," I whispered to Micky as Etherington blathered on about the importance of moral fibre during times of adversity.

"Can you drop it?" he hissed back. "It was a one-off."

"No, I can't drop it, and I bet Mum won't either when I tell her."

Micky narrowed his eyes and was about to say something, but we suddenly became aware that Etherington had stopped mid-sentence. He was standing at the front of the class, nostrils flared as he eyeballed the rows of kids. "Who dares to speak over me?"

I looked at the floor, hoping he wouldn't spot me.

"It were Ronnie Smith, sir!" Arthur Davey shouted, a smug smile on his face which I could have cheerfully knocked right off him.

Lugs did a huge sigh and looked up at the sky like he was thinking, here we go again. Micky didn't look thrilled about the prospect of taking another caning on my behalf either. I couldn't let it happen, not again, but before I had a chance to speak, Mr Etherington said, "I see there is no honour amongst thieves, Mr Davey."

Arthur's brow crumpled in confusion. "Sorry, sir?"

"How quickly you give up your fellow student, Mr Davey." Mr Etherington clasped his hands behind his back and began walking through the rows of kids. "Let us hope that when our men are on the front line they do not cave as quickly as you."

"I...I don't follow, sir," Arthur stuttered.

"Moral integrity, Mr Davey!" Mr Etherington boomed. "Do you know what that means?"

Arthur's eyes flashed from Graham to Harry, but he wasn't going to get much help there. "No, sir."

"Courage to live by your principles! You will know it when you see it!"

Arthur didn't look any clearer.

"Moral integrity!" Etherington boomed again, and then let the words hang in the air for a minute or so. Kids were looking

93

at each other, not quite sure what was going on. I don't know who was more confused by what had just happened, me or Arthur Davey.

Etherington nodded to Miss Grimshaw, turned on his heel and headed inside.

Miss Grimshaw blew her whistle, then bellowed, "Everyone to class. No dawdling."

"Did Etherington just call Arthur out for snitching?" Lugs asked as we walked up the stone steps into the building.

"You know, I think he did," Micky said.

"I'll be blown," Lugs said.

Micky looked at me. "Seems even Etherington knows snitching is wrong."

"Alright," I said. "I'll keep my mouth shut. But no more early morning bike rides." To be honest, I'd already decided that I wasn't going to get rid of Johnny by telling Mum about Micky going out on his bike. I needed more on him than that. I'd have to be patient and, with that dodgy Mr Dimes fella showing up with warnings of being nicked, I felt like it would only be a matter of time before Johnny's secrets caught up with him.

Waiting was something that everybody seemed to be doing back then. For all the promise of war, to me, it seemed like it had never really got going. Sure, Germany had invaded Poland, but that was miles away. Still, people seemed to think it was going to happen at some point and by the end of February, even more kids had left for the countryside. I didn't get it myself – a single bomb was yet to fall on London.

It must have been troubling Mum, because one morning, after a long shift at the hospital, she sat us down at the kitchen table and tried to ask us if me and Micky wanted to go to the countryside too.

"They're saying Deptford, what with it being so close to the river, is an area of concern," she explained.

I could see what she was saying – there were loads of factories along the banks of the Thames. After Chamberlain had made his announcement back in September, more and more of them had switched over to making weapons for the war effort, and the Thames itself was like a big transportation artery for the city of London. Still, the threat of something that may or may not happen wasn't enough to make me want to leave.

"No chance," I said. "Who'll look after you and Mrs Green if we're not around?"

Mum smiled. "You make a very strong case and though it would be hard, I'm sure Mrs Green and I could muddle through without you."

"Why muddle when you don't have to?" I asked.

Micky clearly wasn't keen either. "Nothing down in the countryside for us, is there?"

We heard the front door open and a moment later Johnny swanned in to the kitchen.

"Hello, hello!" he said and planted a kiss on Mum's cheek.

He opened up the cupboard and helped himself to some biscuits. He leaned against the sink, stuffing his face and said, "What's going on here then?"

Micky said, "Mum's trying to ship us off to the countryside."

"I'm not trying to *ship them off,* I just think they'll be safer there."

Johnny took the last biscuit from the tin. "If the boys want to be with their mum, let them stay. It's not like they're young'uns is it? They'll be more useful round here."

At the time, I didn't know what he meant by useful, I was more annoyed that his words seemed to be working on Mum and mine and Micky's hadn't.

Mum took hold of Micky and my hands. "If you're sure."

"Yup, we're sure, aren't we Ronnie?"

"Yup," I said.

"Oh, I don't know," Mum said, but then before we could get into it all again, there was a knock at the door, and I got up to answer it. Johnny followed me.

It was Postie Stan.

"Wanted to deliver your post personally today as it will be my last round." He handed an envelope over to me and rolled his shoulders back like he was proud about something.

"I've enlisted and I'm heading off to training tomorrow."

"Is that so?" Johnny said. He sounded right interested, which I thought was odd.

Mum poked her head out the kitchen. "Oh, Mr Stanley," she said. "We will miss you."

"Anyone taken your route?" Johnny asked.

"Think the fella from the Blackheath round is going to cover it. Anyway, must be off."

Mum took hold of his hands. "Now you stay safe, you hear."

We headed back into the kitchen and Micky whipped the letter from my hands. He was all excited, but his face fell when he saw it wasn't from Dad. We hadn't heard from him for ages – his letters had dried up before Christmas. I tried not to think about him and what he might be doing. I'd heard RAF planes had been sent over to France ready to help out if the Germans invaded. Maybe he was there.

Mum fixed us all some breakfast, then she headed upstairs to bed.

Johnny drummed on the table with his hands and said, "Right, I'm off to see a man about a dog. You boys want to join me?"

"Nah, you're alright," I said. "Got school."

"Micky, you coming?"

"He's got school too," I said quickly.

Micky looked uncertain.

"One day off isn't going to kill you, son."

Micky's eyes fell on the letter. Then he looked at Johnny and nodded. "I'll get my coat."

I proper glared at him, slung my gas mask over my shoulder and stomped off on my own.

*　　*　　*

When I got home that evening, ready to tell Mum that Micky hadn't gone to school, Johnny and Micky were already back, and she already knew everything about it. They were all in the front room, Johnny was reading the paper, Mum was reading a book and Micky was lying on the floor reading a comic. Like some happy family.

"You're not angry," I said, annoyance and disbelief rising in me.

"You need to lighten up a bit," Johnny said from behind the paper.

Mum laid the book in her lap. "I wasn't happy, but Johnny explained why and assured me it won't happen again."

"Got myself a job," Micky piped up.

"You what?" I said.

"Johnny's taken on a part of Mr Stanley's post round and I've agreed to let Micky help as long as it's not during school time," Mum explained.

I couldn't think why Johnny wanted to take over the post round. Seemed to me he was busy enough. He must have some reason for wanting to do it though, and probably not a good one.

"Going to pay me three shillings a week," Micky said proudly.

"Right," I said, and stomped off to our room. Johnny was getting his hooks deeper and deeper into my brother, and I was determined to do something about it. I still didn't know what, but I was going to figure it out.

CHAPTER 12

I began to see less and less of Micky over the next few weeks. Every day after school and sometimes on a weekend, he'd go off on his bike doing his post round. He was right pleased with himself now he was earning a bit of cash. He bought Mum some peppermint creams, her favourite. He also bought me and Lugs some pear drops. I ate them, but they stuck in my throat. I had a hunch that what Micky was doing was less than legal, that his deliveries were somehow to do with Johnny being a fascist or a crook, or both. Whatever it was, he and Johnny had Mum fooled and me grasping in the dark for explanations.

Lugs and I were kicking a ball out on the road when he went off one Sunday midway through March.

"Who gets post on a Sunday?" Lugs said, as Micky wheeled his bike past us.

Micky brushed it off. "Too many letters and not enough posties."

"You don't want to stay for a kick about?" Lugs asked.

Micky pushed down on his pedal and called back at us,

"You two play, I've got work to do."

Lugs raised his eyebrows at me. I knew what he was thinking. There was something different about our Mick. He seemed more self-assured, he'd even started walking with a bit of a swagger and I didn't like it one bit.

I didn't really know just how much he'd changed until the next Monday when we had a run in with Arthur, Graham and Harry.

They were waiting for us after school. We'd been expecting it. Lugs had won some marbles off them at playtime, and they were there to see that he handed them back.

"You're a cheat," Arthur called at us as we walked out the school gates.

"He won those fair and square," I said.

"You'll give me back what's mine, Billy Missell!" Arthur shouted back.

I weren't in the mood for a run-in, so I said to Lugs and Micky quietly, "Just ignore them and keep walking."

"Coward, are you, Missell?" Arthur continued. "Just like your old man."

Graham sniggered and Harry said, "Yeah, just like your old man."

It was Micky who reacted first. He stopped and swung round. "He ain't no coward and neither is his dad, he's missing a liver, that's all!"

"Kidney," I whispered.

"Kidney! He's missing a kidney!"

"It's okay, Micky. Leave it. They're only marbles." Lugs turned round, reached into his pocket and pulled out the marbles he'd won. "Have them, if you want them so much."

"That were easy," Arthur said walking over to take them.

"Yeah," Harry said. "Real easy."

Just as Arthur reached out to take them, Micky pulled out the penknife that Johnny had given him for Christmas, flicked open the blade and said, "I'd think twice before doing that if I were you."

Arthur's hand froze in mid-air. Lugs and I looked at each other, both in shock. I couldn't believe what I was seeing. I had to blink a couple of times to make sure I wasn't imagining it.

Harry said, "Hells bells is that a knife?"

Micky said, "No, it's a trombone."

Harry said, "That ain't no flippin' trombone! It's a knife!"

Micky moved the blade towards Arthur. "Still want those marbles?"

"Micky, what are you playing at?" I said, but he ignored me, all his focus on Arthur.

Arthur looked from the marbles back to the penknife then back at Micky.

"If you want them, take them," Micky goaded. "Go on, I dare you."

Panic flashed across Arthur's face. He looked at Micky, then at me, then he turned and ran.

"Yeah, thought so," Micky called after him.

"You're a bleedin' lunatic you are!" Arthur shouted back.

Micky put the penknife back in his pocket and laughed. "Did you see his face! Quaking he was!"

I didn't say anything. If I hadn't been there, I would never have believed it had happened. Our Micky, threatening someone with a knife? It just wasn't like him. I'd thought people couldn't change, but looking at Micky, I knew I'd been wrong about that.

Lugs said, "You shouldn't have done that, Mick."

Micky frowned but the smile didn't leave his lips. "Didn't get your marbles though, did he?"

"Yeah, but I mean, a knife – bit much weren't it?" Lugs said. "They're only marbles."

"Sometimes you just have to show people who's boss." Micky headed off down the road, walking with a swagger and whistling.

He looked just like Johnny Simmons.

Seeing Micky like that, I knew two things for certain. The first was that there was more to Micky's post round than just delivering letters. And second, that I had to put a stop to it.

CHAPTER 13

Mum was getting ready for work when we got home from school. I thought about telling her about the knife incident, but I knew Micky would only deny it, and I didn't want to push him further away from me by snitching.

Vera had come round to fix our supper. She was in a right mood.

"Barely over a shilling's worth!" she said, plonking down two pork chops on the table. "That's all you get for a week! I'll waste away before the Nazis get me!"

More and more foodstuffs were being rationed, but Johnny always seemed to be able to get his hands on stuff if we really needed it. Instead of flowers and chocolates, whenever Johnny dropped by, he'd always bring us sausages or chicken thighs or tongue, which was a lot more than most folks were getting. He didn't say where he'd got it all from and nobody asked.

"We'll just have to be inventive, Mrs Green," Mum said. "There's a lot you can do with vegetables. You keep those chops for yourself. There's some tripe and cabbage the boys can have."

I groaned.

"You'll eat it and you'll be grateful," Mum said and packed off to work.

It took me a while to get to sleep that night. The cabbage and tripe weren't settling in my stomach despite Vera having boiled 'em to death, but that wasn't what was keeping me awake. I couldn't stop thinking about what Micky had done. I'd made him promise that he'd leave his penknife at home in future, like Mum had asked. I told him if he didn't, I'd tell her what he'd done. He'd agreed, but it came too easily, and I didn't believe him.

It must have been well after midnight when I was woken up by noises in the room. Micky was out of his bed, it was hard to see, what with the windows blacked out, but it looked like he was getting dressed. I was going to ask him what the heck he was up to, but I decided not to. I wouldn't get an honest answer – it would be better to find out for myself, so I stayed quiet.

I watched as he put on a jumper and some trousers over his pyjamas, then tiptoed over to his bed. He lifted up his mattress, pulled out something from underneath it and stuck it in his waistband, then crept out the door.

"What are you up to, Mick?" I whispered to the empty room, knowing instinctively it was something to do with Johnny.

The front door opened and closed quietly. I scrambled out of bed and rushed downstairs after Micky. I flung open the front door and saw him cycling off down the street. I took up chase, my bare feet pounding the concrete. I got all the way to the end of Heald Street before I lost him. I stood at the T-junction wondering which way to go, but knowing it was pointless – Micky was long gone. I walked home with visions of Micky getting up to all sorts in my head.

When I got inside, I headed straight for our room and turned on the light. I walked over to Micky's bed and flipped the mattress. On the floor, underneath the bed slats, was a jar of coins. I tipped them onto the floor and counted five pounds, six shillings and four half crowns. I'd never seen so much money. There was no way he'd got that all from his post round – he could have paid for a hundred cinema tickets with that kind of cash. A feeling of uneasiness swelled in me.

There was a piece of paper under the bed too. I picked it up and unfolded it. On the top, in typed writing it said, Certificate of Exemption on Medical Grounds. My heart thudded double time. The certificate looked official, was signed by a doctor and everything – a Doctor Arnold.

I don't know how long I stood there trying to take it all in and piece it all together. I reckoned some men would be willing to pay handsomely for a certificate that could get them out of joining the army. And I also reckoned that Micky was earning himself a fortune supplying them. Doing that sort of thing could land him in a whole lot of trouble with the law.

I looked at the certificate again. "How on earth have you got your hands on this, Mick?"

But I knew there was only one answer.

CHAPTER 14

When Micky got back, about an hour later, I was waiting for him on his bed with the jar of money, the certificate in my hand and a whole load of words ready to explode from my mouth. He jumped when he saw me. For a split second, he looked guilty, but his expression was quickly replaced by one of annoyance.

"What are you doing sitting on my bed in the middle of the night? You almost gave me a heart attack."

"What am *I* doing? You're kidding right?" I said.

"Don't start, Ron," he said. "I'm tired and it's late."

"I don't believe this!" I said. "You disappear in the middle of the night, and I find this stuff under your bed and you're acting like nothing has happened – that I'm the one in the wrong."

"Nothing *has* happened," he said.

"Then where've you been?"

"Out and about." He sat down on the bed next to me and pulled off his socks.

"Micky, tell me, please. First the penknife, now this. Tell me what's going on, or I'll tell Mum. I'll tell her everything."

"Didn't think you were a snitch, Ronnie."

"I don't care if I am! I'm worried about you! Micky, you're my little brother, we stick together, remember?"

He sighed. "Fine, I'll tell you and it really isn't anything bad."

"Clearly this post round you've got isn't a real post round."

"It is, ask anybody on the street! I've just been doing some favours for Johnny, that's all. He needed someone he could trust."

I held up the certificate. "Favours involving this?"

"Yeah, all I'm doing is delivering them. There's nothing dodgy about it. Johnny helps out a few doctors, getting certificates to men who aren't fit to fight. You know what the post can be like. If anything, what I'm doing is a good thing."

"So why the secrecy? Why at night?"

"People aren't always in during the day. And it's not just at night, I deliver in the mornings too."

"Why can't Johnny do it?"

"He's busy and also no one's going to jump a kid, are they? Johnny reckons there are some bad sorts who would be after certificates like that one."

I turned the paper over in my hands, sceptical. "So, you're telling me this is genuine, then? This Thomas Rose of number 35, Shooters Hill really only has one eye?"

"I guess. Haven't delivered it yet, have I?" Micky pulled off his jumper. "Johnny pays well."

"I've seen. Pay's usually good if you're up to something dodgy. You're going to get yourself into trouble."

"Ronnie, you worry too much. What trouble can I get into delivering letters? Just think of it as a better paid paper round. If you want, I could find out if you could work for him too?"

I thought about the conversation we'd had building the shelter. How he'd said he'd have me working for him. Whether he'd planned this from the start. "I'd never work for him, and I don't think you should either."

"I don't care what you think," Micky said and kicked me off his bed so he could put the jar and the certificate back under the mattress.

"Then maybe you'll care what Mum thinks," I said.

"Fine. Tell her. Johnny will back me. Turn off the light, Ron. I need some sleep."

Head raging, I did as he asked, then climbed back under my covers.

I didn't say anything else. I was so cross – he was acting like what he was doing was nothing, but I didn't believe a word of it. There was no doubt in my mind that Johnny had Micky working outside of the law. Surely, certificates weren't delivered by schoolboys. I thought about everything I knew about Johnny – how he managed to get stuff that should be rationed, that warning from Mr Dimes about treading carefully and now the certificates, it was only pointing in one direction – Johnny was a criminal.

"Tell you what," he said. "Tomorrow, I'll get us some more

sweets with my earnings, maybe some sherbet lemons, would you like that, Ron?"

I said, "You're alright, Micky. Don't think I could swallow them."

I couldn't figure out what was bothering me most, that Micky was working for Johnny or that, all of a sudden, I felt like the younger brother.

Whichever it was, I knew I had to get Micky off that post round. I was going to show Mum the exemption certificate first thing in the morning.

CHAPTER 15

Micky wasn't there when I woke up. I checked under his mattress and the certificate and his stash of money were gone. I kicked the bed, annoyed that I'd lost the evidence. I heard laughing coming from downstairs. It was Mum and Johnny, and the sound of it annoyed me so much that I decided to hell with it, I was going to tell her even if he was there.

I burst through the kitchen door so hard it bounced on its hinges.

"Ooh, someone isn't a morning person," Johnny said.

I didn't even look at him – didn't want to lose my nerve. "Mum, I need to tell you something. Something important about Johnny and our Micky."

Mum turned round from the sink. "What is it, love?"

"Yeah, what is it?" Johnny said – that fake concern back in his voice. "If there's something troubling you again, let's hear it." He raised one eyebrow, daring me to go on – he knew what I was going to say. I realized Micky must have warned him.

I took a breath and blurted it out anyway. I couldn't see him wriggling out of this one. "Micky went out late last night on his bike."

"I know," Mum said. "He told me already and we have already had words with him about that."

I was stunned – on the back foot – but I wasn't going to give up. "But did he tell you what he was delivering? He's delivering *exemption certificates*, Mum. Selling them on and making a packet!"

I expected that to land like a bomb, but it didn't.

"I know, he showed me, and Johnny explained."

"Course he did," I snapped.

Johnny leaned forward. "Ronnie, your brother is helping out. We're not selling them – we're being paid for doing a job. I know he shouldn't do it at night, but there are men who need those certificates."

"Fake certificates you mean? 'Cos I don't know why Micky would have earned five quid if what he was doing was legal."

"Five quid!" Johnny laughed coldly. "The lad's paid a couple of shillings a week a best!"

"That ain't true! I know what I saw! He's a liar. I bet there isn't even a Dr Arnold."

Johnny suddenly leaped to his feet, knocking his chair over. It made me jump – Mum and Micky too. Johnny leaned over the table, his face red, eyes wild with rage, and jabbed his finger at me. "You need to watch what you're saying about me!"

"And you need to get out of my house!" I yelled back, sounding braver than I felt.

"Stop it! Just stop it! Both of you!!" Mum cried.

I stared Johnny down, my chest heaving, wanting him to hit me, so Mum could see who he really was. But I think he knew that, because he dropped his finger and, smoothing his shirt, he sat back down.

"Sorry, Cathy, I shouldn't have reacted like that."

I was still glaring at him, my breathing loud in my ears. Mum put her hand on my arm. "Ronnie, you need to calm down. I don't know what you think you saw, but I do know there is a Dr Arnold. He works at the hospital."

"I've been working with him to get the certificates to people who need them," Johnny added, the shadow of a smile on his lips.

That threw me for a second – made me doubt myself.

"This Dr Arnold has to be bent too then!" I said, desperate to make Mum see what was happening.

"Ronnie, enough!" Mum said. "I've known Dr Arnold for years. He's an upstanding pillar of the community and I will not have you saying bad things about him. Now I know you're looking out for your brother, but you cannot keep making unfounded accusations about people. We need to band together at times like these!"

I looked from Mum to Johnny, the desperation in me unravelling into resignation.

"So that's it then?"

"Yes," Johnny said, holding my gaze. "That's it."

"Do you want some breakfast?" Mum asked, but I was already storming out of the kitchen.

I made my way over to Lugs's, wanting to rant to him about what had happened. I was chuntering away to myself about the injustice of it all and I must have been blind with anger, because I almost walked straight past him. As it happened, Lugs was heading over to mine.

"What's up with you?" he asked.

We sat on the pavement, and I told him everything – about the post round and the money, the medical exemption certificate.

"This Dr Arnold has to be in on it too," Lugs said.

"That's what I said! But Mum reckons he's the good sort."

"Where did you say that one-eyed fella lives?"

"Up on Shooters Hill."

"Reckon we should go and pay him a little visit. That way we'll know for sure if Johnny's pulling a fast one."

"That is an excellent idea," I said, jumping to my feet.

It took us an hour and a half to walk to Thomas Rose's gaff. The whole way I was convinced that we'd turn up, see him with two perfectly functional eyeballs and I'd be able to go back to Mum and tell her that Johnny had been lying to her. I'd drag Mr Rose back with me if I had to.

When we reached number 35 Shooters Hill – a small, terraced house with a front door that opened right out onto the pavement – Lugs said, "So how we going to do this? Should we find some spot to hide and spy?"

"Nope," I said and knocked on the door. I didn't want to wait around. The sooner I had the proof I was right, the sooner I could rid my family of Johnny Simmons.

Lugs shrugged. "Fair enough, the direct approach could work too."

A couple of seconds later the door swung open and there standing in the doorway, was a man in a filthy white vest, brown trousers and an eyepatch on his right eye.

"What?" he barked.

I didn't say anything. I was too stunned. I'd been so sure I was right.

"What do you want?" he repeated.

Thankfully, Lugs spoke because I still couldn't find my voice. "Are you Thomas Rose?"

"I am, who wants to know?"

"And you have just the one eye, do you?" Lugs said tentatively.

"You knock on my door to ask me that?" he growled, his one visible eyebrow lowering.

"Pretty much," Lugs said, then grabbed my arm and we raced off down the road as Thomas Rose shouted after us threatening to tan our backsides.

When we were far enough away, we slowed to a walk. I felt a bit sick. I booted a stone down the road. "I was sure I was right," I said.

"I dunno what to say," Lugs said.

"I still reckon Johnny's up to something. Even if he's not

selling on dodgy medical certificates, I'd bet both my legs he's a fascist. No way that newspaper accidentally ended up in Micky's comic, and all that stuff he said to me about the war being a Jew's quarrel." The words rushed out of me, hot and angry.

"You need to be careful," Lugs said. "You don't want to get yourself on the wrong side of someone like him."

I sighed. "Think it's a bit late for that."

CHAPTER 16

Over the next few months, Micky continued with his post round. His "patch" – that's what he called it – had grown and so too had the space between us. Sometimes he'd head up into the city or out west to make his deliveries. I tried to follow him a few times, but I couldn't keep up with him on foot. I kept my ear out whenever he and Johnny were talking, but Johnny knew better than to say anything incriminating round ours. Whenever I had a chance, I checked under Micky's bed, hoping to find evidence that he was up to something bad, but he never put anything back under there again. I had nothing on them, at least nothing that would convince Mum, and Johnny and Mick were doing a good job of keeping it that way.

Mum was fine with him making his deliveries as long as he wasn't missing school. He did, but I couldn't say anything about that, because I was skipping school too. I could see how that would play out – Micky would tell her he was doing it for a good cause, and me, well, I was doing it because I just didn't want to be there.

See, Lugs and I had become big on plane spotting. We'd take off up to Blackheath hoping to see Hurricanes and Spitfires, Blenheims and Tiger Moths and the occasional Avro Anson, on training missions or making their way across the sea to Europe. We got good at identifying them – Spitfires with their elliptical wings, Hurricanes with a deeper body than the Spitfire, the Tiger Moths with their open cockpits, Blenheims with two engines and a long blunt nose and the Avro Ansons with their bulky fuselage and low set wings.

"Go on, give the Hun hell!" we'd yell at the tops of our lungs. Sometimes, we'd chase them down the street. Other times, we'd just stand there and gawp. It was an incredible feeling, looking up at the sky as they passed over. There were times they flew low, and you could hear the rumble of a bomber's engine so clearly it almost felt like it was coming from inside your bones. More often, they'd be further off in the distance. They almost looked like starlings then.

It was the Hurricanes I liked best. I'd often wonder if Dad was flying one of them. If he was looking down at me at the same time I was looking up. I'd always watch the Hurricanes until they disappeared out of sight. When the distance between us became as big as the sky.

It was late Spring when I first felt the war finally closing in on us. Winston Churchill had been made Prime Minister in May, and it felt like there'd been a shift when he'd taken charge.

Don't think there was a person in Britain who hadn't listened to the first speech he made on the wireless. The Germans were storming through France, but Churchill said we would stand side by side with the French and wage war until victory was done. Mum and Vera listened, all glassy-eyed, cups of tea untouched in their laps, unspoken fear thickening the air, as our new PM talked about the struggle for right and honour, life and freedom. *Conquer we must, and conquer we shall*, he'd said, and I knew he was talking about Hitler and the German army, but all I could think about was Johnny.

One day, right at the end of May, a Wednesday, I think, Lugs and I skipped school again and went down to the Thames. We'd heard that the river was full of boats heading off to Dunkirk and we wanted to go take a look. Allied troops had got trapped in France, the German army was giving them a bit of a pasting on all accounts, and we'd sent a load of boats over to bring our boys back.

We watched all manner of vessel – from ships right down to little fishing boats and barges – head off along the Thames, it were quite the spectacle. Lugs and I waved at the captains and cheered when they sounded their foghorns. I kept thinking that Micky were mad to miss it. He was too busy – working apparently.

When Lugs and I had grown hungry, we decided to go back to mine. Mum was at work and there was a half a potato pie left over with our names on it. As we walked down Watergate Road back from the river, Lugs let out a low whistle.

"Look at that motor, Ron!"

Parked on the side of the road was a Rolls Royce. The very same one I'd seen on Christmas Day. My heart did a heavy thud in my chest when I clocked who was standing next to it, his bike balanced between his legs.

"Is that *Micky*?" Lugs said. "Who does he know with wheels like that?"

"That Mr Dimes I told you about."

An arm came out of the window holding a large brown envelope. Micky took it, stuck it down the back of his trousers and tore off.

"What do you think he's up to?" Lugs said.

I watched my brother disappear round the corner, a weight in my stomach as I remembered Dimes talk of a *big job*. "Something for Johnny."

That evening, when we were brushing our teeth, I confronted Micky about what we'd seen. He said, with an air of superiority, "It's *top secret*, Ronnie."

I spat some foam into the sink. Looked at my brother's reflection in the mirror. "So, you don't know then?"

"Johnny says it's something that's going help us. Something to do with the war effort."

I tried not to sound too sceptical, because I wanted Mick to talk. "Like what?"

"I dunno, do I? It's *top secret*." Micky stuck his toothbrush in

119

his mouth and spoke as he brushed. "But Johnny's got friends in high places."

"Like that Mr Dimes?"

I let his name hang in the air, waiting for Micky to react, but he gobbed a load of toothpaste into the sink and shrugged like it was no big deal. "Him and others. Johnny wants to do his bit to help any way he can." Micky ran his toothbrush under the tap, then threw it in the holder. It clinked the china – a bell marking the end of our conversation.

"Yeah, Johnny's a regular saint," I said after Micky had left. What could a fascist like Johnny possibly be doing to help the war effort? Whose side was he even helping?

On a Friday, a week or so later, on one of the days we'd actually gone to school, my worries about what Micky was mixed up in got bigger. Johnny showed up at the gate with Micky's bike and a bag. It was larger than the one Micky usually carried, and I reckoned my brother had definitely moved on from the exemption certificates.

Lugs bellowed over to them. "'Ere, what you got in the bag, Micky?"

"He's taking medicine round to some old folk, if you must know," Johnny yelled back. He gave Micky a nudge. "Helping the elderly, ain't that right?"

"Yeah, that's right," Micky said.

I didn't believe a word of it.

120

Johnny clapped his hands together. "Right, as scintillating as this conversation is, we've got things to do."

"You reckon they're up to something?" Lugs said as we watched them head off down the road, Micky pushing his bike.

"Yeah, I do." I grabbed Lugs's arm, realizing this may be my chance to find out what they were up to. "Let's follow them."

Lugs shrugged. "Sure, why not?"

We waited a bit, so they were far enough away not to notice, then started after them.

We hung back, ducking behind walls and fences if we thought they were going to turn round, which, fortunately, they never did. It was kind of exhilarating tailing them like that.

"Bit like spies aren't we, Ron?" Lugs said as we jumped into someone's garden and peered over the wall.

From there, we watched as Johnny carried on up Evelyn Street and Micky steered right and teared off down Grove Street.

"Who do we follow?" Lugs asked.

"Johnny, we won't catch up with Micky on his bike."

We followed Johnny all the way to the Chichester Arms.

"What do we do now?" Lugs said. Two kids couldn't exactly stroll into a pub unnoticed.

The windows were blacked out, but I spotted one where the blackout paper was peeling away from the glass. I pointed at it. "Let me get on your shoulders."

Lugs ducked down and I climbed on. It took him a while to straighten up.

"'Ere what you been eating, bricks?" he said as he staggered all over the pavement.

"Where you goin'? The window's that way!" I said as he stumbled into the road.

Eventually, he got me to where I needed to be, and I climbed up him, so I was standing on his shoulders, and I peered in through the gap.

"What can you see?"

I scanned the room and to start with, I couldn't spot Johnny anywhere. "A few blokes, all wearing black shirts. Some playing darts, some drinking."

Lugs wobbled underneath me. "Black shirts? Ronnie, I think we should go.

"Hang on...he looks familiar!" I said.

"Who?"

It took me a moment to figure out where I knew him from. "You're not going to believe this!"

"What?" Lugs hissed.

"It's that Thomas Rose and he looks like he's got two functioning eyes to me!"

"You sure?"

"He ain't wearing an eyepatch and he's just scored a treble twenty with one dart, so I'd say pretty sure."

"You're kidding!"

"I'm bleedin' not! I knew it was a scam! Wait! I see Johnny. He's with some big fella sitting in the corner."

"What they doing?"

"Having a pint."

"Can I let you down? I want to get out of here."

"Just a minute. I want to see who he's with." I pressed my nose to the glass, trying to get closer, willing the guy to show his face.

But then Johnny looked up, directly at me.

The shock of it caused me to leap back, which caused Lugs to stagger backwards, then forwards and slam me into the glass. It wasn't pleasant at the time, but lucky he did because I just had time to see the big fella turn round.

It was that Mr Dimes again.

Having slammed me into the window, Lugs sort of crumpled beneath me and we both ended up in a heap on the floor.

I jumped up quick and pulled Lugs to his feet. "Run! I think he saw me!"

CHAPTER 17

We didn't stop running until we got back to Lugs's place and collapsed on the pavement outside his, trying to catch our breath. Lugs lives a couple of roads down from ours in a two-up, two-down with a small garden, the back of which was taken up mostly by the Anderson shelter. It was too small for a shelter really. Most people on his street went to the public one under Burton's clothes shop on the high street. But Lugs's mum had said that if she was going to be blown up, she wouldn't be dug out from under a pile of men's underpants.

I was buzzing with excitement at the discovery that I'd been right about Thomas Rose and his faked medical exemption certificate. I thumped my hand into my fist. "I knew it! Didn't I tell you!"

I looked at Lugs expecting similar enthusiasm, but he looked awful. Even though we'd been running all the colour had drained from his face.

"You alright?" I asked.

"You said there were guys in the pub wearing black shirts," Lugs said quietly.

"Yeah, some of them, I think. It was a bit gloomy, hard to tell. Why?"

"*Blackshirts*, Ronnie!" Lugs said and I suddenly realized what he was getting at. I'd read about the Blackshirts in the paper just the week before but hadn't put it together when Lugs had said that name at the pub. The headline had caught my eye because it mentioned Oswald Mosley. What with him being a fascist and a Nazi sympathizer, Churchill reckoned Mosley and his Blackshirt lot were a security risk as they wanted the Germans to win the war. A bunch of them had been imprisoned to stop them helping out Hitler. The article had gone on to say that the support for fascism was on a steep decline, although, I now realized, it was still simmering away in a pub in Deptford.

"Blackshirts are fascists," I said.

Lugs swallowed, then nodded. "I thought they'd been banned, but I reckon we might have been spying on one of their meetings."

"Strike a light, Lugs! Should we tell someone?"

"Who?"

"I dunno. Your dad?"

He laughed, but it was a sad kind of laugh. "You think my dad can stop the BUF?" He looked down at the ground. "I don't want to get him involved – it would be too dangerous – they hate people like us, Ron."

I realized then how big of an ask it was and that it had been wrong of me to suggest it. "'Course. Sorry."

Lugs nudged me, gave a weak smile. "Besides, he wouldn't be happy to find out I'd been hanging out at the Chichester Arms. But maybe you should tell your mum. You don't want Micky mixed up with that lot."

I thought about it, played it all out in my head. "Johnny will either deny it, or say he was minding his business having a pint and didn't realize he was surrounded by a load of fascists." The weight of another realization hit me. "And if I tell her about Thomas Rose, Johnny will probably say it was a case of mistaken identity. All I've got is my words. I need actual proof if she's going to believe me, or he'll talk his way out of it."

"You could go to the police?"

"That could end up with Micky in trouble. He'd never forgive me for that."

"I dunno what to suggest," Lugs said.

I didn't either. I mulled it over in my head, trying to come up with a plan, but I couldn't think of anything Johnny couldn't squirm his way out of or that wouldn't land Micky in trouble.

"Do you think Johnny saw us?" Lugs said, breaking the silence.

"I dunno, maybe."

"So that Mr Dimes character is the one we saw with the Rolls – the bloke who turned up at yours at Christmas?"

"Yup, he showed up to tell Johnny to keep out of trouble."

Lugs sat up. "Hey, do you think that's why he's got Mick

doing these dodgy deliveries – so he doesn't have to?"

"You could be right there. He said he was working on something big."

"And if he's a fascist too…" Lugs trailed off.

"Yeah, I know. I haven't a clue what's going on, but whatever it is, it ain't good." I sighed, wondering where Micky was – what he was doing, what trouble he could be getting himself into. I covered my face with my hands. I'd really thought I finally had Johnny, but all I'd done was confirm what I suspected. It wasn't enough to convince anybody else.

"Let's go inside," Lugs said. "I'll show you a trick I'm trying to teach Tiger."

I took my hands away and frowned. "Can cats do tricks?"

"At the moment, my answer to that question is no, but I'm optimistic that Tiger will be the first."

When we got inside, Lugs's dad was sitting in his armchair, staring at the wall, with what looked like a letter in his lap.

He smiled when he saw us, but he had this far-off look in his eye. "Billy, Ronnie, come sit with me. Tell me, how was your day?"

I couldn't ever remember a time when my dad had asked me to sit with him, or about my day.

"It was fine," Lugs said leaving out the part about us spying on a pub full of Blackshirts. "You alright, Dad? Just you don't look that happy."

Lugs's question turned out to be an invitation to his dad to drone on about the wrongs of war. He talked on and on about the devastating loss of life in Europe. The futility of it all.

"France can't hold on much longer. The Battle of Britain is coming, Churchill says so himself. May God help us." He sniffed so hard that his nostrils flared. Then, he closed his eyes and sat completely still.

Lugs and I just stood there awkwardly, waiting for him to say something else. But he didn't, so we just snuck outside to the shelter.

"Blimey, Lugs, your old man's a bit doom and gloom, isn't he? From what I've heard, Dunkirk was a victory. All them boats we sent over to get our boys back from them French beaches – unbeatable, that's what the paper said."

"I know. Imagine living with him."

Tiger strolled in, and Lugs bent down and scooped him up.

"He's a proper softy now," Lugs said as Tiger fought to get free. Lugs gave him a kiss on the head and got a scratch on the cheek back. He didn't seem to notice though. Think he'd got used to it.

"Yeah, seems real soft," I said.

"Told you that all he needed was a little bit of loving."

"Let's see this trick then."

Lugs held Tiger on his lap and said, "Tiger, paw."

I didn't think a cat could give someone a look that said *naff off*, but Tiger managed it.

Lugs tried a few more times before he gave up and said, "It's a work in progress."

"I'll say," I said.

A rat scurried past the shelter entrance. Lugs quickly put

Tiger on the ground. "Go on! Get it, Tiger! Have the blighter!" But Tiger just sat down and started cleaning himself.

"He's a pacifist, like your old man," I said

Lugs rolled his eyes. "Can you blinkin' believe it."

That evening, Mrs Missell insisted on giving me my tea. She lit some candles and said a blessing in Hebrew over them, and Mr Missell blessed the bread and some raisins in water. I asked if they did that for every meal, and Lugs's mum said they only really did it on Fridays and Mr Missell told me he'd usually say a blessing over some wine too, but they didn't have any, what with there being a war on. Hence the raisins.

"We're not really a religious family," Mr Missell said. "We only started doing the blessings after war was declared. I guess some things make you reach for your faith." He squeezed Mrs Missell's hands. "And we are lucky that here, we are able to."

I wasn't completely sure what he was talking about, so I nodded and smiled. Then we tucked into cabbage, potatoes and liver, followed by something she said was a mock banana but that tasted like parsnip with a tiny bit of sugar. It wasn't horrible, but it wasn't a banana by any stretch of the imagination.

It was halfway through this questionable pudding that Mr Missell made a sudden announcement. It kind of came out of nowhere but, thinking about it, he'd probably been trying to find a way to say it all evening. He'd been quiet and hadn't really touched his food. I'd put it down to it being pretty inedible, but it was clearly down to something else.

He dropped his spoon, and it clattered against his bowl.

Mrs Missell said, "Frank, whatever is the matter?"

I thought, I know what's the matter, this ruddy parsnip-banana.

Mr Missell looked his wife in the eyes and kept his gaze steady. "I've been conscripted. I leave next week."

"But the tribunal..." Mrs Missell said. "I...I thought you'd explained your reasons."

"I shall serve in a non-combat role. A stretcher bearer or some such. It is either that or prison, Elsie. I have been told I must go, so go I must. A stretcher...that I can bear. It is arms that I won't."

Mrs Missell started crying. I didn't really know where to look. I was about to have my last mouthful of suspicious banana when Mr Missell had made his announcement. In the circumstances, I didn't know whether I should eat it or put it down. So, I just held it there, hovering in the air.

Eventually, I put the spoon down and said that I'd best be heading home. It didn't feel right to be intruding on family matters. I quickly thanked Mrs Missell for the food and left fairly smartish. Lugs saw me out. I couldn't really read the expression on his face. He opened the front door for me and handed me my gas mask. "See you, Ronnie."

"See you, Lugs."

I started off down the road, then stopped and turned round. He was still there, watching me from the doorstep. "You're okay, aren't you, Lugs?"

He shrugged. "Yeah, I'm okay. Is what it is, ain't it?"

I stuffed my hands in my pocket. "Yup, it is what it is."

"At least I can look Arthur Davey in the eye now."

"You sure can."

I thought about going over and giving him a hug, but that just wasn't something we did. Instead, I stuffed my hands in my pockets. "Right, best be off."

Lugs nodded.

I only went a couple of steps before I stopped and turned round again.

"You know, I meant to say earlier that I think there was one time, back in the shelter, when Tiger lifted his paw when you asked. Ever so slightly, but I think he did."

"Yeah?" Lugs's face lit up. "You think?"

"Yeah, definitely."

Lugs smiled, then said quietly, "Thanks, Ronnie."

I gave him a nod, then started the walk home. As my feet pounded the pavement, I couldn't stop thinking about Mr Missell. I would never have told Lugs this, but before that evening, I'd thought of his dad as a coward.

But I was wrong about that.

Mr Etherington said we'd know moral integrity when we saw it.

It was courageous to march onto a battlefield with a gun in your hands, but treading that ground without one, I realized, was even braver.

CHAPTER 18

When I got home, I paused on the doorstep and listened out for Johnny's voice. Trying to work out what I was walking into was something I used to do when Dad was still around.

I opened the door, the house was quiet, and relief washed over me when I saw that Mum was on her own in the sitting room. She was asleep in the armchair. For a moment, I thought about waking her up, telling her everything, but instead, I covered her up with a blanket, gave her a kiss and went upstairs.

Micky was reading a comic on his bed, but he shut it as soon as I walked in.

"Got a message for you from Johnny." His voice sounded strange, not like his, colder.

I sat down on my bed, pulled off a shoe and tried not to sound worried. "Go on."

"He says if he catches you following him again, he'll break your legs."

I dropped the shoe on the floor. I couldn't believe the words that were coming out of my brother's mouth. "Break my legs? Micky, can you hear yourself?"

"He doesn't mean he'll *actually* break your legs."

"You sure about that?"

"It's not right, Ronnie, spying on another man's business. All he's doing is helping this family and you're treating him like some kind of criminal!"

"I saw that Thomas Rose, and you know what? He's got two perfectly good eyeballs. Johnny's a criminal, Mick and he's trying to turn you into one too!"

"Thomas who? What are you talking about? I'm helping Johnny delivering things to people who need them, that's all."

"He's a fascist, Mick! He was in the pub with a load of them!"

"You're boring me now. I'm not going to listen to you bad-mouth him. He's not a fascist, he just has ideas and opinions."

"And what about you, Mick? Do *you* have ideas and opinions too?"

Micky didn't answer, he just rolled over to face the wall, pulling his blanket tight around him. I got into bed and stared up at the ceiling and silently seethed at how Johnny had wormed his way in to my home, and in to Micky's head.

Eventually, the summer holidays came, I was pleased as it meant a break from Etherington and Arthur Davey. Micky was pleased because it meant he could work more. I barely saw him. When he wasn't out on his bike, he'd spend his time with

Johnny. Mum didn't mind, think she was just glad Micky had someone to look up to. I wanted to tell her that that someone was a raging fascist, but unless she saw him goose-stepping down the street, saluting like a Nazi, she wouldn't have believed me. I'll give it to him, Johnny was clever. He never dropped the act when he was round ours and he treated Mum like a queen.

Lugs and I tried to follow Micky a few more times, hoping to get some actual evidence of his wrongdoings, but we didn't stand a chance keeping up on foot. Lugs suggested I should try asking him what he was up to again, but I knew he would lie. Back then, Micky was almost a stranger.

It was towards the end of August, I reckon, because we'd had a few weeks off from school by then, when I came downstairs to find Mum sitting at the table, white faced and white knuckled as she gripped hold of the newspaper.

"You alright?" I asked.

"Course I am, love." She gave a weak smile and put the paper down. "They sure are giving it to our boys out on the south coast."

"They're getting closer, aren't they?"

Mum didn't answer, she didn't need to. I knew what was going on. Everyone did. Hitler was bringing the battle to Britain. The war was in the sky over the channel. The German air force, the Luftwaffe taking on the RAF. Taking on Dad.

I turned the paper round so it was facing me. There, on the front, was a squadron of RAF Spitfire planes over the Kent coast. Twelve of them, in perfect formation.

"Do you ever think about him?"

"Who, love?"

I didn't need to say, she knew who I meant.

"Yes. Sometimes. Do you?"

"Nah, not really." I sighed, then said quietly, "A bit."

"It's a strange feeling, to think of him up there, protecting us," she said.

"Shame he didn't know how to do that when he was here."

"He does love you, you know, Ronnie. I know you had it hard. But he does love you."

I looked out of the window and forced back the tingling feeling behind my eyes. "He had a funny way of showing it."

"That hasn't changed."

"What do you mean?"

"I think that's what he might be doing now. Trying to show us in the only way he knows how."

"By fighting?"

"By fighting."

I looked back at the headline on the paper.

BATTLE OF BRITAIN RAGES ACROSS SOUTHERN SKIES
Churchill's Tribute to Spitfire and Hurricane Heroes
"Never in the field of human conflict has so much, been owed by so many to so few."

"He could be talking about Dad, couldn't he?" I said quietly.

Mum took my hand in hers. "Yes, love, he could."

CHAPTER 19

The first Saturday in September started off as a good day. Johnny wasn't over and Mum didn't have to go to work, and she'd decided that she wanted to do something with me and Micky. When we plodded down for breakfast, she was at the cooker, frying kippers and singing away to herself. I wouldn't say she's got the best voice in the world. I remembered Dad used to say what she lacked in talent she made up for in enthusiasm and smiles. Then I got a bit cross at myself for thinking about him again.

Mum had pinned her hair up and put on her nice frock, the one with the little flowers on the hem. She had her butterfly brooch pinned to her collar.

"Morning," I said. "Why you all dressed up?"

She turned round, fish slice in her hand. "The mood took me. What do you say we forget that there's a war on, just for today?"

I sat down at the table. "Suits me."

There'd been a few light air raids that week. German planes

flying over London heading to bomb airbases and factories. Four times the air-raid siren had rung out. Four times we had gone to the shelter and four times we'd come out again to sleep in our more comfortable beds. The first time it went off, Vera had come running round to ours in a right flap. She were dripping wet and had nothing on but a towel and her gas mask. Micky and I had walked straight out the shelter and agreed that we'd rather take our chances with the Nazis.

"We should go to the Palladium!" Mum said. "It's been ages since we went to the pictures together."

"It's called the Odeon now," Micky reminded her.

Mum set our kippers and bread in front of us. "We'll go for pie and eels after. Just the three of us, what do you say?"

I shovelled in some kipper. "Sounds good, Mum."

"Don't speak with your mouth full, Ronnie. Honestly, I could never take you anywhere nice! Micky, what do you think?"

"Dunno, said I'd help Johnny out with some deliveries. Old people depend on me for their medicines."

"You always have deliveries," I said.

"What can I do? Johnny says I'm a real asset."

"You're a real ass."

"Ronnie! Don't be mean to your brother. It's wonderful you've found a way to make some pennies, but I shall tell Johnny myself you can't help him! Not today! I shall put my foot down! He's had more than his fair share of you of late." She walked up behind Micky, put her arms round him and hugged him, quite aggressively, truth be told. "You're mine and I'm claiming you back, this instant!"

Micky almost choked on his kipper. "Fine! Fine! I'll come!"

She let go and kissed him on the cheek. "You've made your mother very happy!"

He'd made me happy too, but I said, "Yeah, delighted you can spare time away from helping all the old folk," in a bit of a sarcastic tone.

Mum said, "Nothing but niceness today, Ronnie." Then she sat down at the table and kept looking from me to Micky, with this huge smile on her face.

"What?" I said. "Why are you grinning like that?"

"Just appreciating my boys, that's all."

"It's a bit off-putting when we're trying to eat," I said. "Could you appreciate us a little less obviously?"

"Yeah, rein it in a bit, Mum," Micky said.

She picked up a bit of one of my kippers and threw it at me. It bounced right off my nose.

"I shall not rein it in, you little blighters!"

I picked up the kipper from the table and put it back on my plate. "And you said you couldn't take *me* anywhere nice."

"Today is about the three of us," she continued, "and if I want to smile at you, or tell you how much I love you, or hug you in public, then I shall."

"You're not serious about the hugging in public thing, are you?" Micky asked.

"I am," she said. "Deadly."

*　　*　　*

Just William was playing at the Odeon. It was nice to lose myself in someone else's story for a while. Mid-way through, Mum leaned over and whispered, "This William's a bit of a rascal, he'd better not be giving you two ideas." I didn't like to say that I had my suspicions that our Micky could probably teach William a thing or too.

When the film finished, we watched some footage of Spitfires and Hurricanes engaged in dogfights over the channel with the *Messerschmitts* and *Junkers* 88s of the Luftwaffe. The government thought it was a good idea to show people how well our boys were doing, and some people would go to the cinema just to watch the war reel at the end. Every time a German fighter plane spiralled down towards the sea in a plume of smoke, the cinema would erupt with applause. And every time a Hurricane filled the screen, I'd sit forward in my seat to see if I could spot Dad. When I looked across at Micky, he was doing the same.

When we came out, blinking in the late afternoon sunlight, I thought that the low growl of engines I could hear was still in my head from the film. Then I noticed everyone in the street had stopped still. They were all looking up.

In the distance, the sky was filled with the black silhouettes of squadron upon squadron of German bombers.

I tugged Micky's arm. He stopped rabbiting on to Mum and fell silent.

Hello, Hitler, I thought. *You took your time.*

Mum gasped, "Lord help us!" and grabbed our hands just as

the air-raid siren went off. She tried to drag us down Deptford High Street – I guess she was headed towards the underground shelter at Burtons. But my feet struggled to move. The sight of all those planes was incredible. Dreadful, but incredible. The sheer number of them. Waves of them, layered on top of each other, as if stretching down from heaven. I reckoned there were squadrons of *Junkers* and *Dorniers* and *Heinkel He 111s* with their escort fighter planes, the *Messerschmitts*. Some were flying so low I could almost make out the crosses on their wings.

"Will you two stop looking at the sky with your pie-holes open and start moving!" Mum said, pulling our arms.

"But look at 'em all," I breathed.

"They'll pass over, won't they?" Micky said.

Mum cast a glance upwards. "I blinkin' hope so."

Mum tried her best to hurry us along, but I think both Micky and I were paralysed by the sight. Not from fear, but from a sort of terrible curiosity. For us, the war had finally arrived.

When we got inside the shelter, it was a bit chaotic. We found ourselves stuck behind a woman struggling down the steps into the dark with her massive bagwash sack.

"Do you have to bring that down here?" one old fella shouted from the bottom of the steps. "Cramped enough as it is."

"I'm not having my whites dirtied up by the Hun," she snapped back.

Two lads came thundering down the stairs whooping and pushed past us.

"Oi! Watch it!" Micky said but they just laughed and said, "Oi! Watch it!" back.

I recognized them, but not from school. Not sure they went to school at all, to be honest. I'd seen them most Saturdays working round Deptford docks delivering sacks of coal in an old pram to the boat workers. They were covered in soot, not a bit of them was clean. The bagwash lady turned round, clocked them heading towards her and panicked. She let out a very wobbly wail and tried to leg it down the stairs. Don't think she could see where her feet were going over the bag though and she sort of stumble-ran down the last few steps. Then she fell. Quite spectacularly. She landed on top of her sack with a whoomph, and it burst open, and her whites spilled out onto the floor. The old fella helped pull her to her feet. It took him a few goes, but he got her vertical in the end.

"Where are the little scoundrels?" she barked, her head whipping around, but they were long gone, hidden in amongst the crowd. All that was left was two pairs of black footprints on one of her sheets.

"Bloody Hitler's gonna pay for this!" she said.

Not everyone out on Deptford High Street had decided to make for the shelter. Some must have headed home – others maybe took their chances out in the open. Still, it was busy enough. Near us was a group of women clutching shopping bags of groceries and a group of elderly men who looked like they had just staggered out of the Prince Regent.

All the benches had been taken up, but eventually, we found a spot in the corner against the reinforced concrete wall and sat down and waited. There must have been a hundred-odd people down there, packed together. It smelled dank, and the few lights were weak and kept flickering on and off, which added to the tension.

It wasn't long before we heard the booming sound of an explosion. Hush fell over everyone in the shelter. All eyes wide and looking upwards.

Then another boom and another.

CHAPTER 20

I'm ashamed of myself now – of the excitement I felt. I could see the fear in other people's eyes, I heard their breath quicken at the sound of plane engines droning overhead. I saw mothers cling to their children, I felt Mum's cold clammy hand in mine. I saw Micky's body stiffen with the sound of each blast, and my heart raced, but not with fear. With excitement – a long-owed debt finally being paid off.

Another *boom, crump, crump* – getting louder.

"That didn't sound far away," one woman whispered.

"That'll be the other side of the river. God help them," one of the old drinkers said.

His pal nodded. "Sounds to me like they're bringing the fight to the dockyards."

And then the shelter fell silent again. We'd always known, hadn't we, that Deptford would be a prime target for the Nazis? Or had we known but chosen not to believe it?

Another explosion. The bagwash lady shut her eyes.

Then another.

"That's five," Micky said.

"They drop in sevens," I said. Two more then.

The next two explosions sounded further away.

"The Isle of Dogs is taking a hammering," a woman said.

The sound of another explosion. Close. So close the ground trembled, and dust fell from the ceiling. People gasped. Bagwash lady covered her mouth to stifle a wail. Another wave of bombers must be passing over.

Another boom. Close.

And another. Closer.

And another. Closer still.

Then came the distant *ack-ack* sound of the anti-aircraft guns that were stationed at Mudchute. We were giving it back to them at least.

Now the *crack, crack* sound of firing. Ours or theirs or both? I thought back to the footage of the dogfights and pictured Hurricanes and Spitfires dancing through the sky, circling the Luftwaffe, taking them down.

I thought of Dad. Of how he could be up there, right now. Fighting for us.

I tugged Mum's arm. "Can we go outside and have a look?" I asked.

"Can you go outside and have a look? No, you ruddy can't!" Mum said.

"Just want to see what's going on. Just a quick look, that's all."

"That's all? I do not believe what I am hearing!" Mum said so loudly, she drew a few looks. Then she hissed, "You'll stay down here until the all-clear is sounded."

I huffed and slumped back against the wall. What was the point of a war if I wasn't going to be able to see any of it?

"You can huff all you want, you're staying put."

After an hour or so, the anxious silence in the shelter began to ease. The sound of bombs grew quieter. People started moving about again and striking up conversations.

The old fella who was leaning against the wall next to us said, "Probably moving up the country, or turned back." He smiled and I saw he was missing his front teeth. "They'll sound the all-clear siren in a couple of hours, I'm sure."

"Better get comfortable," Mum said, then she turned round and started chatting with the bagwash lady, telling her that a good boil wash and some bleach would see her sheets right. Micky began tying and untying knots in his shoelaces. The old guys got out a pack of playing cards.

I tapped Mum on the shoulder. "I need a wee."

"Sorry, Rosie, my boy seems to have forgotten his manners," she said, then turned to me. "You're not going outside for one. There's a loo over there."

The loo was a large tin bowl, a lot bigger than the chamber pot at home. It was on the other side of the shelter behind a fence panel. It took me a little time to get things going, think I suffered from a bit of stage fright what with there being so many other folk around. When it did happen, I peed all around the bowl in a satisfying circle. As I buttoned up, the stairwell out of the shelter caught my eye.

I glanced over at Mum – she was chatting away. I could go – if I was quick.

I took the stairs two at a time.

Someone yelled up at me, "Where you going, lad? There's a war going on out there."

"I know," I called back. "And I'm missing it."

I burst onto Deptford High Street, wondering if it would even still be there. It was deserted, all the shops were shut up and no one else was around, but other than that it looked the same as before the bombing had started. The sky though – that was different – smoke almost completely blotting out the sun.

My head swiped to the left at the sound of engines. Two Hurricanes chasing down a *Heinkel* that looked like it was on its way home. A *Messerschmitt* joined them, firing its guns. The Hurricanes split and circled back round, swooping and swerving in and out of the vapour trails and tracer smoke. They came back behind the *Messerschmitt*, the *rat-tat-tat* of their guns firing.

"Have him!" I shouted. "Go on! Have him!"

The *Messerschmitt* soared upwards, taking a higher path, but the Hurricanes pressed on. I watched them, heart racing, chest heaving, as they disappeared out of view.

I wanted to stand out there longer, but I knew I'd better get back before Mum noticed and blew a gasket. I turned back and that's when I noticed someone on the other side of the street.

Johnny Simmons.

He was coming out of the shuttered grocers, a bag slung over his back.

"Johnny?" I shouted.

He froze. Just like you would do if you'd been caught doing something you shouldn't.

"Quite the display, weren't it?" he shouted over. "Had to take a look for myself."

"Sudden desperate need for some spuds?" I shouted back.

His eyes narrowed. "Something like that. Now why don't you get yourself back underground. I wouldn't want something to happen to you. There's a good chance you could get hurt out here and we wouldn't want that, would we?"

I didn't move. "You threatening me, Johnny?"

"You're not as stupid as you look." He grinned.

A bomb exploded down by the wharf and Johnny jumped – his cool exterior momentarily shaken. He was scared. That much were obvious. He pulled his bag up on his shoulder, looked anxiously up at the sky then down the street. "See ya, Ronnie," he said, and then he ran off.

No, I thought, *I see you.* Then I ran back into the shelter, my heart hammering in my chest like gunfire.

CHAPTER 21

When I got back down into the shelter, my heart was still pounding. Micky looked up from re-tying his shoelaces and said, "You took your time."

"Turned out it was more than a wee." A lot more.

"Oh, Ronnie. Spare us the details," Mum said.

I settled back into my space in the corner, my mind racing with images of fighter planes and gunfire and smoke, but mainly of Johnny. He'd been up to no good, I were certain of that. Probably on the rob when no one was around to see him. While men risked their lives in the sky and on the battlefield, he was out there, on the take – stealing from his neighbours. Johnny really was the worst type of criminal and I seemed to be the only one who could see it. The anger rose up in my belly, hot and alive. My fists balled. The urge to hit something – anything – was overwhelming.

"Ronnie, love?" Mum was looking at me, the worry clear in her eyes. "Ronnie, what's wrong?"

I exhaled deeply, trying to let the rage out. "Nothing, I'm fine."

"Really? You didn't look fine."

I let out another breath. "Really."

She studied my face, then stroked my cheek. Her touch was so gentle, and I felt myself relax. "Ah, there you are," she said. Her face was close to mine. I could see the yellow flecks in the blue of her irises.

"I'm fine," I said again. I wished so much that I could tell her what I'd just seen, and that she'd believe me.

"It's hard this," she said, looking round the shelter, "but we'll get through it, together."

I nodded. "I know."

"There's my lad. But you didn't half look like your father just then." Mum smiled, then turned back and started talking to Rosie again.

As the sound of the bombing faded away and then disappeared into nothing, the atmosphere in the shelter relaxed further. People were chatting on, some even managing to raise a laugh. But I kept thinking about Johnny. About Dad. About me. How Mum had said I'd looked like him. How that troubled me.

Just under an hour later, the all-clear siren went off. Everyone sighed with relief at the exact same time, and it seemed as though the walls of the shelter expanded with our communal release of breath.

We waited in line as people filed out of the shelter. As we climbed up the steps, a woman grabbed Mum by the shoulder. She was smartly dressed and didn't sound like she'd been brought up round Deptford.

"That butterfly brooch," she said. "My mother had one just like that. She brought it with her when she moved from Poland."

Mum touched it. "It's lovely, isn't it?"

"Hers went missing. Stolen, we think."

"What a shame. This was a Christmas gift," Mum said, like she was trying to prove she weren't the one who nicked it.

The woman nodded, her eyes still on the brooch. "I must say it does look remarkably similar."

"Mum," I said, "Do you think J—"

She cut me off. "I'm sure many were made."

"Yes, perhaps," the woman said, then made her way out of the exit.

Out on the street, the smell of burning hung heavy in the air. As talk of the damage that had been sustained along the Thames made its way through the crowd, people started to drift down the road towards the docks to look for themselves. Mum, Micky and I found ourselves drawn to do the same. A few houses in streets nearer the river had taken a battering. Windows smashed, roofs caved in, chunks blown off the side so you could see right into people's bedrooms.

By the water, the crowd gathered, mouths gaping.

The warehouses that hugged the river on our side had copped it. Fires had broken out everywhere. The long necks of cranes bent at painful angles. A boat, loaded up with sandbags, had come off its moorings and had drifted out into the Thames.

The Isle of Dogs was ablaze. The whole of the other side of the river, an angry orange glow stretching as far as the eye could see. We watched on as small fires turned into bigger ones. Firefighters ran around with hoses, trying to put them out, but each time they seemed to get a blaze under control, it would reignite, and the flames would seethe again. Smoke billowed upwards blanketing the air. The acrid smell of cordite was sharp and pungent, even from where we were standing.

Mum clutched her chest and when she spoke, her voice caught in her throat. "Those poor souls. Those poor, poor souls."

We stood for ages, Mum, Micky and I, trying to take in the scene. The total destruction. We were there, right opposite it, seeing it with our own eyes, but still, it was hard to believe.

Eventually, Mum said, "Let's go, I can't bear to look a second longer."

We walked back along the High Street. Mum was quiet, occasionally she'd look down at her brooch, and I wondered if she might suspect something. But at that moment, Micky and I, well, we couldn't stop talking about the fires and the broken buildings and how close it had all been. We blathered on with the same sort of excitement that we usually reserved for talking about football.

Suddenly, Mum stopped dead in her tracks and shouted, "Enough!"

She startled us. I guess we had forgotten she was there. "Just enough," she said again, quietly this time, "this isn't a game." She looked tired. The brightness she'd had in her eyes that same morning gone.

Micky and I gave each other a look.

I struggled to think of something to say. Something to make Mum feel better.

Then Micky said, "Pie and eels. We should get pie and eels."

Mum said, "Pie and eels?" like she'd never heard of the things.

"Yeah," I said. "Like you wanted. I'm starving, aren't you?"

Mum thought about it. "I suppose I am."

When we got home, my belly and my mind were full. We were all dog-tired. Amazing how an afternoon doing nothing in an underground shelter can take it out of you. Micky and I went up to our room. Mum tried to make a cuppa, but the water was off – probably from fighting all the fires, and the gas wasn't working, so she took herself off to her room instead.

With Mum having a lie down and safely out of earshot, I said, "I went outside during the raid. I went and had a look."

Micky stopped fiddling with his penknife and looked up. "You didn't! What did you see?"

"Dogfight between some Hurricanes and a *Messerschmitt*. It was incredible, Mick!"

I spread my arms out and swooped round the bedroom.

"They were darting this way and that, showing the Hun what for!" I jumped up on the bed and pretended to fire. "Bang! Bang! Bang! You should have seen it, Micky!"

"You should have told me you were going."

I sat down next to him. "And maybe you should finally tell me what it is you really do for Johnny. The planes weren't the only thing I saw outside the shelter."

"What do you mean?"

"Johnny was there too."

"So?" Micky shrugged, but I could tell by his face he might know something, or he was interested at least. "Probably just doing what you were doing – having a look at the action."

"He came out of the grocers."

"That don't mean nothing! Could have just been taking shelter or something."

"He was on the rob, Micky. Is that what he's got you doing? Stealing from folk? I'm not buying the *helping old people* line."

"I'm not stealing from anybody. I drop off stuff, that's all. And Johnny isn't a thief either."

"You heard what that woman said about her brooch."

"You're adding two and two and getting a sack load of rubbish, Ron. Like Mum said, there are probably loads of those brooches knocking about."

"I'm adding up more than two and two. I'm adding up the grocers, the brooch, the exemption certificates, that Nazi newspaper, the Blackshirt meeting I saw in the pub, Mr Dimes, and *you*. I'm adding up you."

"What do you mean *me*?"

"I mean how you've changed, Mick."

"So that's what it's all about? You don't like that Johnny and I get on. You're jealous."

"That ain't it at all," I said, although maybe it was a bit. I wanted my brother back.

"You're seeing problems that ain't there. Johnny has this family's best interests at heart."

The frustration built up inside me. "Flamin' heck, Micky! What is it going to take for you to realize that Johnny is bad news? No matter what I tell you and Mum about him, neither of you will believe me. He's a criminal. I know in my heart of hearts he's a criminal and I know whatever he's got you doing for him is wrong. Why can't you see him for what he is? He's a criminal and a flamin' fascist to boot! Why won't you believe me?"

Something about the expression on my brother's face hit me like a blow to the stomach.

"But you know what he is, and you don't care, do you?"

CHAPTER 22

Micky didn't get to answer me because, for the second time that day, the air-raid siren rang out. The vivid orange glow from the other side of the river flashed in my mind and an unsettling sense of dread tugged at my bones. The Germans were coming for us again.

Mum was in our room a few seconds after the siren began to wail. "Get up!" she said, even though both Micky and I were already standing. "Grab your gas masks and go!"

We didn't hang about, not this time.

When we got downstairs Johnny was already heading out the door.

"When did he get here?" I asked.

"Stop asking unnecessary questions and get yourself in that shelter," Mum snapped.

We hurried outside and arrived to see Mrs Green's backside disappear through the door.

"Where's Johnny going to go?" I asked as we piled in, and Micky clambered onto his bed.

Mum jostled me further inside. "There's room enough. You and Micky will have to top and tail on his bunk."

I didn't much like that idea, I think my expression must have said that too because Mum said, "You can wipe that look off your face, sunshine. We wouldn't even have an Anderson shelter if it wasn't for Johnny."

Johnny ruffled my hair. "You'll be fine. You're only small." Then he climbed onto my bunk and winked at me.

Just great. Having to sit an air raid out with Johnny Simmons was not top on my list of plans for that night.

I opened my mouth to ask him if he didn't have other shops to visit, what with everyone being out the way, but the sound of planes grinding overhead stopped me. It made my insides freeze to be honest. In the distance came the boom of heavy bombs, quickly followed by the rapid vicious firing from fighter planes. Then the *crump, crump* of anti-aircraft guns.

"Sounds like they mean business," Johnny said, crossing his arms behind his head. "I'd settle in for a long night of it."

Vera pulled her knitting out of her bag and began frantically click-clacking away. "Talk is that the invasion has started. All them fancy folk are alright in their big houses in the country. It's us regular people who will be the ones who'll suffer."

"I should have insisted you boys go," Mum said, her voice cracking. "What was I thinking, keeping you here for this?"

"You could have insisted all you like," I said, "we wouldn't have left you."

Vera's knitting needles stopped at the sound of a bomb

whistling outside. We looked at each other anxiously and I held my breath, waiting for the explosion.

When the boom came, it rumbled through the air. It was so much louder there, in the shelter than when we were underground at Burtons. The noise vibrated right through you.

"If you hear the bombs scream or whistle," Vera said, her knitting needles starting up again, even more feverishly, "they ain't destined for you."

Micky looked at her, his face pale. "Is that true?"

"Oh yes, lad."

Vera's knitting needles stopped clacking for a second time, and she looked upwards. I found myself doing the same – don't know what either of us thought we'd see through an iron roof. But the sound of another bomb was unmistakable. It was whistling louder this time. It sounded nearby.

"God help us!" Vera wailed as she jumped from her bed and stuck her head under Mum's bunk.

Johnny bolted up – his eyes wild. "You said we don't have to worry about the whistlers!"

The whistling stopped. In silence, we waited for the boom, each of us trying to work out how close it was.

"It's not for us," Micky said, like he was trying to make it true. "It's not for us."

"It can't be for us," I said. "My last sight on this earth cannot be of Mrs Green's backside."

Micky managed a snigger and Vera shouted from under the bunk, "I heard that!" just as the bomb found its target – which sounded to me like it was a way away.

Not that Johnny seemed to realize that. He got to his feet and started turning in circles. "But that sounded close. Didn't that sound close?" He couldn't keep the fear from his voice and, for some reason, that made me feel braver.

"Soil and corrugated iron, that's all that's separating us from the might of the Nazi planes. Hope you built this shelter solid," I said.

Another boom.

Johnny whimpered. I wanted to laugh, but I'd scared myself too with my shelter comment.

"The shelter's solid," Mum said. "The best in the street, isn't that right, Mrs Green?"

"I bleedin' hope so!" Mrs Green said, crawling back from under the bunk. "Can't stay bent under there all night with my knees. Cathy, be a doll and help me up."

With a bit of effort, Mum got Vera back on the bed and she started up her knitting again. Johnny began rocking back and forth which made the whole bunk creak. Between the clack-clacking and the rocking, the two of them made the atmosphere pretty intense.

Eventually, Mum persuaded Johnny to lie down. "Your heart!" she said.

"What about it?" he snapped, all agitated.

"All this stress, it's no good for your heart," she put her hand on his knee. "You must try and rest. Nurse's orders."

He took to the top bunk and didn't move and didn't speak for the rest of the night, which was no small mercy, in my opinion.

*   *   *

Wave after wave after wave...we listened to the sound of planes ploughing overhead. It was like the whole of the German air force had taken to the sky that night. The rattle of gunfire was continuous. The deafening sound of explosion after explosion after explosion.

Micky and I ducked – don't know why, instinct I suppose – when the shelter was pelted with shrapnel.

"Sounds like hard rain," Vera said, rescuing her knitting from the floor, where she'd chucked it in fright.

Hour after hour, bomb after bomb whistled through the air. And with each one came the agonizing wait while we tried to work out if it had gone off. Where it had gone off. If it was on a timer. Then the deafening boom. The sound of falling brick and metal. Trying to figure out how big it had been.

In the early hours of the morning, Micky and I somehow managed to snatch a few minutes of sleep. At some point, his hand had found its way into mine. I don't remember it happening, but I was glad that it had. I hadn't wanted to share the bunk with him, but having him there so close, made me feel better. Our sleep, though I was grateful for it, was light and fretful and we both jerked awake to the sound of yet another ground-rattling explosion.

"That one was near, weren't it?" Micky whispered to me.

I didn't answer. We both knew the Luftwaffe were right there on our doorstep.

CHAPTER 23

Eight hours the Germans came at us. The all-clear siren didn't sound until five-thirty in the morning. It's hard to explain how I felt that night. How, after the initial couple of hours of terror, we almost got used to the sound of destruction around us. The silence after we heard a bomb fly, the relief when we knew it had fallen on some other poor blighter. The guilt at having felt that way.

Johnny got down off my bunk and stretched. His hair was stuck up at all angles and he looked dog-tired. I suppose we all did. But while the rest of us looked at each other with the bond of people who had been through something and come out the other side, Johnny struggled to look anyone in the eye.

We stumbled outside into the dark of the morning. Heston Street had survived that day. Windows had broken, roof tiles had fallen and shrapnel littered the pavement, but the houses were still standing.

A group of men in volunteer firefighter uniforms ran down our street, I suppose heading somewhere that had fared far worse.

An air-raid patrol warden stopped to talk to us. The ARP that was printed on his helmet was hardly visible under all the brick dust. "Don't go far," he said. "Reports of unexploded bombs round Deptford. Stumble into one of those and it will blow you sky high."

Vera said, "The only place I'm going, is to my bed."

The air-raid warden looked Johnny up and down. "Good night, was it, safe in your shelter?"

"He'd be out there if he could." Mum looked cross. "He's got a bad heart!"

The warden raised an eyebrow. "Righty-ho." Then made his way down the street.

"Pompous git," Micky muttered, then caught a clip round the ear from Mum.

Johnny put his cap on his head and shoved his hands iln his pocket. "Cathy, thanks for the hospitality, but I best be going. Work to do."

Mum frowned. "But you heard what the pompous git said, unexploded bombs."

"Oh right, so it's okay for you to say it!" Micky said but Mum ignored him.

"Johnny, I really think you should stay here." She had her serious face on. "It's not safe."

"Tell you what, if I see an unexploded bomb, I won't step on it. How's *that*?"

His words came out sharp. Think Mum was a bit taken aback. She folded her arms to show him leaving was not acceptable, and neither was his tone.

I think Johnny realized he'd shown a little of his true self, and he forced his face into a smile. "Sorry, just tired that's all." He kissed Mum on the cheek, then said, "I'll pop back this afternoon. You get some rest. Don't worry, I'll be careful." Then he turned to Micky, "See you later, Micky." He jumped over the wall and headed off down the road with slightly less swagger than usual.

"I'll tell you something," Vera said as she headed off to hers, her knitting bag bundled up in her arms. "If I can't make a cup of tea when I get in, I'll commandeer a plane and bomb Hitler myself."

More and more of the neighbours started to emerge from their shelters and houses and Mum went off to chat over the night's events with them in the middle of the street.

Micky suddenly shouted, "Cripes! My bike!" and dashed over to see if it had been damaged.

A bit of shrapnel, lodged in the grass, caught my eye. I bent down to pick it up. It was still warm to the touch. It had cut down deep in the ground and it took some will to pull it up. Eventually, I wiggled it free. I turned it over in my hands. Don't know what it was about it, but holding it made me feel alive. Almost like it was a reminder that I'd survived. Proof that I was part of the war.

"My bike's fine," Micky said. To be honest, I wished it'd been blown to bits. That would have slowed his deliveries down. He bent down next to me. "What's that you got there?"

162

"Shrapnel," I said. "Reckon it's a piece of anti-aircraft shell that our boys must have fired off to welcome the Germans."

He tried to snatch it from me. "Gerroff! Get your own, not like there's a shortage. Look at the place!"

We spent much of that morning, first in our garden, then working down the street, collecting fragments of shells and scraps of iron. The bigger it was, the better. Our knees were scratched to pieces by the time Mum called us in for our lunch. Micky and I both found a box to put our collections in.

We were upstairs looking through our new treasures when we heard a knock at the door.

"Hiya, Billy, love, I hope you took care getting here, there's unexploded bombs about."

I shouted down the stairs, "He's alive, isn't he?"

"Alright, you cheeky so-and-so," Mum bellowed back. "The boys are up in their room."

Lugs thundered up the stairs and burst through the door.

"Germans didn't get you then?" I said.

"Nope. It was a bit of a rough night though, wasn't it?"

"Just a bit," Micky said.

"Mum was in a right mood the whole time. Water came up through the floor of the shelter again last night. She had a right go at Dad for digging it too deep, even though he wasn't there to hear it."

"Heard anything from him since he left?" I asked.

Lugs bit his lip and shook his head.

Micky and I didn't say anything – really, what could we have said?

Lugs was the one who changed the subject. "Heard Jerry dropped incendiary bombs all over the park. Burned it to bits."

"We've been collecting shrapnel," I said, nodding towards my box. "Want to see?"

"Nice," he said, but he stayed in the doorway, like he didn't want to stay long. "Actually, I came round to ask for your help."

"Go on," I said.

"Tiger did a runner. Don't know where he is. Thought you might come out and help me look for him."

"He get scared off by the bombs?" I asked.

Lugs ran his hand through his hair. "Nah, would you believe it, but he shot off after a rat."

"He picked his timing!"

"I know, the rascal."

"We'll come, won't we, Micky?"

Micky put the lid on his box. "Sure."

"Thanks. I know he's just a cat but it's not his fault there's a war on."

We headed downstairs to go and look for Tiger. Johnny Simmons came in through the front door as we were grabbing our gas masks.

"You off out, Micky?" he said.

"Thinking of it, why?"

"Need you to do something for me that's all."

"He's busy," I said. "Come on, Micky, let's go."

Micky hesitated. I looked him right in the eye. "Micky?"

"Sorry, Lugs," he said, "if you don't find him, I'll come out tomorrow."

Lugs, who had sort of pressed himself back against the wall, as far away from Johnny as possible, said, "No bother, Mick."

But I wasn't going to let him off the hook so easy. "Micky, you already said you'd help Lugs. You going to let him down?"

Lugs said, "It don't matter, Ron."

"Yeah, it does," I said, keeping my eyes on Micky. "So, you coming?"

Micky stared back but didn't say anything.

Johnny put his hand on Micky's shoulder. "Go with them if you want."

"Nah, Johnny," Micky said. "I'll come with you."

"That's a good lad," Johnny said. Then he looked at me. "Off you go boys. Go and play."

I shook my head, then turned away from Micky – I couldn't bear to look at him no longer. When I walked out, I slammed the door behind me.

We spent a good couple of hours walking the streets trying to find Tiger. There were houses with broken windows, one with the whole front blown off, like a doll's house, with its innards exposed to the air. We saw families carrying what was left of their belongings under their arms, heading off to find

165

somewhere else to stay. It was hard to look at the destruction. The war that I'd been waiting for had arrived and it was more terrible than I could ever have imagined.

In the end it was Lugs who suggested we call it a day, which I was relieved about. He sat down on the pavement and said, "I'm too tired to keep looking. Didn't get much sleep last night."

I sat down next to him. "I'm sure Tiger will be alright. He's a very clever cat." I wasn't sure that was true, but I wanted to give Lugs some hope.

Lugs let out a weary sigh. "Ugh. School tomorrow. Can you believe we still have to go?"

"You never know, maybe it'll be blown up in the night."

"Fingers crossed, hey?"

We wandered back together, and Lugs peeled off when we got to the end of his road. We were saying goodbye when Lugs said, "Hey, isn't that Micky going like the clappers on his bike?"

I looked down the street and sure enough, Micky was bombing towards us.

"Oi, Micky!" I shouted but he didn't stop.

"I'd better go," I said, starting to run after him. "Find out what's up."

I ran all the way back to ours. When I got home, Micky's bike was lying on the ground, wheels still turning.

Vera was propped up against the fence, cigarette in hand. "Your brother seemed in a hurry. What's up with him?"

"I dunno," I said, "but I swear I'm going to find out."

I ran up the stairs to find my brother sitting on the bed, chest heaving, eyes full of fear and his arm clutching his side.

"Micky?" I said. "What's going on? I think it's time you started telling me the truth."

CHAPTER 24

I stood at the end of Micky's bed waiting for him to answer. My mind turned over all the possibilities. He'd got caught thieving – or maybe someone turned him over knowing he might be carrying an exemption certificate. Perhaps Johnny or one of his Blackshirt buddies had roughed him up to get him to do what they wanted.

Micky sniffed, wiped his eyes. "Nothing. Came off my bike, that's all."

"Your cheek's swelling up something rotten. It looks like you've been in a fight."

"I told you, I fell."

"That's the story you're sticking to, is it?"

"It's not a story."

I let out an exasperated yell. Right then, I really wanted to knock some sense into him. But then I remembered what Mum had said about me looking like Dad, and I took a breath. "I can't help you if you're not honest with me, Mick."

"I don't need your help," Micky shouted back.

I took another breath and calmed myself. "I think you do, and I'm just going to sit here until you tell me what's going on." I folded my arms and sat cross-legged on my bed and stared at him.

"What? You're going to just sit there looking at me?"

"Yup," I said. "All day if I have to."

Micky rolled his eyes. "Suit yourself."

I would have stayed there all day too, but I heard Mum and Johnny talking to Vera outside.

I looked at Micky, all bashed up and bruised and something inside me snapped. I jumped off the bed, threw the door open and took the stairs two at a time. I burst in to the front garden and shouted, "You need to leave our Micky alone."

Mum spun round, confusion on her face. "Ronnie, what are you talking about."

"Micky's been beaten up and it's got something to do with Johnny – I'm sure of it."

"Micky's been beaten up?" Mum said, her face etched with concern.

"I haven't! I fell off my bike!" Micky came charging out of the house after me.

When Mum saw him, she covered her mouth with her hands. "Micky, love!"

"Blimey, Micky, are you alright, son?" Johnny said.

"No, he isn't, thanks to you!" I shouted.

"How's him falling off his bike anything to do with me?" Johnny jabbed his finger in my face. "You need to watch that mouth of yours." I felt the anger vibrating through me, and before I knew what I was doing, I'd shoved him with both hands, hard in the chest. It was like pushing a brick wall. He didn't even move. I tried again, then again, pushing him as hard as I could. I was so angry. I couldn't stop.

"Ronnie, stop it! What's got into you?" Mum cried.

I swung round and looked at her, angry tears prickling my eyes. I proper shouted at her then. "Why can't you see? Why can't you see what he's like? Micky, tell her! Tell her what's going on."

Mum said, "Micky, I need you to be honest with me. How did you get hurt?"

I stared Micky right in the eyes, pleading with him to speak up, to tell the truth, but he looked straight back at me and said, "Like I said, I fell off my bike."

It felt like my whole world tilted on its axis.

He'd chosen Johnny over me, and the pain of knowing that was almost unbearable.

I charged past him – Johnny was saying something and Mum was shouting after me, but I couldn't hear them. I thundered up the stairs and threw myself on my bed. Then I sobbed. I really sobbed.

The door opened half an hour or so later. Mum came in with a cup of tea. She handed it to me, then she sat down on the end of my bed. "Ronnie, what's wrong? I'm worried about you. Why are you so angry?"

"I hate him, Mum. I really hate him."

She closed her eyes and let out a long, heavy sigh.

"I understand that it's hard, but not everyone is like your father. You've never given Johnny a chance."

"He doesn't deserve a chance."

"Everyone deserves a chance." She sighed again. "I know it's difficult for you to trust people, with how your father was. Micky didn't see everything, you shielded him from a lot, so maybe he finds it easier to let Johnny in."

"But Mum he—"

Mum, put her hand on my face. "Ronnie, I want you to listen to me. You've been doing an awful lot of talking, been making all sorts of accusations and I'm trying to understand why you're behaving like this. We've talked and decided that Johnny's going to go away for a little while."

"You've told him to leave?"

"No, it was his idea. He has some work to do and we both hope that, over the next few weeks, you can find a way to get past this vendetta you have against him. And Micky won't be delivering any more letters or medicine."

"Johnny won't like that."

"That was Johnny's idea too. It's clearly worrying you, and Johnny and me are worried too. The streets aren't safe for him to be cycling about on."

I couldn't quite take in everything Mum was saying.

"But you must promise me something. You have to work on your anger. Shoving Johnny, shouting at me like you did, it's not like you. I won't have it, not in my house. Not again."

I thought of all the times I'd heard Dad shouting at her, how I hated him for it, and I felt a wave of shame wash over me and the tears started to fall again. I didn't want to be anything like him. "I'm sorry, Mum, truly I am."

Mum took the cup from my hands and placed it on the bedside table. Then she pulled me back into a hug and rested her chin on my head. "We all get angry, Ronnie, and sometimes it's right to be. Sometimes things happen and the only thing you can do is feel angry. Take this war, my goodness, if I could tell you how angry I am about it. How angry I am that it's robbing you and Micky of your childhood. There are days I feel like I could run out into the street and throw rocks into the sky and scream about how unfair it all is! But see, it's not the anger that's the problem, it's when you let it overcome you. And you, my sweet, courageous boy, aren't the sort to let anything overcome you."

She kissed me on the head again. "Now, what do you say we forget about all this? Why don't you get yourself into that bathroom and freshen up?" She held up my hand in front of my eyes. "You could grow spuds under those fingernails! What have you been doing, scratching around in the dirt?"

I shrugged. "Pretty much. Micky and I were collecting shrapnel this morning."

"I hope you're being careful. Now, I'm going to send Johnny up. He wants a quick word with you before he goes and Ronnie, try to be nice for me."

I nodded but my insides twisted at the thought. I went to wash my hands and when I got back to my room, Johnny was sitting on my bed, waiting for me. I took a breath and stepped inside.

"Close the door," he said. "You and I, Ronnie Smith, need a word."

CHAPTER 25

I pushed the door shut, my hands already shaking. As soon as I turned round, Johnny had me up by the collar and pinned against it.

"I seem to remember you've found yourself in this position before."

Even though I knew he wouldn't be able to do much to me with Mum downstairs, my heart still hammered against my ribcage.

"All I want, Ronnie, is for us to get along." He leaned right up close to me, his hot breath hitting my face. "While I'm away, I want you to adjust your way of thinking. Maybe try and be a little bit more like your brother. 'Cos I won't be so reasonable if you keep stirring up trouble when I get back. I'm going to be involved in important things for important people and I don't want you sniffing around messing things up. Do I make myself clear?"

I croaked out. "Crystal, Johnny. Crystal clear."

"Good." He dropped me back to the floor. "Now get up and

slap a smile on that miserable mug of yours, because what we're going to do is go downstairs and make like happy families for your mother."

I glared up at him, wishing I was brave enough to ask him what important things he was up to and for what important people.

"I said *smile*."

I forced my lips to turn up at the edges.

"That's more like it."

He followed me down the stairs and called out, "Cathy, love, I'm off."

Mum ran to the front door and Micky slunk into the hallway behind her.

"Everything okay?" Mum asked hopefully.

Johnny ruffled my hair and slung his arm over my shoulder. "Everything's just fine, isn't that right, Ronnie?"

I felt the bile rising in my stomach. "Yeah, everything's great."

Mum's whole face beamed with happiness when I said that, and it broke me inside a little. I caught Micky looking at me, but he immediately turned the other way. He knew I was lying.

"Right then," Johnny said, planting a kiss on Mum's lips. "I'd best be off. Important things to be getting on with. I'll see you in a few weeks." Then he looked at me and said, "See ya, Ronnie."

I swallowed. "See ya, Johnny."

*   *   *

That evening, I pushed my cabbage around my plate – I didn't have much of an appetite after my run-in with Johnny. I tried to take comfort in the fact that he'd be gone for a few weeks – that Micky wouldn't be out doing his deliveries any more. But the knowledge that he'd be back made it hard to feel too happy. And when he did come back, what then? Would this important thing he was up to involve Micky? Was it something to do with the Blackshirts? A feeling of helplessness started to creep in at my edges.

The sound of the air-raid siren jolted me out of my thoughts. Mum laid her knife and fork on her plate and took a deep breath. "Come on."

"We could stay and finish it?" Micky said.

"No, I'm not going to be found dead with my head in a plate of cabbage and liver," Mum said. "Bring it with you, we can eat it in the shelter."

Vera must have had the same idea because she came round with a half-eaten cabbage and potato pie. "Jerry don't half know how to ruin a mealtime," she said as she settled into her bunk. Then she clocked our Micky – took in his bashed-up face. "That must have been some fall."

He shrugged. "There's worse happening out there."

Vera nodded at the truth of that and shovelled some pie into her mouth.

Mum looked up at the roof of the shelter "Thought they'd give us an evening off after the performance they put on last night."

But as the first wave of bombers ploughed overhead, something told me that the Germans were only just getting started.

It was early when the all-clear sounded. It had been another rough night, where the terror had ebbed and flowed and peaked and subsided only to peak again later. Nobody moved for a while after the siren had sounded. We all just sat there, trying to put the pieces of ourselves back together again.

Eventually, Mrs Green slapped her thighs and said, "Better go see what the damage is."

On shaky, tired legs, we filed out of the shelter and breathed a sigh of relief to see that our houses had escaped the bombing. It was a bright morning, the birds were tweeting and, despite the smell of smoke and destruction in the air, to me it felt like a glorious new day. We'd survived another raid and, in that moment, I felt that we would also survive anything Johnny could throw at us. He was gone, which meant that I had some time to win my brother back. Telling Micky who Johnny was hadn't worked, but maybe reminding Micky who *he* was would. He was my brother, even a German *Sprengbombe*, I decided, couldn't break that bond.

"Is that birdsong?" Mum said, looking up.

"Sparrows, I think," Vera said.

A small smile crept across Mum's lips. "How lovely."

Heston Street was lucky again, but we could see the flames

from a house a couple of roads down, and there was no pretending that London hadn't been pummelled severely in the night.

"We should collect up some things – spare pots and pans, clothes, that sort of stuff – and take it round to them," Mum said.

"That'd be nice, Cathy," Vera said. "Let's do it."

"You're alright to watch the boys tonight?" Mum said. "I'm starting lates again."

I hated the thought of Mum being in the hospital, away from us. Micky must have been thinking the same because he said, "Do you have to go?"

She stroked his cheek. "You know I do. The hospitals are busier than ever at the moment. I have to do my bit and you two have to do your bit too, by not playing up for Mrs Green, understand?"

"They wouldn't dare," Vera said, "or I'll bash them over the head with my frying pan."

We all laughed, but I wouldn't have put it past her.

"Right, I'm going to collect some stuff together then try and get some sleep before work. Boys, you might get an hour in before school if you try now."

"School? Are you serious? After what we've just been through," Micky said.

But it wouldn't wash with Mum. "We have to keep going. I'll be damned if Hitler steals your education too."

Micky and I went up to our room and laid down on our beds.

"We okay?" I asked.

"What, after you lost me my job?" Micky paused, then said, "Yeah, we're okay. Pleased to have a break to be honest."

I sat up. "A break?"

"You know...from all that cycling."

The way he said it – a weary sigh under his words – made me think he meant more than just the cycling, but I didn't want to push it and put him on the defensive. Maybe I was reading too much into it, but it felt like the smallest of admissions that he knew things he was doing for Johnny weren't right. It gave me hope that Johnny's hold over Micky wasn't as strong as Johnny seemed to think. I had two weeks to show my brother how life was better when Johnny wasn't around.

The thought brought me some sense of peace and my eyelids became heavier. I looked over at Micky, he was rubbing his eyes and yawning. I reckon we were both out for the count in seconds.

Mum came blustering in what felt like only minutes later. "Get up!" she said, "you're going to be late."

"But we've only just this moment laid down," Micky groaned and stuck his head under his pillow.

I scooched myself down under the bed covers too in protest. Three seconds later they were whipped off.

"It's been over an hour! Up and at them!" Mum said, causing both Micky and me to groan some more. "Breakfast is on the table, but I think you'll have to eat it on the way."

Micky and I dragged ourselves out of bed and started to get changed. I watched as Micky whipped his pyjama top off and quickly put on his shirt, but he wasn't quick enough to stop me seeing the bruise on his side. It was big and a deep, deep purple. He caught me looking.

"Vera's right, that must have been some fall," I said. "At least that won't be happening again now you're not delivering."

Micky just nodded – I could tell he didn't want to get into it again.

"*And*," I said, more cheerfully, "you might even have some time to knock about with me and Lugs."

"I suppose I will," Micky said.

I grinned. "Want to look through the shrapnel, take some of it to school?"

Micky smiled. "Yeah, alright then."

Before we went downstairs, we both selected some of the best bits of shrapnel we'd collected the day before and put them in our gas-mask boxes. Then we grabbed some bread and a small chunk of cheese that was pretending to be breakfast and made our way to school.

"Not taking your bike?" I asked as Micky followed me down the path.

"Thought I might walk with you."

I opened the garden gate and did an elaborate bow. "Consider me delighted." He rolled his eyes, like he thought I was joking, but I think we both knew I wasn't, not really.

We strolled together, eyes on the ground looking out for any bits of nice-looking shrapnel. I kept looking over at Micky – just feeling happy he was there.

"What's with the stupid grin?" Micky asked

"Just a pleasure to be in your company," I said, putting on a posh accent.

Micky shook his head, but he was smiling too.

Neither of us were in a particular hurry that morning, and by the time we arrived at school, both my pockets and my heart was full, but the playground was empty.

"Guess we missed roll call," I said.

"He can't give us a hard time for being late today, under the circumstances," Micky said.

"Who knows with Mr Etherington?"

When we got into class there was about half the number of kids usually there. Some had been evacuated and some had stopped seeing the point of school when there was a war on, and I didn't like to think about the reason why some others might not have made it.

At playtime when we were finishing our milk, I told Lugs that Johnny had cleared off for a while and he told me that Tiger had finally found his way home.

Lugs leaned against the school wall and let out a long sigh. "Pleased to hear that, Ronnie, right pleased. I was thinking both you and Micky looked a bit chirpier."

We watched Micky making his way over to us, a smile on his face, hands stuffed in his pockets. "Hoping that with Johnny out the picture Micky might see sense," I said.

"He will," Lugs said with a confidence I was grateful for.

"I'm pleased to hear about Tiger too," I said. Then, as Micky had just got to us, I added, "Lugs's cat came back. 'Ere, do you think he caught the rat he went after?"

Lugs shrugged "Not sure. I'd like to think so, but he put a dirty oil cloth down on the front doorstep so I have my suspicions he might have spent his time thinking he was killing that."

"Probably having one eye don't help," Micky said.

"Mum weren't too happy with the oily pawprints all through the house. I pointed out that the people round the corner didn't even have a house any more, but she said, if a bomb were to drop on us, she would not have all and sundry commenting on the state of her carpets."

"Sounds like something our mum would say," Micky said.

Once we'd put our empty milk bottles back, Micky and I got out our shrapnel collection for everyone to see. Lugs and a few of the other kids had some of their own to show – I didn't stop to think that it was funny we all had the same idea to collect it. I suppose us kids were natural collectors. In the summer girls would gather up daisies and string them round their necks, in the autumn it was all about conkers. I suppose the war was its own kind of season, a season that brought with it deadlier but no less covetable trophies. Soon there was a group of us sitting crossed-legged on the floor passing around our riches. It didn't take long before Arthur and his goons sauntered over.

"What you got there?" Arthur said.

"And before you say a trombone," Harry piped up, "I know it ain't."

"It's bits of a trombone actually. It was blasted apart in an explosion. Made a hell of a racket apparently," I said.

Lugs looked at me out of the corner of his eye.

"You're lying," Harry said, though his tone suggested he wasn't sure.

Graham looked up at the sky, his hands on his hips. "Course he's lying. He's trying to make you look a mug again."

Harry jabbed his finger at me. "Are you making me look like a mug, Smith!"

I held my hands up. "Nope. You take care of that all on your own."

Harry took a step towards me and rolled up his sleeves. "Why, I ought to—"

"Ought to what?" Micky said.

Harry shrank back, which was something, considering he was almost twice the size of our Micky. I guess the penknife incident had left something of an impression.

"So, what is it then?" Arthur asked, crouching down.

"Think it's a bit of a shell nose cone," Lugs said.

"*Nose cone?* Trade you?"

"For what?"

Arthur rummaged in his pocket. "This. It's a bit of a *Messerschmitt's* belly, I reckon."

"Pull the other one," I said. "That is not a bit of a Messerschmitt's belly."

"It is!"

I held out my hand. "Let's have a look then."

Arthur hesitated, then handed it over.

"Reckon I've got a sharp eye for decent shrapnel," Arthur said.

I turned it over in my hands, then grinned. "This isn't a bit of Jerry fighter plane," I said. "This is part of a Heinz soup can."

That caused some laughter – even from Graham and Harry. "It isn't!" Arthur shouted back.

"Look at the corner, you can see a part of the Z."

"That's a bit of swastika," Arthur said.

I pulled a face. "What, *that* small?" Micky grinned at me, and I couldn't help but grin back, not just because I was getting one over on Arthur, but because Micky was with me and part of it.

Arthur looked closer as more kids started sniggering.

"No...it's definitely..."

I saw the exact moment Arthur Davey realized I was right, his face sort of collapsed in on itself, like week-old flan. It was pretty satisfying.

"Tell me about that sharp eye of yours again, Davey?" I said.

Arthur closed his hand round his soup souvenir, took a step back, then launched it over the school wall.

"I'll tell you what," he said, his cheeks flushed either from embarrassment or rage – probably both. "You against us."

"It's always us against you," Lugs pointed out.

"But this time it's formal."

"Do I have to wear my Sunday best?" I asked.

"I don't think my mum will let me wear my Sunday best if it's not a Sunday," Harry said.

"For Pete's sake!" Graham said.

Harry opened his mouth, but before he could say anything Graham said, "And if you ask me who Pete is, you're out of the gang. For good this time."

Harry shut his mouth.

"We challenge you to a shrapnel competition," Arthur continued.

"A what?" I'd thought he was hankering for a fight. Maybe it was knowing Micky could be a bit free and loose with a penknife that had put him off. Or maybe it was the fact that there was enough fighting going on already. Either way, I was relieved when he said, "Whoever gets the best collection wins."

"Wins what?" Micky asked.

"The other gang's collection and…"

"And what?" Lugs asked.

"Dunno, what's the most valuable thing you own?"

"My cat," Lugs said, "but you're not having Tiger."

"We don't want your mangy cat," Arthur said. "Think of something else."

I suggested some comics but that didn't seem to go down well.

185

"Nah," Arthur said, "it's got to be better than comics."

"What about your bike, Micky?" I said, thinking that it was a good prize and also thinking that I wouldn't care too much if we lost it.

"No way!" Micky said.

"Come on, we're bound to win, he thought a Heinz Oxtail soup can was a *Messerschmitt* bomber."

"Was it oxtail?" Harry said wistfully. "That's my favourite."

Everyone ignored him.

"What are you offering up then?" I asked. "Just so we know if the bike's worth the risk."

"We're not risking my bike," Micky said.

"A go-kart!" Arthur said. "We put up Harry's go-kart."

"It's not my go-kart! It's my older brother's! And I can't ask him because he's in the middle of the North Atlantic fighting German U-boats!"

"Perfect," Arthur said.

"Why's that perfect?" Harry asked.

"Because he's not going to need a go-kart in the North Atlantic, is he?"

"S'pose not."

"So that's a deal, our go-kart for your bike," Arthur stuck out his hand.

I looked at Micky. "We won't lose."

"Or are you scared, Micky Smith?" Arthur said.

Micky nodded at me, I clasped Arthur's hand, and the deal was sealed.

CHAPTER 26

As we headed back inside for lessons, Micky chatted on about the shrapnel he wanted to find, saying how good it would be if we actually found some real *Messerschmitt* belly – with a swastika on it. I laughed, imagining Arthur's face, but as I followed him into the classroom, all I could think about was how I could almost feel Johnny's grip on him weakening. The bet had pulled Micky right back to me and Lugs.

After school, Arthur suggested a time limit of two weeks for the competition. I thought about it. It was two weeks before Johnny would be back. I reckoned a fortnight shrapnel hunting with Micky would be enough time to get him back on side.

"Two weeks it is," I said. Then we drew up a score sheet for the different pieces of shrapnel and what we thought they would each be worth. Shell nose cones and tail fins were classed as top rate. The more rings on the nose cone the better. Anything that was still hot got extra points. The bigger the piece the more valuable it was. German bomb fragments were better than British anti-aircraft shells. Any identifiable marks and the more intact the piece was, the higher it would score.

Once we were all happy with the score sheet, Lugs said, "We should have team names."

"Yeah," Graham said.

"We'll be called Arthur's Army," Arthur said.

Graham and Harry weren't keen.

"I've got a great one!" Harry shouted. He held his hands out in front of him and parted them in the air and said, "The Mighty Blasters!"

Arthur and Graham looked at him open-mouthed.

"Because we'll blast through the streets collecting the wreckage of bomb blasts!"

"That's good," I said. "And you're already known for the mighty blasts that come out of your backsides too!"

Graham swiped Harry round the head. "Idiot."

"What about The Wreckers?" Arthur said.

Graham nodded as he considered it. "Yeah, The Wreckers, I like that."

"Because we'll trawl through the wreckage and wreck your dreams of winning," Harry said.

Arthur and Billy looked at him open-mouthed again.

"What? I said something stupid, didn't I?" Harry said.

"No, what you said was genius," Billy said. "That's why we're shocked."

Somehow, our name, The Shrapnel Boys, was decided upon. I don't remember who came up with it. Micky would have you believe it was him, but I don't suppose it matters who it was.

All I do remember is that those two weeks when we were scavenging for shrapnel and Johnny was out of the picture might have been my happiest time of the war.

There was another heavy raid that night. To take my mind off what was happening, I tried to focus on all the shrapnel we might find the following morning. Mrs Green was in one of her chatty moods. Maybe that was her way of dealing with the horror that was happening on the other side of the corrugated iron.

She click-clacked away at her knitting and only stopped talking when she jumped at the sound of the nearby explosions.

"I know you're worried, but your mother is a brave girl. And you two boys will have to be brave too."

"We know," I said.

"I hear Lewisham Hospital has extra strong walls."

It was a nice thing for her to say, but we knew it wasn't true.

"How was your day?"

"Pretty good," I said.

"Yeah, pretty good," Micky agreed.

"Stay out of trouble?"

"Yup," Micky said and, for the first time in a long time, I knew he was telling the truth.

"Good. My day has been a trial, thanks for asking. An hour I queued up at the butcher's this morning. I don't have time to be standing in line for one measly sausage and a bit of brisket. You know, I'm sure I saw Mr Brown give Martha Trimble an extra lamb chop too. Think he's taken a shine to her. I was a looker too when I was younger, you know."

"Were you?" I said, probably sounding more surprised than was polite.

Her needles came to a halt, and she glared at me. "Deptford May Queen in 1894." An explosion went off adding a certain amount of terrifying drama to her announcement.

"Blimey! That was last century," Micky pointed out when the ground had stopped shaking.

"I'm well aware of that," Vera said, her knitting needles starting up again. "That's when I first met my Bert, God rest his soul." She sighed. "Oh, to be eighteen and in love again."

Rather than continue with that conversation, Micky and I lay back in our bunks, listening to the barrage of noise from both outside and inside the shelter. I wondered how Lugs was getting on with only his mum and Tiger for company. How they must feel thinking of Mr Missell overseas somewhere, facing the enemy with nothing to protect him but his courage. I thought about Dad and what he might be doing. If he was in the sky right at that moment.

Mr Missell and my father were two very different men. One fighting, the other not, but both trying to show who they were when it really mattered. Others might not agree, but to me, Lugs's dad was a hero. And I couldn't help but think of my dad as a hero too. But it was hard to know if that was right. I'd seen my father. *Really* seen him. He could take on the form of a monster. How was I supposed to feel about a man like that?

CHAPTER 27

The next two weeks took on a familiar pattern, with everything focused on the competition. At night Micky and I huddled in the shelter listening to the hard rain, imagining all the pieces of tail fin and nose cone we might find, and trying not to think about where they were coming from. Then in the mornings, we'd search for valuable shrapnel on our way to school and do the same again on the way home.

When we did get back to ours, our spoils of war clinking in our pockets, we'd head straight to the shelter. Didn't seem much point going into the house when we'd only have to turn out again when the sirens sounded. Life fell into a strange sort of normal – school, shelter and shrapnel hunting, and I loved that Micky was melded into it. And even though we were battling against them, The Wreckers and us had found some sort of mutual respect. If a tasty looking bit of shrapnel was found, sure the other gang would be annoyed, but we'd all acknowledge the importance of the discovery and congratulate the finder.

When it came to shrapnel hunting, the mornings were always the best. In the morning you were more likely to find hot bits. We'd wrap those up in a couple of pairs of old socks to try and keep the heat in and then run like the clappers to present The Wreckers with the evidence. Our most precious pieces were kept on us at all times, in our pockets or in our gas-mask boxes. The rest we kept in a box in our bedroom.

Tiger had taken to following Lugs about. He'd often be there at the school gates waiting, although he'd pretend like he wanted nothing to do with Lugs whenever he tried to pat him. He'd follow along behind, making out like he didn't want to be there, that he'd just happened to be in the area, but that cat had fallen in love with Lugs. It's easy to see why.

Mum weren't all that keen on our shrapnel collecting. Said she'd heard horror stories about kids cutting major arteries or picking up live bombs, but everyone was doing it round our way, so she couldn't really stop us. Besides, we weren't stupid enough to go handling anything dangerous. We were knowledgeable – we knew what was what.

Mum did lose her rag one morning early in October though, when she found Micky standing over the cooker.

"I DO NOT believe what my eyes are seeing!" Mum yelled.

I ran into the kitchen, keen to find out what was going on. Micky had the look of someone who had been caught with his hand in the sweet jar. The wooden spoon he was holding was hovering over Mum's biggest cooking pot. On the side next to the cooker were a couple of pairs of socks and a few of Mum's tea towels.

Our Micky wasn't one for cooking, so I was immediately curious.

"What you doing?" I asked.

"The child has lost it!" Mum said. "Well and truly lost it!"

I peered into the pot then looked at Micky and smiled. "You, Micky Smith, are a genius!"

"I can think of lots of words for him right now," Mum said. "And genius is not one of them! Not even close!"

Micky ignored her and said, "I thought if we heated the bits up, we'll get extra points!"

"You're scratching my best pot!" Mum said.

I laughed. "Who has a *best pot*?"

"I do! Well, I *did*! Get that rubbish out of it."

Micky and I both looked at her, appalled. "This is not rubbish," I said. "This is highly valuable shrapnel."

"Highly valuable *hot* shrapnel," Micky added.

Mum threw her arms in the air and did a massive huff. "I give up! There's a war on and my children are cooking metal." Then she went and sat down on the sofa and closed her eyes.

Micky and I each grabbed a handle of the pot and tipped the hot mangled bits of metal out onto the socks and tea towels. Then we bundled up our packages and legged it to school.

On the way, I said to Mick, "I know there's a war on and all, but life don't feel too bad, does it?"

"If you say so," Mick said.

I hadn't spoken to him much about Johnny since he'd left. I guess I was scared of how Micky might take it – that if I lectured him, he would back away or leap to Johnny's defence. But with the shrapnel radiating heat in our back pockets, I felt this warm togetherness, that made me think I could bring him up.

"It's alright with just us, though. You, me and Mum?" I let the unsaid *without Johnny* hang in the air between us.

"Yeah, it's alright with just us," Mick said. He rolled his eyes, but he was smiling.

"That stuff Johnny was into, the robbing, the deliveries – those fascists he knocks about with, it's not you. He's not a good person, Mick."

Micky's jaw tensed. "Well, he ain't here now, is he?"

"But he'll be back, what'll happen then?"

"He might not be." He swallowed and looked away. "People leave, Ron, it's what they do."

"And sometimes, it's better when they're gone," I said, unsure whether we were talking about Johnny or Dad or both.

Micky looked down at the ground. "I guess."

My heart ached for him. He deserved a proper dad, a decent guy, like Mr Missell. But I couldn't offer him that. I put my hands on his shoulders to stop him walking.

"I won't leave. You, me and Mum – we stick together. The three of us."

Micky looked up at me and quietly said. "Okay."

I smiled, hoping it would make him feel better, then ruffled his hair to lighten the mood. "How about we run the rest of the way to make sure this shrapnel doesn't cool down before we get there?"

"Alright," Micky said.

"Last one there smells of Hitler's underwear!" I said and charged off with Micky chasing after me.

Lugs couldn't believe it when we showed him our warmed treasure. Neither could The Wreckers.

"Touch it, go on," Micky said.

Arthur put a finger on one of the scraps. Then he put his hand on his hips and nodded. "It's hot alright. Extra point for The Shrapnel Boys, note it down, Graham."

Harry produced a bit of shell fin for The Wreckers. It wasn't big and there was some debate as to whether it actually was a bit of fin, but we let them have it because we'd been a little creative with the truth ourselves.

"Think that makes us even score-wise," Arthur said.

"Give over!" Micky said.

"Reckon he might be right," I said, because at that moment, I didn't want our competition to stop.

I wonder if maybe Arthur thought the same because he said, "You're alright, Smith. Still my sworn enemy, but you're alright."

We were so busy chatting that we hadn't noticed the rest of the school had already lined up and Mr Etherington was making his way over to us. We scrambled to put the shrapnel in our gas-mask boxes and stuff it in our pockets, but he'd already seen.

"To your feet!" he barked.

We all jumped up.

Mr Etherington waved his cane at our gas masks. "Tip it out, all of it."

Reluctantly, we did as he said.

"Empty your pockets."

"But sir—" I said.

"Do it!" he barked, then turned and shouted, "Miss Grimshaw, bring me a box."

Miss Grimshaw disappeared inside, then reappeared moments later with a cardboard box. "In here," Mr Etherington said, pointing at it.

Harry stepped into the box.

Mr Etherington looked at him aghast. The rest of us tried to stifle our giggles, but the sight of Harry Scott standing in a box was too much.

"Not you, you imbecile! The shrapnel!"

Harry stepped back out. "Sorry, sir. When you said *in here*, I thought you meant us."

"Why would you think that?" Mr Etherington blasted.

"Dunno, sir. Thought you'd come up with another one of your weird punishments. You know, like when you'd cane Lugs and Micky when Ronnie did something wrong."

We all snickered again, but Harry did have a point. I wouldn't have put it past Etherington to get us all to stand in a box. He'd had me standing in the corner once with a dunce's cap on my head for misremembering my nine-times table.

"Silence!" Mr Etherington bellowed.

We tried our best to be silent, but you know when you've got the snickers in you and there is no way they're going anywhere but out? Well, that happened to all of us that day. We couldn't stop laughing even though we knew we'd be for it.

Mr Etherington huffed and puffed but he didn't seem to know what to do about a group of children spluttering with laughter. Scared children, angry children – yes, he knew what to do about those. But ones bent over double giggling – those he was far less experienced with. He stood there looking outraged for a bit. Then said, "For goodness' sake! Pull yourselves together! There's a war on!"

I don't know why, but that just made us laugh even more.

"Ridiculous! The lot of you! Get that scrap in the box. I'm sending it to be melted down for the war effort," he said and then stormed off.

We watched him stomp back to school as best he could with his bad leg. Then we all looked down at the pile on the floor and our laughter died down.

"Come on," I said. "Better do as he ordered."

"It's all our best bits too," Lugs said as we started chucking it in the box, slipping a few of our most cherished pieces into our pockets.

Harry kissed an almost complete bit of nose cone, that was too big to hide, and said, "You were my favourite."

When it was full, we stood over the box. I know it would have looked like worthless junk to most people, but to us, it meant something. I dunno, maybe finding it and claiming it as ours had given us the feeling we had a little bit of control over something. I guess we needed that when we were powerless over everything else.

We were quiet for a bit, all feeling this strange sense of loss – daft really.

Then Harry said, "I really thought he meant for *us* to get in the box," and we started laughing again.

CHAPTER 28

After Mr Etherington confiscated our shrapnel, we didn't give up on our battle. If anything, we got into it even more.

We knew we couldn't take our findings in to school, so we set about finding ourselves somewhere else to meet.

"What we need is a den," I said, as the six of us wandered down the road after school. I had my arm slung over Micky's shoulder and Tiger was prowling along behind like he had nothing better to do.

"What we need is a den *each*," Arthur said. "We're still sworn enemies, remember?"

"Don't worry, I haven't forgotten."

"There's a couple of houses a few streets from the docks that took a hit. The front's off them both, but I reckon the downstairs looks perfect for what we need," Graham said.

"Let's go and check them out." Lugs turned to Tiger. "You coming?"

Tiger tilted his head and stood there like he was considering it.

"Nobody's forcing you," Lugs said and set off. Tiger waited for a bit, then followed.

Graham had been right. The houses were perfect for what we needed. Not that you could really call them houses. A better description was piles of rubble. The fronts were open to the street and parts of the ceilings had fallen down. There was a big chunk of the interconnecting wall missing – you could see right through one sitting room into the other. There was a family photo on one of the walls. A mum and a dad and two girls in their Sunday best. Smiles on their faces from another time. I didn't look at it long. Maybe I should have done. Maybe we should have stopped to think more about the people who'd lived there before we claimed the houses as ours. But we didn't. Thinking about sad stuff like that wasn't the way to survive. It's best to close yourself off to some things.

The Wreckers took number 27, and we took number 29. We scrambled over the wreckage, making seats out of burned bits of wood.

"'Ere, we've got a sofa!" Harry shouted over from their house, "or what's left of one."

Lugs climbed up the remains of our staircase. "Just popping upstairs," he said, which was a joke because there was no upstairs.

"You lot shouldn't be playing in there!"

The voice caused me to jolt with a start. I pulled my head out of a broken kitchen cupboard and saw Mr Etherington standing in the road, a pitchfork in hand.

Surprised, Lugs dropped the brick that he was about to throw, and we all looked at each other, slight terror in our eyes, until Graham shouted back, "Not at school now, sir!" and we realized he was right.

"That may be so, but I am still in charge of your welfare, and it is not safe to be larking about in a bomb site!"

"This ain't a bomb site," Arthur said. "These are our dens. You live round here, don't you? Makes us practically neighbours."

Graham held up a battered-looking kettle. "We'd invite you round for a cuppa, but the stove is on the blink. You could try number 29."

"Sorry, we're all out of tea, and cups." I tried the tap. "And water. Maybe another time, hey?"

Mr Etherington turned a very deep shade of purple, made a few blustery noises, then stomped off.

"We're going to be for it at school!" Micky shouted through to Graham and Arthur.

"Worth it to see his face," Arthur yelled back.

"Here, fellas, watch this!"

Through the gaping hole in the wall, I could see Graham lashing a rope up over one of the ceiling beams that had survived the bombing, and he began swinging about on it like an ape. Arthur had a go next and then it was Harry's turn.

"I have to see this," Lugs said, and we went outside to get a better look.

Someone probably should have realized what would happen, but we were having too much fun.

Harry grabbed hold of the rope and started making a noise like Tarzan. He'd only done two swings when there was this almighty creak, then a deep groaning sound.

"Get out!" Arthur shouted and he and Graham dived out into the street.

Harry said, "Uh-oh," which seemed like quite a subdued reaction in the circumstances. Then he disappeared under a pile of plaster and wood and a great big puff of dust and dirt as a section of the ceiling gave way.

"Harry!" Graham shouted.

We all dashed over and started pulling the debris off him.

"Is he dead? He's got to be dead," Micky said.

"Shut up, Micky, and help!" I yelled.

We worked together to move a great big piece of plaster. Underneath lay Harry, covered in dust and completely motionless.

Graham bent down and shook him. "Harry! Harry, can you hear me?" His voice was cracking a little. I'd never seen Graham Talbot looking so scared. Guess I hadn't reckoned The Wreckers were such great mates with each other as me, Micky and Lugs were.

We flashed each other anxious glances as Arthur and Graham bent down over Harry.

Graham tried again. "Harry! Please, say you're okay. You need to be okay. Harry, can you hear me?"

Harry's eyelids sprang open, his eyes looking brilliant white against the greyness of his dusty skin.

I let out a huge breath in relief.

"I'm not dead," he said, "and I'm not deaf, and there's one other thing I am not."

"What's that?" Graham asked.

"I am NOT having another go on that stupid rope swing."

Graham laughed but I saw there were tears mixed in with it.

"Think he's okay," Arthur said, smiling.

We all helped to get Harry to his feet and he gave himself a shake, like a very dusty dog. "That turned out to be less fun than it looked," he said, glancing at the rafter.

"Thought you were a goner," Micky said. "When that ceiling came down, I thought that's it, no more Harry Scott."

Harry grinned, then touched his split, bleeding lip. "Take more than that to finish me off!"

"You really are a wrecker," I said.

Harry beat his chest. "I am," he said proudly. "I am Harry Scott the invincible!"

We all whooped and cheered, and Harry bowed, and I guess we did all kind of think we were invincible too. Thing is, that's not how war works.

The next morning was a Saturday, the fifth of October, I think. Despite what had happened with the rope swing and Mr Etherington hanging around, we'd decided that our new dens were still fit for purpose, and we agreed that The Wreckers and The Shrapnel Boys should meet after lunch, so we had time before the night raid to check over the shrapnel we had found. It would also give us the morning to have a scout about.

As soon as the early morning all-clear had sounded, Micky and I went outside to wait for Lugs. We were in the road, turning over the rubble, but it was slim pickings. Vera came back from speaking to one of our older neighbours, who she checked in on from time to time, and started relaying the gossip about some Mrs Kirkley or Kirtley who had been up before the courts for showing a light. I was making all the sounds of someone who was listening, but I wasn't really paying much attention, until she mentioned Johnny.

"Will he be back this way soon?" she asked and took a long pull on her cigarette.

I shrugged, my shoulders tensing at his name. If he kept to his word, Johnny was due back any day.

"Dunno," Micky said, then shoved a piece of mangled metal under my nose. "'Ere Ron, think this is anything?"

I didn't answer because I was taking in how disinterested he'd been about Johnny.

"So?" he pressed.

"I think you might have something good there," I said.

He scrunched up his nose, not convinced. Then stuffed it in his pocket.

"Oi-oi!" We looked up to see Lugs striding down the road, a pleased look on his face and something black and heavy in his arms. Tiger was behind him, snarling away.

"What you got there, Billy, love?" Vera asked, lighting her

third cigarette in what seemed like as many minutes.

"A magnet," Lugs said proudly.

"It's the size of a brick!" Micky said, impressed.

"Found it down by the docks."

Vera rolled her eyes and headed back inside.

"Micky, Ronnie, I've had an absolute corker of an idea. That go-kart will soon become property of The Shrapnel Boys, I'm telling you!"

"Go on then," I said, "let's hear it."

CHAPTER 29

At the time, Lugs's idea seemed to be one of pure genius. The plan was for Micky to ride his bike through the bomb wreckage with the magnet tied round his waist. We all reckoned that we'd cover loads of ground in no time and the magnet would pick up all the bits of shrapnel and we would be saved the bother of having to scratch around in the rubble.

We decided to head down to one of the roads by the docks, because that's where most of the destruction was and therefore the best of the shrapnel. I looped some rope round Micky's middle and tied it tight, then Lugs tied the magnet to the end of the rope.

"You done a decent knot?" he asked me. "Don't want it coming loose."

I yanked it to show it was secure.

"Good," Lugs said. "Micky, you ready?"

Micky nodded and grabbed the handlebars of his bike. "Roger that. Smith number one is ready for take-off."

"Smith number two," I corrected.

"We'll run along behind and shout when you've picked up enough." Micky looked at me, rubbing his hands in anticipation.

"Got it," Micky said.

"Okay, off you go!"

Slowly, Micky made his way down the middle of the road, swerving to avoid any craters as the magnet bounced about behind him. A few people stopped and laughed, a few stopped and shook their heads, disapproving. But we weren't worried.

"It's working!" Lugs said as we watched the shards of metal collecting on the magnet. "It's actually working!"

We jogged along behind until we'd decided we'd collected enough and then shouted for Micky to stop. We sat on the edge of the pavement picking through the bits. Those that were worth keeping went in a bucket, those that weren't we chucked. And then we'd go at it again.

"The Wreckers aren't going to believe how much we've collected!" Lugs said all excited.

"This is an absolute belter of an idea," I said.

We decided to give it one more go, before we headed back for lunch. I'd said Lugs could come back to ours as Mum had gone to the shops in the morning to get our weekly rations and I reckoned she'd be okay about feeding Lugs too.

Micky tore off down the street, with the magnet trailing behind and us struggling to keep up with him. Lugs and I were getting a bit tired, and our thoughts had turned from shrapnel to our stomachs. Micky picked up a few nails and other bits that didn't look very interesting and I was beginning to think we'd had the best of the shrapnel for the day. Then, instead of carrying on down the road, Micky cut over the corner of a pavement and down the back of the warehouses, guess he thought there may be more shrapnel closer to the river.

Lugs and I chased after him as he wove into one of the abandoned buildings through a damaged doorway, then emerged through another door further down.

He pedalled along the alley until, suddenly, he jerked backwards. Something had clanged onto the magnet, and it must have been heavy because Lugs and I heard the noise from the end of the road. Micky dragged it along for no more than a metre until it held him back like an anchor and he ground to a halt.

Both Lugs and I stopped still. The thing that Micky was now attached to was big. And torpedo shaped.

My knees went weak.

"FLAMING HECK!" Lugs shouted, finding his voice before me.

"D…D…DON'T MOVE!" I finally managed to bellow, because Micky had succeeded in magnet-ing himself to what looked very much like an unexploded bomb. A fifty-kilo high explosive by the looks of it. If that thing went off it would blow him and half the street sky high.

Micky turned round to look behind him. When he saw what was on the magnet, he immediately turned a translucent white colour and let out a terrified whimper.

"I said don't move!" I yelled at him.

"W…what do I do? I think I can hear it ticking."

I held out my hands. "Don't panic. Stay calm."

"Easy for you to say, you're not the one attached to a bleedin' bomb!"

"I can't look! I can't look!" Lugs said, in quite a high-pitched voice, which did nothing to help calm the situation.

I swivelled round desperately looking for help, but we were in an alley between two large warehouses, and nobody was about. Micky was about fifteen metres from us – the bomb a metre or so behind him, propped up at an angle against a brick. "Lugs, go for help. We need a bomb disposal team here and fast."

Lugs nodded, took one last look at Micky, then stumbled off over the rubble.

"Micky, you need to untie the knot round your waist, carefully and then slowly walk to me."

"How can I do that? I'm holding on to the bike! I think I'm going to throw up."

"You're not going to throw up. Lower the bike to the ground, carefully."

Micky did as I asked and placed the bike on the floor.

"Great, you're doing great!" I said. "Now, untie the knot."

Micky nodded. He tried to reach round to the knot on his back, but I could see by the way his hands were trembling that he was going to struggle.

"I can't do it." Sweat was beading on his forehead – tears were spilling out of his eyes. "Ronnie, please, help me."

"I'm coming over," I said.

I took a deep breath. I was vaguely aware that some people had gathered at the other end of the alley. I could hear voices but not what they were saying. It was probably something along the lines of *Look at that kid attached to that stonking great bomb!* I took another deep breath. Then a third.

"Ronnie, are you coming or what? Or are you just going to stand there panting?" Micky blubbed.

"I'm coming." Slowly, I made my way over, picking through the bits of debris. I edged past the bomb, not wanting to disturb it. It was a green-grey colour, with yellow stripes on the tail fin and the letter *I* painted in black on the shell. If it had been stood on its end, I reckon it would have reached up to my elbow. I didn't know how much time we had. I'd heard that some unexploded bombs could lie dormant for weeks, months even – if they weren't disturbed. I suspected that Micky dragging it across the ground probably wasn't a good thing.

I made it to Micky and said, "Right let's get this thing off you, shall we?" and started trying to loosen the knot. My own fingers were trembling too, and the knot was so tight.

"I don't suppose you have your penknife to hand?" I asked.

Micky gave the smallest shake of his head.

I tried to break the rope with my hands, but it was hopeless.

"It's not working!" Micky said, panic rising in his voice.

"Stay calm," I said. "It's only rope, we can do this."

I looked over at the crowd. I could see Lugs waving his arms around wildly.

"I think Lugs has found help," I said. "I'm sure the bomb disposal guys will be here soon. They deal with these things all the time."

"A kid attached to a bomb by a magnet?" Micky said.

"Maybe not that exactly, but they're experts, they'll know what to do."

Micky's breathing was getting fast and shallow. He started pulling at the rope. Tugging it.

"Micky! Don't!" I said. "You might set it off!"

Micky calmed down and I tried the knot again, but my fingers were trembling even more ferociously, and I was sweating so much, I struggled to get a grip. I was so focused on what I was doing, I didn't notice a man approach, until I heard two footsteps right behind me. One strong. One laboured.

"Do not move."

I looked up. I couldn't believe my eyes.

"Mr Etherington?"

Seeing him there was almost as surprising as the bomb that Micky was umbilicalled to.

"It's ticking, sir!" Micky sobbed.

Mr Etherington bent down, unwrapping a leather case as he spoke, "I want you both to listen to me carefully."

"Y...yes, sir," Micky said.

"I need you to stay very still, Michael." Mr Etherington pulled out a sharp blade and then, very carefully, cut the rope. His hands didn't even shake.

I exhaled. "You're free, Mick. It's going to be okay."

"I want you both to walk, steadily and slowly, all the way to the people at the end of the road. Go."

Micky took a couple of wobbly steps. I grabbed him under his arm to help. Then, keeping my eyes on the crowd, we started walking. After a couple of metres, I think Micky had recovered considerably because he ignored the instruction to walk steadily and suddenly legged it.

I was about to do the same when I remembered Mr Etherington. He was still there, with the bomb. I turned round. He was kneeling and it looked like he was trying to unscrew the bomb's base plate.

"Flippin' heck, sir! You know that's a bomb?"

"I'm well aware it's a bomb, Smith."

"I wouldn't touch it if I was you," I said. I couldn't believe that he hadn't just walked away. "Seriously, sir, what are you doing?"

"I'm going to take a look at this bomb and hopefully neutralize the fuse."

I blinked, surprised at how knowledgeable he sounded. "Do you think that's a good idea, sir? Maybe it would be better if we just legged it out of here."

He spoke without looking up, his eyes fixed on the bottom of the bomb. "Contrary to what you may think, Master Smith, I was not injured by a garden fork. I led a bomb-disposal unit during the Great War."

I didn't know what to say.

"On your way, Smith."

I started heading towards Lugs, Micky and the others. Then stopped and said, "Thanks, sir."

Mr Etherington, didn't reply, just gave the tiniest nod of his head.

CHAPTER 30

Micky, Lugs and I watched through the banisters as Mum brought a cup of tea to her mouth. Her hand was shaking and the liquid was sloshing about inside. Vera was sitting next to her, her hand on Mum's knee.

Mum put the tea down, undrunk. "When I think of what could have happened..."

"Honestly, silly little blighters!" Vera said. "A magnet round his waist! Of all things! What a ridiculous idea!"

"It wasn't *that* ridiculous, Lugs," I whispered. Lugs had been giving himself a hard time about what had happened, but it wasn't his fault, he weren't to know that our Micky would lash himself to a high explosive.

"If Mr Etherington hadn't been there..." Mum continued.

"Now, that *was* a surprise," Vera said. "Heard he'd defused it before the bomb disposal team even arrived. I suppose we should be grateful. If the lads hadn't have found it, it might have gone off and more lives could have been lost."

"See," I whispered to Lugs, "we're practically heroes."

We all knew that wasn't true though. If anyone was a hero, much to my astonishment, it was Mr Etherington.

Vera pushed down on the sofa with both hands and got herself up with a groan. "You stay there, Cathy, I'll fix the boys their lunch."

We crept back upstairs so Mum didn't hear us and had a look through the shrapnel we had collected in our bucket. It wasn't bad. A couple of incendiary bomb shells, a few fragments of anti-aircraft shells, something that looked like it might have once been part of a bomb fuse – that could do us well.

"All looks a bit pathetic compared to what Micky found," Lugs said.

I laughed. "Can you imagine what The Wreckers would have said if we'd shown up with that!"

After lunch, we headed to the dens with our bucket of finds. The Wreckers were already there. I knocked on what was left of the door frame of number 27 and said, "Anybody home?"

Arthur said, "Visitors, how nice. Graham, put the kettle on."

Graham clattered about a bit in what was once the kitchen, then said, "Fraid we're all out of tea."

Arthur sighed. "Well, offer them a beer then."

"Beer!" Harry said. "We don't have any of that either..." Then he grinned and shook his head, "Oh, you're being sarcastic, aren't you?"

*   *   *

We gathered round what Arthur called the lounge area and Lugs, Micky and I told them all about what had happened with the bomb in the warehouse and how Mr Etherington had defused it. Micky couldn't help but exaggerate a bit. He left out the part where he was scared and crying for me to help him. Didn't really mention me at all. But the bomb was now a hundred kilogrammes big and the ticking could be heard all the way down the street. The Wreckers lapped it up, but it was the part about Mr Etherington that they struggled to believe. The part that was actually true.

"Ethers?" Arthur said. "Nah, you're having us on!"

"I swear to you it happened," I said. "He said he worked on bombs in the Great War, and it didn't half look like he knew what he was doing."

"If it's true, I guess that makes old Mr Etherington a bit of a hero," Billy said.

"But he's a bully," Harry said.

"Yeah, he is," I said, "but I guess people can be both."

Harry frowned, like he was trying to make sense of what I'd said. I didn't blame him – it was hard to get your head around. I'd been wrestling with the same thing for ages.

"Right, let's get a look at what you've got," I said and tipped our shrapnel out onto the floor.

"Gor blimey, you've got loads!" Harry said.

"The magnet worked pretty well, to start with," Lugs said.

We spent some time going through our finds, arguing over the value of each. Once we'd reached an agreement, we put our collections into our safe places, then spent a bit of time jumping about and playing war in the rubble until we were interrupted.

"Alright, lads? Thought it was you."

I knew whose voice it was immediately and, for the second time that day, my insides froze.

Lugs shot me a concerned look. There was Johnny larger than life. His hair slick with Brylcreem and a look of purpose in his eyes.

Micky dropped down from the bit of crumbling wall he was standing on. For a moment he didn't move, then he dashed over to Johnny. "Johnny, you're back!"

I stood up, arms crossed – a weight as big as a fifty-kilo bomb in my stomach.

"Just on my way to the Chichester Arms. What do you think of the threads?" Johnny held the jacket of what looked like a new and expensive suit out wide and spun round.

"Nice!" Micky said.

"Business," Johnny said, with a cocky wobble of his head, "is booming."

"That's great, Johnny, really great," Micky said.

My brother had been sucked back in immediately and completely. I felt the helplessness creeping through me. I really thought I'd done enough to get my brother back. Watching him now, I knew hadn't. I'd convinced myself that with Johnny out of the picture for a while, Micky had remembered who his true friends were. Who his family was. Seemed he hadn't remembered either.

Johnny nodded over towards The Wreckers. "Why don't you introduce me to your pals?"

Micky said, "Okay, Johnny. They're The Wreckers. That's Arthur Davey –"

Arthur held up his hand.

"And the blond one's Graham Talbot and the big lad, that's Harry Scott."

"Nice to meet you boys. The name's Johnny Simmons. If you're ever looking to do something more financially rewarding with your time than scrabbling about in the muck, you let me know. I've got some big things happening and I could use some strapping-looking fellas like you."

I stood there, rooted to the spot, watching it all unfold in front of me. I was shouting at myself inside my head, telling myself to do something to stop what was happening, but I couldn't speak, couldn't even move.

"Yeah?" said Graham, picking his way through the rubble towards Johnny. "Paid work? What sort of stuff?"

"Bit of this, bit of that. Deliveries and collections mainly," Johnny said, and my heart sank. He narrowed his eyes. "You the trustworthy sort?"

"We sure are," Graham replied.

"You speak to Micky then – he'll tell you it's a sweet deal."

"We'll do that, sir!" Arthur said.

Johnny slung his arm over Micky's shoulder. "You happy to get back on your bike, be in charge of some new recruits, Mick?"

"Course I am," Micky said, his chest puffing up.

"Good lad," Johnny beamed. Then he looked at me. "Happy to see some kids round here know to seize an opportunity when it's offered to them."

I felt the anger and desperation building in me. But every time I tried to say something, an image of Johnny with his hand at my throat came into my mind and my voice disappeared with it. So I just stood there, glaring at him. He smiled back. He knew he was getting to me, and he was enjoying it.

"You, you with the ears," Johnny said, looking at Lugs. "Invite's open to you too."

Lugs took a step closer to me. "That's awful kind of you, Johnny, but me and my ears decline."

"Suit yourself," Johnny said.

It was at this moment, that Mr Etherington appeared from the alleyway down the side of the houses. He had a spade in his hand and was wearing wellingtons. Guessed he'd been down his allotment again. Usually, I would have made some joke about taking care around his spuds. But not that day.

Etherington stopped in his tracks when he saw us. Thought he might be able to have a go at us for clambering around in the bombed houses again, but he wasn't looking at us. He was looking at Johnny.

"*You*," he said, fixing him with a glare.

Johnny, for a moment, looked a little rattled, but then a smile found its way to his face. "Hello, sir." Johnny said. "Been a while."

I looked from Mr Etherington to Johnny. Did they know each other?

Mr Etherington raised his spade. "You stay away from those boys, you hear me?"

Johnny's eyes narrowed, but the smile stayed. "Your days of telling me what to do are long gone."

"I mean it!" Mr Etherington shouted, his face flushing red. "Stay away from them! I don't want any of your Blackshirt nonsense around here!"

I shot Lugs a look. Mr Etherington knew that Johnny was a Blackshirt?

Johnny took a step towards him. "Calm down, old man, wouldn't want you giving yourself a heart attack now, would we? I'd be watching that mouth of yours too. And these boys, well, they're good friends of mine, isn't that right?"

None of us said anything. I think we were all too shocked by what we were seeing.

Mr Etherington held his spade out in front of him, more like he was using it for protection than to attack. "Go on, off with you! Should be locked up with the rest of them!"

The spade wavered about in front of him and, for the second time that day, I saw Mr Etherington in a different light. He hadn't been frightened by the bomb, but there was something about Johnny Simmons that was scaring him.

Johnny must have sensed that because he laughed. "How the tables have turned."

"Rotten to the core, you are! Now get away!" Mr Etherington spluttered.

I gawped at Mr Etherington, listening to him saying all the

things I wanted to say. Confirming everything I knew. Reigniting my determination to get Johnny out of our lives for good.

Johnny held up his hands. "I was about to go anyway." He pointed at Micky. "See you later, Micky lad, and I'll tell you what I've got planned."

Johnny winked at Mr Etherington, then walked off down the road whistling. Mr Etherington planted his spade on the ground and rested on it for a moment.

"You alright, sir?" I asked.

He straightened himself up. "Lord knows I've tried my best to teach you boys, but if there is anything you learn from me, let it be this – stay away from that man."

"Know him, do you, sir?" Arthur said.

Mr Etherington gave the smallest of nods. "Oh yes, I know him." Then he shuffled off down the road with us all standing there watching him leave.

When he turned the corner, Arthur burst out laughing. "What the heck was that about?"

"He's full of hot air that one," Micky said.

"Don't you think maybe we should listen to what he said?" Lugs said. "He called him a Blackshirt – you know, a fascist."

"They're not proper fascists, though, are they?" Graham said. "My dad says they make some good points about stuff."

"Like what?" Lugs snapped. "About hating Jews?"

Graham pulled a face. "Nah – about putting your country first."

"Lugs is right, Graham," I said, throwing my arms in the air, in disbelief. "The Blackshirts are proper fascists and I can't see how they can be putting our country first if they are backing the Nazis." I grabbed my brother's arm. "Micky, come on! Didn't you hear what Etherington said? Surely, you can see now that Johnny is dangerous."

"What's this?" Graham laughed. "Didn't think I'd see the day when Ronnie Smith listened to Mr Etherington!"

"Tell you what, any man that can get that kind of reaction out of old Ethers is alright with me! Did you see him shaking?" Arthur said.

"Mr Etherington saved Micky's life today!" I said.

"That may be so," Arthur said, "but Johnny's offering us paid work, and I'm not going to turn that down." Arthur slung his arm round Micky's shoulders. "Come on, Micky, tell us more about this job for Johnny."

The Wreckers crowded round my brother, pelting him with questions about Johnny Simmons and the kind of money he might pay them. I think I knew then that our games were over. In the space of a few minutes, Micky had become the new leader of The Wreckers, and The Shrapnel Boys were down to just two.

CHAPTER 31

I didn't much fancy hanging around after Mr Etherington had left, and Lugs was keen to leave too. I could tell that Johnny's resurfacing had rattled him. We loitered about for a bit, trying to hear if Micky was going to tell the truth about what it was that he did for Johnny, but he was spinning the boys the same old yarn he'd spun me. That it was just like working a better-paid paper round.

"Wanna come back to mine for a bit?" Lugs asked as we watched Micky larking about with the others.

We only had an hour before we needed to get back home ready for the night raid. We were well used to the routine by then.

"Yeah," I said.

Lugs draped his arm over my shoulders as we headed off under a sky that was darkening like a fresh bruise. "Do you want to talk about what just happened?"

I shook my head. I couldn't face it. "Not really."

Lugs whispered something under his breath that I didn't quite catch. I raised an eyebrow. "What was that?"

"Just said a little prayer asking that when the bombs fall tonight if they were to pick out Johnny Simmons, instead of some other poor soul, I'd be awfully grateful."

"If you're praying, don't you think you should ask for the bombing to stop completely?"

"Tried that. Didn't work. Come on, I'll show you Tiger's new trick."

"What is it this time? The can-can? Juggling? Walking the tight rope?"

"He's getting better at those," Lugs joked, "but the new trick he's perfected is what I call the sand-mat death gaze."

"What's that then?"

"He's taken to standing and glaring at the new sand mat Mum got to put out incendiary bombs. I think he thinks it's a new pet and he ain't so happy about it."

"What are we waiting for? Who doesn't want to see a one-eyed cat glaring at a sack of sand."

Lugs wasn't lying, Tiger was standing on the doorstep of number 39 Oscar Street in some kind of Western stand-off with the mat.

Lugs stood with his hands on his hips and shook his head. "Reckon he's been there for hours, daft moggy."

Lugs and I went and sat in the shelter and Mrs Missell brought us out a piece of her mock apricot flan in two metal bowls.

"She's real into her experimental ration cookery," Lugs sighed.

I took a spoonful. "It's carrot, isn't it?"

Lugs nodded sadly, spooned in a mouthful, swallowed and then said right apologetically, "'Fraid so, Ron. 'Fraid so."

When we'd finished, I put my bowl on the floor, laid down on the bunk and sighed.

"Ready to talk?" Lugs said.

"No. Maybe. I don't know." I let out a frustrated puff of air. "You saw Mick, how pleased he was to see Johnny. Suckered straight back in."

Lugs shook his head and did a long sigh himself. "What do you think it is – this plan of Johnny's? All his talk of something big happening has got me right worried."

"Me too. S'pose I could try talking to Micky about it, but I don't think he'll tell me, and I think he's even less likely to listen to me now he's got a *team* round him."

"They dropped us pretty quick, didn't they?" Lugs said.

"They sure did."

We both fell silent. Lugs' brow was crumpled, either in thought or worry – maybe both – and I fought against the tears that were threatening to form in my eyes.

"You know," Lugs began, "having the others involved might be a good thing."

"How's that then?"

"Not talking Harry down – I like him, truth be known – but I reckon you ask Harry the right question in the right way, and you might be able get the inside scoop on what's going on."

225

I sat upright. "You, Billy Missell, are a genius."

"Steady. Last time we thought that Mick ended up attached to a high explosive."

"True. But *this*...this is good!"

When I started to head back home, the light was fading fast and there was a chill to the October air. I walked quickly. It felt like it had been a long day and the thought of yet another night of broken sleep in the shelter weighed heavy on me. I suddenly felt tired, so, so tired.

I think maybe my tiredness was what stopped me from noticing the boy on a bike a few metres in front of me. I didn't clock his uniform – the blue jacket and blue cap. Or the leather bag that would have bounced up and down across his shoulder. Nor did I see him get off his bike and open our gate. I didn't hear what he said to Mum either. The first thing I saw when I opened my eyes to the world around me, was the look on my mother's face.

It's a look I can't ever forget.

She was clutching a telegram.

The telegraph boy said, "Truly sorry, missus," then nodded at me when he walked past.

The air-raid siren started up, but neither Mum or I acknowledged it.

Mum held the telegram in her hands. We both stood completely still, almost as if we were frozen in time.

"Mum?"

"I can't," she said, her eyes not leaving the telegram. "If I read it, it will make it true." She spoke so quietly it was hard to hear.

I put my hands on top of hers. "You can't change the truth." I slid the telegram out from her fingers. "I'll read it."

She looked in my eyes and nodded.

Vera's front door swung open and she burst outside, a sandwich stuck in her mouth and her knitting under one arm. She took the sandwich out and said, "Don't dally, Jerry are on their way." Then stuffed it back in.

Mum and I didn't respond.

"What are you waiting for? A written invitation?" Vera said, her voice muffled by the bread. Her eyes then fell on the telegram, then the sandwich fell out of her mouth.

"Oh goodness," she said and took a step back, her head bowed. "Oh, Cathy."

"Go on, Ronnie," Mum said.

"From Air Ministry Adastral House, Kingsway. Deeply regret—" I stopped, the words catching in my throat and blurring on the page. I blinked, took a breath and pushed down the emotions that were climbing up through me. "Deeply regret to advise you that your husband PLT/OFF George Robert Smith is reported missing in action presumed dead as a result of air operations on the night of 27/28th/ 9/40 STOP The Air Council express their profound sympathy STOP."

The air-raid siren must have still been wailing, but I can't remember hearing a thing, except the drumming of my own

227

heart in my ears. The world had changed and the memory of a chance I hadn't taken swelled in my mind. I never forgave him. And now it was too late. *Presumed dead.* Everyone knew the word presumed was unnecessary.

Mum stood opposite me, her chest rising and falling rapidly as her breathing quickened.

Her knees buckled but she grabbed the door frame and stopped herself falling. She pushed herself forward, staggering past me and along the path, her eyes fixed straight ahead.

Out in the middle of the street, with the drone of German bombers in the distance, she let out a deep groan – stuttering and painful. Then she fell to her knees, and clutching her stomach shouted, "God damn you, George! God damn you!"

I pushed away my own feelings and stuffed the telegram in my pocket. I ran over and dropped down beside her. She turned to me, her face tight and unfamiliar. I realized it was not sadness she was feeling, not then anyway. But anger.

"Why?" she shouted. "Why does he get to hurt me again?"

I didn't know the answer. At that moment, I didn't know anything.

I reached down and picked up a rock from the road. I put it in her hand and closed her fingers round it. She looked at me, confusion in her eyes. "Ronnie?"

"Throw it," I said. "Throw rocks at the sky, Mum, if you have to."

She looked at her hand, gripping the rock tightly now. I put my arms round her and, slowly, she struggled to her feet.

"Throw rocks at the sky," she said, then she leaned backwards and launched that rock straight down the road, and with it soared an almighty scream.

She stood there panting, her eyes closed.

"Good?" I said.

"Another," she said. "I need another."

Quickly, I passed another one to her and she chucked that one too. "That's for you, George Robert Smith!" she shouted. She bent down and picked up three more, throwing them in quick succession.

"This one is for what you did to us!"

"And this one is for coming back changed!"

"And this one, this one is for dying and not being able to come back at all!"

Vera came skittering across, her eyes so wide I thought they might fall clear out of her face. "Cathy, love, whatever are you—"

"Throwing rocks, Vera," Mum said, "and you know what? It feels good!" Mum picked up another one and yelled, "And while I'm at it, this one's for you, Adolf, and your stinking stupid war!"

I picked one up, did a little run up and sent one flying. *That's you for, Dad.* Then I grabbed another. *And that's for you, Johnny Simmons.*

Vera put her knitting on the pavement, said, "Alrighty then," and picked up a rock, chucked it up, caught it, then swung her arm round in two full circles and let it fly. "This is for taking our bacon from us!" she hollered.

Mum and I stood, open-mouthed as Vera's rock blasted through the air. It must have gone not short of forty metres, way further than mine.

She rolled her shoulders. "What?" she said and gave me a wink. "I'm only just warming up."

And so we stood there, chucking rocks at the sky as explosions went off around London and fire and smoke and the *rat-tat-tat* of gunfire filled the air.

We might have stayed there all night had an air-raid warden not come running down the street blowing his whistle.

"Have you lost your minds?" he yelled as he dodged an absolute air-ripper of a rock that Vera had hurled in his direction.

Mum put her arms in the air and spun round. "Haven't we all? Hasn't the whole world lost its mind! Look around you, if this isn't insanity, I don't know what is!"

The air warden spluttered, his thick moustache twitching in disbelief. "Get yourselves in your shelter immediately!" He looked from Mum to me. "Act like a mother, for heaven's sake."

Mum stopped still.

I think I might have actually snarled at him when I said, "She always acts like a mother. The best mother, you furry-faced buffoon!"

Then Mum said, "Ronnie, where's your brother? Where's Micky?"

And that's when I realized, Micky hadn't come home.

CHAPTER 32

"Ronnie, where's your brother?" Mum repeated, trying to keep her voice steady even though her rising panic was obvious.

"I don't know. He should be home. He knows to come home in time for the raids," I said, already defensive.

"Well, he's not here now, is he?" Mum said, her voice growing louder.

It felt like she was blaming me and even though I was blaming myself too, I said, "I'm not his keeper, am I?"

"You're his older brother, Ronnie!" Mum shot back.

"Like that matters to him!" I said, the worry and unfairness causing me to shout. I'd tried to be his older brother, really, I had, but I wasn't enough.

"Where did you last see him, love?" Vera asked, putting her hand on my shoulder.

The gentleness and concern in her voice, took all of the anger out of me. "At the dens—"

"*What* dens?" Mum said.

I looked at the floor. "We've a couple of dens in some bombed-out houses round the back of the warehouses. We've been meeting some other lads there."

"Have you indeed?" Mum said.

There was a sharp, impatient cough.

We all swung round to see the air-raid warden. "I must insist that you get in your shelter, immediately!"

I think we'd all forgotten he was still there. Mum looked at him like she'd never heard anything more ridiculous in her whole life.

"I can't very well get in the shelter when I'm missing one of my children!" Then she marched off down the street.

"Madam!" the warden shouted after her. "Where do you think you're going?"

"Where do you think, Timbuktu? I'm going to find my son!"

"We are in the midst of an air raid! The Hun are in the very skies above our heads!"

"Are they? I hadn't noticed," Mum barked. "Vera, would you take Ronnie inside?"

I ran after her. "Not a chance, I'm not letting you go alone and besides, you don't know where the dens are."

Mum stopped, but I gave her one of my stubborn looks.

"Fine," she said, setting off again. "But if you get yourself blown up, Ronnie Smith, I will be furious with you, do you understand?"

The war continued to rage in the skies above us as Mum and I ran through the darkening streets of Deptford. When we got closer to the docks, we saw more and more fires breaking out. The Germans were dropping incendiary bombs again. They were a favourite of theirs. The high explosives were to open buildings up and create maximum damage. The incendiary bombs were to build on the damage further by starting fires within.

"It's those up ahead on the right," I said to Mum as we rounded the corner.

When we got there, Mum climbed over the gate shouting, "Micky! Micky!" but there was no answer.

She turned round to look at me. "Where else could he be, Ronnie, think!?"

"I...I dunno. Maybe out working for Johnny?"

"Johnny would never have him working out in this! Who was he with?"

"Arthur, Harry and Graham," I said.

"We'll have to try theirs, see if he went back with one of them."

"Arthur lives on Carriage Way, by the train station."

Mum nodded and set off.

It took us about ten minutes to get to Arthur's. Mum slipped in the mud as she raced to get to the shelter and banged her knee, but if it hurt, she didn't show it.

We shouted through the door of Arthur's shelter, but his mum said that Micky wasn't with them.

"Arthur," Mum said. "When did you last see him? Please, I just want to find my boy."

Mrs Davey opened the shelter door. She was a small timid-looking woman, with dark circles under her eyes and wrists so frail they looked like they might snap. "Arthur," she said, "tell the lady what she wants to know."

Arthur's face appeared in the doorway. "I don't know anything. We left him at the dens, he said he was heading home."

At the sound of another bomber, Mrs Davey's eyes glanced at the sky overhead, "You should come in," she said.

"Thank you, but no," Mum said, turning to me. "Let's try your other friends."

"If you're talking about Harry and Graham, they won't be at theirs," Arthur said. "They go to the shelter in the crypt at St Marks."

"Thanks," I said.

"Hope you find him!" Arthur called out as his mum pulled him back inside.

"Maybe we should head home?" I suggested as we head off again. "He might be back by now."

"No, I want to check St Mark's first."

We raced down the street, keeping our eyes on the floor so we didn't trip over any debris. To get to St Mark's we had to double back past our house. It was when we were heading past the end of our road that we heard a shout over the noise of the bombing.

"Cathy!"

We both stopped to see Johnny and Micky heading towards us.

"Micky!" Mum shouted.

Relief flooded through me first, quickly followed by anger.

Johnny and Micky jogged over to us. Johnny was dressed in an auxiliary fireman's uniform. I didn't know Johnny was a fireman, and the uniform looked strange on him. Like it didn't quite fit him properly. Micky, well Micky looked different too. His face was a grey-white and he wouldn't look at me, just kept his eyes glued to the floor.

Mum grabbed hold of him by the arms and shook him, so he'd look up at her.

"Where have you been?" she blared in his face, then, before he could answer, she pulled him into a tight hug and said, "We were so worried." Then she gave him another shake. "I'm so cross with you!"

The whistle of a bomb came from over to the left. It sounded close. Our eyes flashed in that direction.

"Come on," Johnny said, grabbing Mum by the arm. "We'll tell you where we've been back in the shelter."

As we raced to ours, I said to Micky, "This better be good, Mum's furious."

If he heard me, he didn't answer.

When we opened the door to the shelter, Vera jumped up. "Oh, thank heavens! I've been going out of my mind here on my own!" She held up her knitting. "Look at this! I've been dropping stitches all over the place!"

Mum sat down on her bunk, looking utterly exhausted and bereft and relieved all at once. Johnny plonked himself next to her.

"Before you start on," he said. "Micky's been safe the whole time. I've kept an eye on him."

He said it so casually, like we were stupid to be making a fuss.

Mum looked so tired. "Later," she said. "You can explain it all later. Right now, there's something that Micky needs to know." She held her hand out. "Ronnie, can you please give me the telegram?"

CHAPTER 33

Micky didn't say anything after Mum told him about Dad. He just climbed up into his bunk and turned to face the wall. He hadn't actually said a word since we'd found him.

"Shock," Vera whispered, but I had a feeling that it was more than that. Something had happened when he was missing. I was sure of it.

"The lad'll be alright," Johnny said. "It's not like his old man was around much anyway. And from what I've heard, it doesn't sound like he was much cop as a father when he was here."

What Johnny was saying was true, but those words, coming out of *his* mouth, ignited the rage inside me, like an incendiary bomb amplifying a fire. I grabbed the side of the bunk, my fingers digging into it. "Whatever he was," I said, my voice trembling with rage, "he died a hero. He died trying to protect us."

Johnny held his hands up. "Woah! Sorry – my mouth, it just runs away with me sometimes. Was just calling it how I see it, that's all."

"It's nothing to do with you!" I spat. Every word that came out of his mouth, made me hate him more.

Mum said, "Quiet, Ronnie, your brother's asleep."

"There's a flaming war going on outside and you think *I'm* going to wake him up?"

"Don't talk to your mother like that!" Johnny barked.

"She's *my* mum and I'll talk to her anyway I like," I said, which weren't what I meant at all. I just wasn't thinking straight.

"Not when I'm around you won't!" Johnny said.

Vera hoisted herself up onto her feet. "Sandwiches," she said. "I think maybe now is the time for some sandwiches. I can't be doing with a battle in here as well." She batted my legs. "Move your knees, Ronnie." Then she bent down and pulled a couple of sarnies out of her knitting bag. "Spam or cheese?"

"I'm not hun—"

She rammed one into my mouth before I could finish speaking.

She forced one on Johnny too. He and I sat eating the sandwiches, glaring at each other from our bunks. I ate quickly and angrily.

"Now that's better, isn't it?" Vera said.

Only Mum nodded.

She waited until we'd finished eating, then said, "What happened tonight, Johnny? Why were you with Micky?"

"No big story," Johnny said, dusting the crumbs off his lap. "Micky lost track of time playing in that den of his. I saw him when I was heading out, part of the volunteer fire services now, see?" He patted his uniform proudly. "I took him to the nearest communal shelter and when I had a moment, I fetched him and brought him back here. I knew you'd be fretting."

Mum nodded, taking him at his word. "Thank you. He was lucky you spotted him. Next time, Ronnie, you bring your brother home with you, please?"

She said it gently, but I still felt that she was making out it was all my fault.

"I'm going to sleep," I said and climbed up and wriggled in next to Micky.

I lay there for a few minutes, I didn't think I'd be able to drift off, my insides were burning with frustration. I heard Johnny whisper to Mum. "He's still got an attitude that one. It bothers me, how he is with you. Thought he'd sort himself out after our little chat."

Mum whispered back. "He's a good boy. He's just had a lot to deal with that's all. His relationship with his dad...well it was a difficult one. Don't think badly of him. He'll be grieving."

Johnny grunted and said something like *that may be so*, but I'd stopped listening. At the mention of my dad, all the anger had burned itself away and all that was left...well I couldn't figure that out. A nothingness? A numbness? Every time I pictured him in his RAF uniform, a sadness crept in, but I couldn't keep hold of it for long, even though I think I wanted to. I couldn't forget who he'd been when he was around. I wasn't grieving. I didn't even know how to start. I glanced over at Micky, wondering if he felt the same. It was dark, but I could make out that he was awake by the tears that were rolling down his cheeks. I didn't feel sad that he was crying. I was jealous that he was able to.

When the all-clear sounded the following morning and we all clambered out of the shelter, no one spoke. There had been almost thirty days of night raids and exhaustion throbbed deep in my bones. Vera went back to hers, with only a nod for goodbye. It was a Sunday, which I was grateful for, it meant I could go back to bed. Mum, Micky and I all headed upstairs, each of us barely able to lift our feet to the next step, and Johnny took the couch.

When Mum woke me up, I saw Micky wasn't in our room.

"What time is it?" I asked.

"Nearly three in the afternoon."

"No, really?"

"Must have needed it." She handed me a glass of milk and brushed her hand through my hair. "How are you feeling?"

I shrugged.

"Better for a sleep, I imagine?"

"I s'pose. Where's Micky?"

"Johnny's taken him out. Something about helping him with some work." She rolled her eyes. "Honestly, the hours that man keeps! But I thought it would do Micky some good to be occupied. You could have gone too, but I thought you needed the rest."

"How was he?"

"Micky?" Mum looked thoughtful. "Quiet. He was quiet."

I nodded.

"His relationship with your dad, it was different to yours. He didn't see everything you saw. His death, it's hit our Micky hard."

I knew what she was saying was true, but her words hurt somehow. What about how his death had hit me? But I didn't know the answer to that myself. I wonder if Mum knew what I was thinking, because she touched my cheek and said, "It will affect us all differently, there's no right or wrong way to feel. You can talk to me about it if you like?"

I didn't want that though, not then.

"I'm worried about Micky, Mum. This work Johnny does... I don't know, I just think it's dodgy."

"Oh, Ronnie, this again?" Mum said. "I know Johnny might have certain ways of getting his hands on stuff he shouldn't, like the odd bit of mutton or a pork chop, but he isn't the only one round here. You know I saw Mrs Rogers from round the way with a whole salmon stuffed up her cardy. Don't know where she got it, and I didn't ask."

I tried to smile but I couldn't.

"Ronnie, my sweet boy, there's so much to worry about at the moment, don't go finding extra things that don't really matter." She sighed, a deep sad sigh. "Lord knows, I can't take any more."

I looked at her for a moment. There were lines on her face

where there never used to be, and her eyes had lost their sparkle. I wondered when that had happened. How I hadn't noticed. I couldn't load any more on her. I'd have to figure out the Johnny situation by myself. Be the man of the house like I'd said I would. I put my hand on her knee. "Are you okay, Mum?"

She smiled. "Oh, you know me, I'm fine."

"Really?"

"Let's just say I don't feel the need to hurl any rocks at the moment."

"I didn't mean to lose my manners with you yesterday. I know what Johnny said about my attitude."

"Think no more of it. Yesterday was quite a day for everybody. Now finish your milk and tidy yourself up." Mum stood up and smoothed down her skirt. "Billy's downstairs, wants to know if you want to go out and play."

"Does he know?"

Mum paused in the doorway. "I told him about your dad. I hope that's okay."

I nodded.

When I got downstairs, Lugs jumped up from the sofa. He had a scratch mark across his cheek.

"Alright, Lugs?" I said. "Tiger been at you again?"

"Wasn't his fault. He's taken to sleeping on me and I bolted up from a dream and scared him. But what about you? Are you alright?" He stuffed his hands in his pocket, then took them out again, then stuffed them back in. "Your mum told me about the telegram."

I looked at the floor, not able to meet his eyes. "Yeah, I'm alright. You know what my dad was like."

"He was still your dad though. You can feel sad if you want."

I wasn't sure that was true – if it was right to feel sad. "I don't know what I want. Do you mind if we don't talk about it?"

"Course."

"You want to go for a walk? Our Micky's not in."

Lugs lowered his voice. "I know. I've seen him. He's with that Johnny and The Wreckers. Saw them talking under the railway arches and I got a feeling. You know? That's why I came over."

"A feeling?"

"Yeah, *a feeling* that they were up to something. They didn't notice me to start with because I was discreet. You'd have been impressed – like a spy I was. Anyway, Johnny was talking to them all serious, and they were all listening real intently."

"What was he saying?"

"Couldn't hear," he grinned. "Can you believe these ears let me down? Anyway, they acted all weird when they saw me."

"Thought you were being spy-like?"

"I was, it was Tiger who gave the game away. Went padding right up to them. That's when they clocked me. They looked real shifty, but then they all smiled, said hi, then just stood there waiting for me to leave. Didn't want to say anything until I was out of earshot, I reckon."

"That *is* interesting, Lugs."

"Came straight over here to tell you. Thought you'd want to check it out."

"You thought right." I grabbed my gas mask off the banister. "Let's go."

I'd find out what Johnny was up to, get proof and get him out of our lives once and for all.

CHAPTER 34

"We're heading out!" I shouted up to Mum.

"Okay, loves. Remember, I'm on nights now for the next few days. Mrs Green will be looking after you."

Tiger was outside waiting for Lugs, even though he pretended he wasn't.

"Think he might want to tag along," Lugs said.

Tiger stalked behind us as Lugs and I walked quickly through the streets down to the railway arches. We didn't even stop for shrapnel. I think we both knew that the game was long over. When we got near to the railway arches, we ducked down behind some bins. They were all still there – Johnny, Micky and The Wreckers with another man who Johnny was talking to. They were a little distance apart from the rest and deep in discussion.

"Who's that geezer Johnny's speaking to?" Lugs asked.

"Dunno." I peeked round the bins to get a better look.

"Big fella," Lugs whispered.

I recognized the wide shoulders and slicked-back hair immediately. "Mr Dimes. Got to be."

He handed Johnny a duffel bag.

"What's in there?" Lugs whispered.

"Helmets?" I said as Johnny opened the bag then proceeded to hand them out to Micky and the others.

"Those are fire warden helmets!" Lugs said, clearly as confused as I was. "What do they want with helmets?"

"Not a clue...oh heck, what's Tiger doing?" The daft cat had prowled right up to our Micky. "He's going to give us away!"

Micky looked up and scanned the area. Lugs and I ducked down behind the bins, making ourselves as small as possible. We waited a few moments – my heart was beating so loudly I'm surprised Lugs didn't hear it. Carefully, I peered round the side of the bin. I let out a breath. "It's okay, they didn't spot us."

"What's happening?" Lugs whispered.

"Johnny and the big guy are shaking hands. I was right, it *is* Mr Dimes." What I saw them do next made me gasp.

"I don't believe it!"

"What? What don't you believe?"

I didn't know whether I should tell Lugs. "They just did that Nazi salute thing!"

Lugs swallowed. "Who did?"

"Johnny and Mr Dimes!"

"What about Mick and the others?"

"Nah, not them." I could only see Micky's face as the others had their backs to us. He'd looked away and stuffed his hands in his pockets when Johnny and Dimes saluted. He knew it was wrong, but he was still there, part of it.

Johnny said a few more things that we couldn't make out and then he and Mr Dimes disappeared. One by one, Micky, Arthur, Billy and Harry put on their helmets, picked up a bag each and took off in separate directions.

"We should follow them," I said, "but we can't follow them all. Maybe we should split up?"

Lugs shook his head. "I'd rather not, Ronnie. Don't feel that safe to be on my own."

"Of course. Sorry. We stay together, but who should we follow?"

I really wanted to follow our Micky but when Lugs said, "Harry. Harry's our best bet," I knew he was right.

Harry headed off in the direction of Blackheath and we followed from a distance. Tiger stalked along behind us for some of the way then disappeared off, think he'd got annoyed by all the stopping and starting. Harry didn't seem to be in a hurry. He paused to look at a blackbird, had a wee down an alley, spent some time looking at his reflection in a blacked-out window while he marched on the spot pretending to be a soldier. That earned him a strange look from some passers-by.

It was during the marching when Lugs said to me. "I'm beginning to think we might have this all wrong. Harry doesn't exactly look like he's about to get involved in criminal activity."

I had to admit that it did seem unlikely at that moment in time, but I knew Johnny Simmons and I knew something bad had to be going on.

"Let's give it a little while longer," I said.

When Harry got to Blackheath, he walked up the hill to one of the posh houses on the edge of the green. Then he sat down on the pavement.

We were about twenty metres away from him, peering round a hedge.

"What's he doing now?" Lugs asked.

"Nothing interesting – chucking stones across the road."

It was beginning to get dark, which came as a surprise to me, but then I had slept most the day. I looked over at the clock on the church steeple. "It's well after five. The air-raid siren will probably go off soon."

"You thinking we should head home?" Lugs asked.

I knew we should, but if there was a chance that I could find out what Johnny was up to, I had to take it. "I'm thinking we should stay here. Wait and see if something happens."

We both looked back over at Harry as he chucked a stone upwards. It came down and doinked him on the helmet.

"He really is a dope," I said, and he chucked another one which also landed on his head. Lugs and I started giggling as Harry chucked stone after stone and got them to bounce off his helmet.

"He's not acting much like he's up to no good," Lugs said. "But it is Harry, I s'pose."

Harry kept lobbing stones onto his own head until the sound of that night's air-raid siren started up and he jumped to his feet.

"You think he's heading home?" Lugs asked.

"Don't think so." Harry was looking up and down the street as though he was expecting someone to show up.

The people in the posh houses started to come outside and head down to their Anderson shelters. Harry scuttled out of sight when the owners appeared out of the house he was standing nearest to.

About twenty minutes later, with the sound of *Heinkel He 111s* and *Dorniers* drawing closer, a man showed up wearing an ARP helmet.

"Who's that?" Lugs asked.

"I don't know, do I? Warden looks like, probably going to send Harry on his way."

The man spoke to Harry, but he didn't tell him to move on. Instead, he took Harry's bag off him, then jimmied open the door and disappeared into the house. Harry stood there, looking up and down the street, like he was keeping guard.

Lugs and I exchanged a look. It was pretty clear something was going down.

Ten minutes later, the man reappeared and handed Harry back the bag, along with a piece of paper.

Harry read it, nodded, then tucked it into his pocket. He slung the bag – which looked considerably heavier than before – on his back and set off down the road.

"'Ere, Lugs," I said slowly as I began to piece together what we'd just seen, "did that air-raid warden just rob that house?"

"Kind of looked like it."

"And has Harry just scarpered with the loot?"

"Kind of looked like that too."

"Is that what they're up to? Mick and the others must all be at different houses, on the rob while everyone's hunkered down in the shelters. Do you think Harry knows what's going on? Or do you think he's swallowed the *just doing deliveries* line?"

Lugs blew out a long puff of air. "It's Harry. Maybe, maybe not. And there might be an innocent explanation?"

The way he said that, like it was a question, made me know he didn't think there would be.

The anti-aircraft gun which was stationed up on the heath started up. The *crump-crump-crump* even louder what with us being so close. The ground shook as a bomb exploded over Greenwich way. Then a *Heinkel He 111*, on a course for the city, flew low over our heads, hounded by a Bristol Beaufighter, it's machine gun rat-tat-tat-tatting. The air rumbled as they passed, and we both ducked instinctively.

"It's getting a bit lively out here," I said. "We should go."

We started legging it back down the hill as the sound of engines and gunfire rolled over the heath.

"What we going to do now?" Lugs puffed.

"I dunno."

"You don't want to call the rozzers on them?"

"Nah, not yet." It was Johnny I wanted to get in trouble. I didn't want to land our Micky or the others in it – there was a chance we might be wrong. Granted a small chance, but a chance, still a chance. "Let's confront Harry at school tomorrow. See what he has to say."

It was a hairy run back home but thrilling too. Sure, I was aware of the danger, and I felt the fear, but it also made me feel alive – being out there while the sky blazed, and the world shook. I was pleased to make it back home though. Vera, however, was not in the loveliest of moods. I bowled in to the shelter, sweating and puffing and full of apologies.

"I'm sorry, I'm sorry, lost track of time."

She folded her arms. "So pleased you've decided to grace me with your presence." She looked behind me. "Where's your brother?"

Before I could say *probably up to no good*, Micky thundered in behind me and chucked his bag on the floor...

"Thank goodness for that," she said. "Both boys accounted for."

"What's in the bag?" I said, wondering if he'd brought his loot back with him.

"A helmet. Been out fire spotting with Johnny," Micky said. "He's training us up to be volunteer fire wardens. Helping out the war effort. Doing our bit."

I laughed coldly – couldn't help myself.

"Have a look if you don't believe me."

I didn't need to look. I could tell by his tone that there was nothing incriminating in there. When I didn't move, he reached forward and lifted up the flap on his bag to show the helmet.

"See?"

"Turning into quite the do-gooder, aren't you?"

251

"Enough of the snark, Ronnie," Vera said. "Your brother's doing a brave and honourable thing."

My blood rushed hot and I muttered, "Yeah, very honourable."

I considered having it out with Micky then and there. but I didn't want to get into it in front of Vera. Besides, I needed time to plan what I was going to do next. I reckoned it was best to keep Micky in the dark about what I knew. I couldn't trust that he wouldn't go straight to Johnny Simmons and tell him I was onto him. I needed to find out exactly what was going on. I needed to talk to Harry.

CHAPTER 35

The following morning, after another night listening to war raging over London, we emerged from the shelter, bleary eyed, to inspect the damage. Incendiary bomb shells littered the road, and we could see a thick plume of smoke billowing upwards from the terraces a few streets over. Mrs Green was on her way back to hers when she managed to trip over a bit of shrapnel. Her legs flew up above her head and she landed on her back with a massive thud, her knitting bag coming down on top of her.

"My hip!" she shouted from underneath the wool balls. "I've gone and done my chuffing hip!"

She was loaded onto the back of an ambulance, puffing away on a cigarette and cursing Hitler whilst the whole street watched on. Mum got home from work as they stretchered her away. "I'm sorry, Cathy! Who will look after the boys now when you're at work?"

Mum took hold of her hands. "Don't worry about us! We'll be okay. It's you I'm concerned about. I'll drop in and see you tonight before my shift."

"I think we need to stay at home today after the trauma of witnessing Mrs Green's accident," Micky said to Mum as the ambulance drove off. "What do you think, Ronnie?"

Normally, I'd agree, but I wanted to get to school to interrogate Harry.

Mum raised an eyebrow. "Nice try, off you go."

"Caught a right eyeful of her undergarments as she fell," Micky said. "If that doesn't count as traumatic, I don't know what does!"

"I said, off you go."

As it turned out, Lugs and I only managed to get Harry on his own when he was on his way home after school. We caught up with him by the railway tracks on Abinger Grove. He was walking along whistling to himself. He smiled when he saw us. "Ronnie, Lugs, you don't normally come this way."

"We wondered if we could have a word," I said.

Harry frowned. "A word?"

"Yeah, we wanted to...ask you about something," I began, trying to think how best to phrase what I wanted to say next.

"We think Johnny Simmons has got you robbing houses," Lugs blurted out.

It wasn't exactly the approach I was going to take but it worked, because Harry said, "How did you find out?" Then he seemed to realize that he'd said something he shouldn't and tried to backtrack. "No! I mean, what are you suggesting? I am highly offended! I deliver stuff."

"We followed you up to Blackheath," I said.

"You did?" he said, his eyes widening. He thought for a moment, then said, "Then you would have seen me collecting something to deliver somewhere else." He nodded, pleased, thinking that he'd got himself out of it.

"Harry," I said flatly. "We saw everything. And 'collecting' something from someone's house while they're sheltering from an air raid, is just another way of saying stealing."

Harry's face fell. "You're not going to go to the police, are you?"

I shook my head. There was no way I was going to drop my brother and mates in it with the law. It was only Johnny I was after.

Harry exhaled. "Good, and the thing is, what we're doing isn't actually stealing."

"How do you figure that?" Lugs asked.

"It's like Johnny says—"

"Oh, this should be good," I muttered.

"We're only taking from businesses and folk with more money than sense. People who don't deserve to have all that stuff."

I was gobsmacked. "Blimey, Harry, have a listen to yourself, will you!?"

Lugs narrowed his eyes. "What *kind* of people of people don't deserve to have stuff?"

Harry shrugged. "Dunno. Rich ones, I guess."

"Harry, what you're doing is wrong. Why does Johnny get to decide who isn't deserving?" I said. "What if you get caught? You'll end up in prison!"

"Nah, Johnny has it all worked out. He knows the best times, best places to hit. No one will suspect us because we're in disguise."

"As fire wardens," Lugs said.

"Yup!" Harry said proudly. "There isn't any risk. The police are too busy, what with there being a war on."

"No risk?" I covered my face with my hands. I couldn't believe he was being so naive.

"Way Johnny sees it, people are blowin' each other to bits on battlefields, so nicking a few bits here and there ain't that much of a big deal. Besides, we're only moving stuff on – we're not actually stealing the stuff."

"Yet," I said. "Do you know where he's sending you next?"

"Nah. He tells us on the night."

"And where do you take the stuff you steal?"

"We give it to Micky and he takes it wherever he's told. Look, are we done here?" Harry said. "Just I ought to be heading home."

I sat down on the side of the road, suddenly feeling exhausted. I suppose I'd known what my brother and the others were up to, but to have it confirmed and then dismissed as not being a big deal was like a punch in the gut. "Yeah, we're done. Do me a favour, don't mention to anyone we've talked."

"Fine by me," Harry said. "Long as you don't tell anyone that I told you what we're doing."

"We won't. But Harry, if ever you want out, come tell me?" I said.

"If ever you want in, you come tell me."

Harry headed off back to his and Lugs sat down next to me. "Well, I guess we know for certain now."

"What I don't get is how Johnny has managed to convince Harry – Micky and the others too – that what they're doing is okay."

"It's not just Johnny though, is it," Lugs said. "It's the war. When the world don't make sense, it's hard to figure out what's right and wrong."

"Maybe. Or is that just an excuse?"

Lugs frowned. "Dunno if it's an excuse, think it's more of ~a reason."

I found myself thinking about Dad. How the Great War had affected him, how its effect was so far-reaching that it had spread its way to this war and had its grasp on Micky. If Dad hadn't ever fought, he would have been different. If he'd been a better man, if he was here, Johnny wouldn't be.

If, if, if.

"How are we going to figure out a way to stop Johnny, without getting our friends in trouble?" Lugs said.

"We're going to have to find out where Micky's taking all the stolen stuff. He must be delivering it somewhere."

"Johnny's place maybe?"

In all the time we'd known Johnny, we'd never been round his. His place was north of the river. He'd mentioned Bow and Hackney before. I didn't think Micky could have made it there and back to the shelter just after me the night we followed Harry.

"No, not his. I think he'll have a base somewhere round here. If we work that out, we can send the police there when we know Micky and the others are nowhere near the place."

"So, you're suggesting we follow one of them to some criminal hideout?"

"I'm suggesting *I* do it."

"Nah, Ronnie, couldn't leave you to do it on your own. Micky's my mate too. Besides, I got my own reasons for wanting Johnny Simmons put away."

"Do you think what they're doing might have something to do with them being fascists? We know Mr Dimes is a Blackshirt and he was there saluting and handing out helmets."

Lugs scrunched up his nose in thought. "Maybe. Not sure how it could be linked though. S'pose it could be to fund their organization? Whatever it is, Micky and the others are up to their eyeballs in it."

He jumped to his feet and pulled me up. "Back to mine so we can figure out how we're going to get Johnny nicked?"

"Thanks, Lugs," I said, suddenly feeling a bit choked up.

"Keep it together, Ron." He slung his arm round my shoulder. "We ain't caught him yet."

"But we're going to," I said, and I really believed it.

CHAPTER 36

The very next day, Lugs and I slipped out the school gates during lunch. From what Harry had told us, I knew the only way to find Johnny's hangout would be to follow Micky when he was delivering the loot to Johnny. Once we knew the location, we could tell the police. We'd do it anonymously, so nothing could be traced back. The idea was that the police would show up and discover Johnny surrounded by stolen goods and he'd be hauled away and sent down for a lengthy stretch at His Majesty's pleasure. At least that's how it played out in my head.

The only problem was that Micky would be on his bike, and I knew from experience that we wouldn't be able to keep up on foot. Which is why, twenty minutes after leaving school, Lugs and I were crouched down behind Harry Scott's wall, ready to break into his dad's shed. We needed wheels and Harry had a go-kart.

"You sure he keeps it in there?" Lugs asked.

"He's not going to keep it in the house, is he? Okay, I'm going to knock to check no one's in."

I knocked on the door and waited. After a few minutes, Lugs popped his head up from behind the wall and I gave him the thumbs up.

Happy that Mrs Scott wasn't in, we went down the small side alley to the shed. When I say shed, it was really some old fence panels covered with a pieced of corrugated iron. Carefully, we moved the two planks of wood that were propped up vertically to act as a door.

"Jackpot!" Lugs said.

Harry's go-kart was green in colour, it had a metal frame with a yellow seat and all four wheels looked to be in pretty good condition.

"Let's get it out of here," I said.

We carried the go-kart out through the gate, just as Mrs Scott burst out the front door. Her hair was up in pipe cleaners, her apron was flapping, and she was brandishing a rolling pin. Got to say, both Lugs and I yelped in fright.

"Oi, you two!" she shouted.

"Run!" I said, and Lugs and I started off down the road as fast as we could. Which wasn't that fast on account of us carrying a go-kart.

"You robbing little blighters!!" Mrs Scott bellowed as we stumbled along the road trying to keep hold of the thing. She launched the rolling pin at us. It Catherine-wheeled through the air, sailed right past my ear and then bounced off the side of the kart.

"Blimey, that was close!" I said.

"What are we doing carrying a flippin' go-kart, Ron?" Lugs said.

"Good point!"

We dropped it onto the ground, I jumped in the seat, Lugs stood on the back, and I pedalled as fast as I could, weaving all over the road, trying to avoid potholes and rubble. It was a right bumpy ride – I thought my teeth might rattle clear out my mouth. Really, Mrs Scott had no chance of catching us, but the idea of it was enough to keep my legs turning like a fighter plane's propeller.

When we got the corner of Tanner's Hill and Heston Street, I pulled in and Lugs and I clambered out the kart and flopped down on the pavement.

"We did it!" I said.

"I'll tell you what, Harry's mum's got a decent throwing arm on her."

"Do you think she saw us?" I asked.

"Probably, but she don't know who we are, so if anyone asks we just deny it. We're going to give it back when we're done in any case."

We hid the go-kart in a bush round the back of Vera's – with her in the hospital, I knew it wouldn't be seen. I'd told Mum I'd stay with Lugs – at his place. She was worried about me being on my own with Vera injured and Micky helping Johnny on fire watch. But that evening, Lugs came over to our shelter, so when Micky went off, we could follow him.

"Your mum going to be okay with you not going home tonight?" I asked when he turned up at the gate.

Lugs shrugged. "She won't be happy, but she always says that if I'm out when the sirens sound I'm to go to the closest shelter and she'll deal with me in the morning. I'll tell her I lost track of time or something and thought it would be safer to stay at yours."

Twenty minutes after the sirens had sounded and the Germans started to drop that night's bombs, Micky put on his fire-warden helmet and got ready to leave.

"I'll be back in a few hours," he said, slinging his bag over his shoulder. "Got to make sure the public is safe."

I wanted to tell him not to go – that what he was doing was wrong, that it was dangerous, but I knew that nothing I had to say would get through to him. As he ducked out of the shelter, I called out to him. "Be careful out there."

He grinned back at me. "Don't worry yourself. I'm lucky, me, remember?"

Lugs, who was pretending to read a comic, said a disinterested "Bye," but as soon as we heard the gate clatter on his hinges, we leaped into action. Lugs followed Micky to the end of the road, while I got the go-kart. I moved quickly – I knew once Micky got going, he was fast.

When I reached Lugs, he was pointing towards Albyn Road. I didn't stop pedalling, he just leaped on the back as I passed.

"Micky went off down Albyn Road, but you're going to have to pick up the pace if you want to catch him."

I pedalled furiously, my muscles burning from the effort. I kept my eyes on Micky's silhouette up ahead and watched as he turned onto Friendly Street.

"This is where Tiger was found," Lugs said.

"On Friendly Street? Was he lost?" I said.

"Yeah, he was, oh, I see what you mean. Ha ha."

At the end of the street Micky took a right onto New Cross Road. The night sky over the river flashed orange and the smell of burning wood, brick and metal rose in the air.

"He's heading up to the Heath," Lugs said.

I groaned, not thrilled at the prospect of pedalling up Blackheath Hill. As soon as the road got steeper, Micky pulled away and I knew we were going to lose him.

"We...didn't...think about the...hills," I said, between breaths.

Lugs jumped off and tried to run after him, leaving me to push on to the top.

When we got there, Lugs was standing hands on his hips, panting.

"Sorry, Ron, I lost him." I looked around but Micky had vanished from sight. I rolled out of the kart and flopped on my back as I tried to catch my breath. From where we were we could see the Luftwaffe were hitting the north side of the river hard.

Lugs laid down next to me. "So, the go-kart has certain limitations," Lugs said.

"This plan isn't going to work. Maybe we need to get a bike."

"Or maybe we're following the wrong person," Lugs said. "We should cut out the middle man."

I propped myself up on my elbow. "You mean follow Johnny? That's easier said than done. It's not like he keeps a regular schedule."

"Next time he's round yours, we'll tail him when he leaves. Now can we get out of here? It's pretty exposed up on the Heath."

Lugs and I were climbing into the kart when, out of the corner of my eye, I caught something whizzing down the other side of the road. I bolted upright. I couldn't believe it.

"It's Micky!" I said.

He'd flown by us without noticing, a bag bouncing up and down on his back. "Quick get in!"

Lugs jumped on the back of the kart, and we set off after him.

"I'll tell you what, Lugs!" I shouted as we began to pick up speed. "Go-karts might be limited in their ability to go uphill, but their ability to go downhill is pretty startling."

We were absolutely rocketing. The wheels were going so fast that I couldn't keep my feet on the pedals. My eyes were streaming from the wind and Lugs was bouncing around behind me, trying to cling on. At one point he had his arms wrapped round my head and I had no clue what was going on.

"We're gaining on him!" Lugs shouted.

I was having a job trying to hold on to the steering wheel because it was vibrating so violently. This was why, despite Lugs shouting, "Take evasive action!" I couldn't steer out of the way of a piece of old fence that was lying at an angle over a bit of rubble.

We shot straight across it, and for a couple of seconds we were airborne. We landed with a right wallop and the steering wheel suddenly wasn't any use at all because it had come away from the axle. Which meant that when Lugs shouted, "Watch out for the wall!" all I could do was shout back, "Abandon kart!"

He dove one way, and I dove the other and the kart rammed straight into a building.

I struggled to my feet and saw Micky disappear round a corner right down the end of the road. We'd lost him. Again.

I staggered over to Lugs. His hair was all stuck back off his head like he'd been in a wind tunnel, and he had a scratch above his eyebrow, but he seemed okay.

"You know what, Ronnie?" he said as he dusted himself down.

"What, Lugs?"

"I think go-karts have a few limitations going downhill too."

"I think you're right about that."

Lugs and I carried the go-kart back to Vera's. The front axle was bent and the steering wheel was no longer attached, but with a bit of work it might be fixable. We sat in the shelter and had some spam sandwiches that Mum had made for us before she went to work. Micky turned up about an hour later.

"Spot many fires?" I asked.

"A few," he said, grabbing a sandwich. "North side of the river are taking a pelting tonight."

"Yeah, we saw," Lugs said. Then his eyes widened, with the realization that he'd pretty much told Micky we'd been outside.

Luckily, Micky wasn't really listening. He'd climbed up onto the top bunk and was too busy stuffing his face. He seemed so okay with what he was doing, it fired me up something rotten. But I knew ranting at him wouldn't help. I needed to be patient. Johnny Simmons himself was going to lead me to where he was storing the loot.

CHAPTER 37

The plan to follow Johnny instead of Micky was more difficult than we'd thought. Mum was put on day shifts, which meant that there could be no leaving the shelter to trail Johnny of a night.

For a week or so, Micky was able to go out with Johnny and the others every night. I imagined them walking around in their fire warden helmets, pretending to spot incendiary bombs until the air-raid siren sounded. Then, when people were hidden away in their shelters, I pictured them sneaking into shops and houses and stealing, and Micky cycling stolen belongings to Johnny's hideout.

Word had begun to spread about the group of lads who were out on fire watch, and whilst Mum was worried about the risk, I could tell she was proud of Micky. She thought he was so mature, first getting a job delivering, now helping the war effort.

"He's a good lad. Knows how to seize an opportunity," Johnny kept telling her and the smile it brought to her face, well, I couldn't be the one to take that away.

Micky and Johnny would leave, and Mum would hug them goodbye, and then I'd have to sit and listen to her talk about how grown-up Micky had become. How Johnny was a good influence on him. Listening to that was worse than hearing the bombs exploding outside.

A head fireman even came in to school and spoke about Micky and the others in assembly. He said it was good to see boys turning into fine young men and they all stood there with their chests puffed up, like it was true. Mr Etherington didn't seem too thrilled about it though. He sat there with a grim look on his face and his jaw clenched every time Johnny was mentioned. Apart from Lugs, I realized, Mr Etherington might have been the only person in the world who knew the true Johnny Simmons. I thought about telling him what Micky and the others were really up to. But I knew he'd be straight down to the police station and my brother would end up behind bars.

On the last evening of Mum's day shifts, she asked me to ask Mrs Missell if I could shelter round theirs, so I wasn't on my own when Johnny and Micky were out. I told her I had, but I knew my chance had finally come. When Johnny and Micky left that night, I was going to follow Johnny to his hideout.

But that day at school, Micky and the others disappeared during lunch.

"Got to be up to something," Lugs said.

I booted the wall.

"There will be another chance," Lugs said. "You should come back, shelter at mine tonight."

"Thanks, but I think I'll go home in case they show up."

"You sure?"

"I'm sure." To be honest, I wanted to be on my own. I was in too foul a mood to be good company.

I knew I'd made a mistake about an hour after the siren had sounded. Sitting in a shelter on your own while the world explodes around you is a pretty lonely place to be. A scary place to be, if I'm honest. I thought I'd got used to the sound of bombs falling on London, but I realized that was because I'd always had people around me. There was a comfort to be found in the clacking of Vera's knitting needles and her idle gossip about the neighbours.

I was wondering whether I should head over to Lugs's, when the door to the shelter burst open and Lugs came bundling in, shortly followed by Tiger.

"What are you doing here?" I said, surprised and happy to see him.

"Mum fell asleep, so I thought I'd drop round – what with you being here on your own and all. I left her a note. She won't be happy when she wakes up, but I thought coming here to check on you was worth an earful from her in the morning. Here, brought you one of her biscuits."

"Thanks, for the biscuit, and for coming." I took a bite. "Carrot again?"

"Got it in one."

"What's it like out there?"

"The usual. Germans still seem to be concentrating on the East End. I took another bite of my biscuit, just as the shelter door burst open for the second time that night. I looked up, thinking it might be Micky, but it wasn't.

"Harry," I said. "What you doing here?"

He had a wild look in his eyes. "Things are going down, Ronnie. Big things."

CHAPTER 38

Harry plonked himself down on the bunk. It was clear he was agitated – his legs were bouncing uncontrollably, and his eyes were darting all over the place. It made me feel nervous. It made me worry for Micky.

"Nice shelter you have here," he said, like he was just round for a chit-chat.

"Clearly you're not here to talk about our Anderson," I said.

"You alright, Harry?" Lugs asked.

Harry shook his head. "Err, not the finest I've ever been, Lugs, no."

"You left school early today. What's going on?" I asked. "Has something happened to Micky?"

"Micky's fine – at the moment." He blew a lot of air out of his cheeks.

"At the moment?" I said.

Harry blew a second gust of air out his cheeks. "We're in trouble, Ronnie. Big trouble. It's all got out of hand, with Johnny, see. I didn't mind to start, just taking things from one place to another. Just moving stuff, that's all it was. That's not a big deal. Johnny said we were just seizing opportunities – if we didn't do it, someone else would."

"Just moving stuff? Harry, we're not talking about moving a pot plant across the room. We already told you what you were doing is stealing."

"Yeah, I realize that now but, Johnny, when he was talking, I dunno…it all just seemed to make sense. You know?"

"He can be persuasive," I said as I sat down next to him.

"But it's not just Johnny now. Seems he works for this other fella."

"Mr Dimes?" I said.

"He's one of them, but Dimes is working for another fella who Johnny says is big business. Proper gangster from the East End I reckon, and they've got us involved in this huge job."

Lugs's eyebrows shot up. "Proper gangsters?"

"Yup, the sort that'll chop your fingers off if you cross them – that's what Johnny told us. Highly connected." Harry's face crumpled. "I like my fingers – I don't want to lose them."

Lugs threw his arms in the air. "Oh, well that's just brilliant that is! You've got yourself mixed up with proper East End gangsters!"

"It's not brilliant!" Harry said. Then he saw our faces and went, "Oh, I see, you know that already. Thing is, I don't want to be involved with this huge job. I don't want to be a crook no more. I want out – told that to Johnny, but he said it don't work like that. That's when he mentioned the fingers thing."

Lugs and I shot each other a look – think we were both rattled by what we were hearing. Things were worse than I'd imagined. Johnny Simmons was one thing, but this was another level and Micky was in deep

"Think of all the things you need your fingers for," Harry said sorrowfully. He held his up and started counting. "Tying shoelaces, doing your buttons up, using a fork, counting!"

"You're not going to lose your fingers, Harry," I said as convincingly as I could.

"You don't know that!" Lugs said, throwing his arms in the air. "Gangsters are always lopping off digits!"

"Oh gawd!" Harry wailed. "Not my digit too!"

"Digit is another word for finger, Harry!" I said, glaring at Lugs so he knew he weren't helping the situation. "Now, everyone calm down. Harry...Harry, stop looking at your fingers and pay me attention. I need you to tell me everything you know about Johnny Simmons and Mr Dimes and this gangster and this huge job, okay? And then maybe we can figure out a way to stop it and save your fingers in the process." I spoke confidently, for Harry's sake, but my mind was whirling. How were a couple of kids from Deptford going to stop a load of gangsters? Gangsters that had connections with an organization of fascists at that.

"Okay," Harry said, nodding.

"Let's start with the job. Tell us what you know."

"It's up in town, a jeweller's. They're going to hit it during an air raid sometime in the next week. There's something real valuable there, apparently. They want us all there to act like decoy runners. We grab a bag and split off in different directions. Only one of us will get the actual loot, the others are just there to act as a diversion. We need to lay low for the night, then meet again the following morning to hand it back."

I rubbed the bridge of my nose, trying to take in everything Harry was saying. He was right, this was big, really big.

"Do you know which jeweller's?" I asked.

"Nope."

"Or where you have to meet?"

"Haven't told us that yet either. Said we'll only know right before. Stop us blabbing, I guess. We're keeping a low profile apparently, no more jobs until this big one."

"What are we going to do?" Lugs asked. "Go to the police?"

I thought about it for a moment. It was a reasonable suggestion. But what would we say? "Dunno, Lugs. What would we tell them? That we think there might be a robbery of a jeweller's, but we don't know which one and we don't know when? They ain't going to believe us."

"So, what *are* we going to do?" Harry asked.

"Not sure yet, but I'll think of something. In the meantime, you're just going to have to act normal. You can't let on that you've told us."

Harry nodded. "Thanks, Ronnie, and I'm sorry about this."

"I know you are."

"Right, better scarper." Harry got to his feet and held out his hand. "You shrapnel boys are alright."

Lugs and I shook his hand, then, after Harry had left, Lugs turned to me and said, "Holy moly, Ron, what we going to do about this?"

I wracked my brains and, though I hated it, there was only one idea I could see working.

"*We're* not going to do anything. But I'm going to join Johnny's gang, that's what I'm going to do."

CHAPTER 39

Lugs stared at me for quite a long time, then finally said, "Join his gang? Are you mad?"

"I need to be on the inside. It's the only way for me to keep an eye on Micky and find out what's going on."

"You can't! You'll—"

"I've made up my mind," I said, cutting him off.

Lugs covered his face with his hands and shook his head. A moment later, he looked up. "I can't believe I'm saying this, but I'll join too."

"But Lugs, Johnny's a fascist. You don't want to be messed up in that."

"My dad didn't want to be messed up in fighting fascists either, but he still went. Guess sometimes you have to do what's right. Even if it scares you."

"But—"

"I've made up my mind," he said – his turn to cut me off.

*　　*　　*

The following morning, we left the shelter and went inside to grab some food, but Micky and Johnny were already in the kitchen fixing their breakfast. Micky was cooking up Mum's last two sausages. Johnny was sitting down at the table. My insides twisted as soon as I laid eyes on him. I saw Lugs flinch when he saw him.

"Alright Micky, Johnny?" I said, trying to be polite. I looked at Micky's bag lying on the floor. "You back home now, Mick?"

Micky nodded. He looked tired – he had dark rings round his eyes.

I sat down opposite Johnny. Lugs sat down next to me, trying to look brave, but he was twitching a little. I didn't blame him – we weren't expecting to have to put the plan into action so soon. But Johnny was there, and our chance was now.

"We want in," I said.

"'Fraid there's only enough for two," Johnny said, as he leaned back and put his boots up on the table.

I looked to Lugs and he gave me a nod of encouragement.

"Not the food. We want to work for you," I said.

Micky looked up from the frying pan, surprised.

"And what if I say I don't need you?"

I shrugged. "That's up to you."

"We don't need him," Micky snapped.

At the time, I thought he just didn't want me around, but I was wrong about that.

"That's for Johnny to decide," I said.

Johnny tilted his head, like he was sizing me up. "Why the change of heart?"

Lugs looked at me wide-eyed, wondering what I was going to say.

I stayed calm, well calmer than Lugs at least. "Been thinking, that's all. About what you said about seizing opportunities."

Johnny looked at Lugs. "This right?"

Lugs gulped and nodded. "Yeah, opportunities, thinking... about them." He wasn't that convincing but Johnny either didn't notice or was too busy enjoying thinking he had the upper hand.

Johnny took his feet off the table and leaned forward. "You know what it is I do, don't you?"

"He knows," Micky said, then looked at me. "Reckon he's always known and up until now he didn't want anything to do with it." He turned back to the pan. "So why now, Ronnie?"

I wanted to shout for *you*, you stupid idiot! But I didn't. "Don't want to miss out on a good thing. Way I see it, a bomb might drop on us at any moment – what does it matter if we steal a few things from rich people who don't deserve it?"

"So, the kid finally comes round to my way of thinking," Johnny said, shaking his head and grinning. "Told you I'd have you working for me, didn't I?"

"You did," I said as evenly as I could.

"You'll have to prove yourself."

"We'll graft for you – won't we Lugs? – if that's what you're asking."

"No, I mean a test. I need you to do something for me. A job."

"When?"

"Today."

"But I thought—" Lugs began. I nudged him under the table. I knew what he was going to say – that he thought there were no jobs until the big one – but Johnny couldn't know Harry had told us about that.

"We'll do it," I said.

The door opened and Mum walked in, looking tired but happy to see us. "What's going on in here, sounded very serious from outside?"

"Me and Ronnie were just making plans," Johnny said. "Thought I might take the boys out for the day."

Mum's face lit up and she looked at me. "Is that so? All of you together? How lovely!"

I had to turn away, it hurt to look at her, knowing the truth of what was happening.

"You get yourself to bed," Johnny said. "Let me worry about this lot."

Mum slipped off her shoes. "It has been a long shift – Mr Abrahams took a turn in the night."

Johnny stiffened. "Mr Abrahams?"

Mum tilted her head. "Yes, *why*?" She spoke with the accusing tone she usually uses when she thinks Micky is flying far from the truth.

"Just don't like to think of you slaving away for the sake of..." he paused, trying to think of a word, "*foreigners* that's all."

He wanted to say *the Jews*. His antisemitism that was always so close to the surface, now seemed to pulse out round the kitchen. Micky glanced at Lugs then turned back to the cooker, shame in his eyes. Lugs didn't say a word, but I don't think I've ever seen someone clench a jaw so tight.

Mum frowned. "What...I...? Mr Abrahams isn't a foreigner. He's lived in London all his life!"

Johnny got to his feet and put his hands on her shoulders. "Cathy, you're a good and kind woman – an angel. An angel too lovely to see the truth of things. Now, you look done in, love. Get yourself upstairs and get some kip. That's an order."

Mum looked like she didn't know what to say. She rubbed her face with her hands.

"Go on, Mum," Micky said. "You look cream-crackered."

Mum nodded, gave Johnny one last uncertain look, then headed off upstairs to bed.

Half an hour later, I was walking up the road with Lugs, an address in my head and a crowbar down the back of my trousers. Johnny had smiled when he'd told us where he wanted us to go, like he was enjoying himself. I should have guessed something was up then.

"I can't believe we're doing this. I really can't!" Lugs kept repeating.

"I know, I know," I said, the panic rising in me too. "But we have to. I can't see any other way. We need to prove ourselves to get on the inside of this jewellery job. We'll just take something small, something that won't be missed."

"It's still wrong though, isn't it?"

"Yes...no...I don't know. Is it wrong if we're doing it for the right reasons?"

"I wish my dad was here," Lugs said. "He'd know what to do."

My steps faltered for a second as the realization hit me that I wished my dad was there too. Whoever he was as a man, I knew that he would never have let Johnny Simmons work his way into our lives like he had. He would have clobbered him one before he even made it through the front door. But I wasn't like that. I wouldn't be like that. I wouldn't let myself be overwhelmed by the anger. I'd sort it out my own way.

It didn't take us long to find the house. Our instructions were simple. Get in, steal something to prove we'd been there, something valuable. He'd told us no one would be in. That the owner stuck to a strict routine and wouldn't be back for a couple of hours.

We knew the area – it wasn't too far from our dens. The street was quiet, I kind of hoped it wouldn't be, so we could go back and say it was too risky. We walked down the row of terraced houses until we found the one we wanted. It was right at the end – a neat little house. Someone had bothered to keep the front yard swept. It looked like the garden wall might have taken a hit, but whoever lived there had cobbled it back together as best they could. Not sure why, but knowing that made me feel even more guilty about what we were about to do.

We jumped over the wall round the back and made our way to the side door. "You stay outside, keep guard," I said. "This was my idea, so I should be the one to do it."

Lugs nodded. "Thanks, Ronnie."

My hands were shaking as I pulled the crowbar Johnny had given me out from my trousers. I stuck it in the doorjamb and gave it one hard pull before I could change my mind. The door swung open immediately and a sick feeling washed over me.

"Crikey!" Lugs said. "You did it!"

We looked at each other, knowing there was no going back now.

I ducked into the house, keen to get in and out as soon as possible. My heart was thudding in my chest, my hands trembling. The side door led into the kitchen. I looked around frantically – at the table, the cooker, the sink. I hadn't got the first idea what to take. I picked up a cup and put it down. That wouldn't satisfy Johnny. I pulled open a drawer. Inside there was one spoon, one fork and one knife. Something felt wrong about leaving a person with no cutlery, so I left those. I raced into the front room. It was dark, the window having been painted with blackout paint, but there was enough light for me to make out there a black suit jacket hanging from a hook on the back of the door, two armchairs – one worn, the other not so – and a small table with two books on it. One was the bible. That made me pause, I tell you. The other was a copy of *The Golden Fleece*. *The Golden Fleece*?

My heart pounded harder. I span round. Was I...?

I dashed over to the mantlepiece and picked up a photo. It was of a woman, she looked happy. And a young man. He looked happy too – I almost didn't recognize him.

"Mr Etherington?" I breathed, my legs turning to jelly beneath me.

I looked up at the sound of the front door bursting open. I couldn't have run, even if I wanted to, because there, holding Lugs by one of his ears, was my headmaster. And he did not look happy.

"Mr Smith," he said.

CHAPTER 40

I didn't say anything. Couldn't say anything. What is there to say when you've been caught red-handed breaking into someone's house? I just stood there with my mouth open and the photo in my hand.

Mr Etherington let go of Lugs's ear and took the photograph off me and set it back on the mantlepiece, pausing a moment to look at the two people smiling back.

"Sit," he said, but Lugs and I just stood there – think our legs were as shocked as our brains.

The second time he shouted, "SIT!" and we both scrambled onto the sofa.

Mr Etherington closed his eyes and breathed deeply, like he was taking a moment to calm down.

"Why are you in my house?" he said, his voice tremoring with anger.

"I...I'm sorry, sir," was all I managed to get out.

"You're sorry? You're *sorry*?"

"Very sorry," Lugs added. "We weren't going to take anything too valuable."

I wasn't completely sure that made things any better.

"Give me one good reason why I shouldn't call the police on you right now."

Lugs began breathing heavily. I could see he was trying not to panic. I was trying not to panic too.

"It wasn't anything to do with Billy, sir. All my idea."

"I don't believe you," Mr Etherington said.

"Honest, sir. It weren't him. It was all my idea."

"Really?"

"Yes, really. Truth is, he wouldn't be here if it wasn't for me."

Mr Etherington studied my face intently for a moment. Then his jaw seemed to relax ever so slightly. "Whoever said there was no honour amongst thieves?"

"Think that were you, sir."

"Indeed, I believe it was. But what I actually meant when I said *I don't believe you*, was that I do not believe breaking into my house was your idea. Come on, who put you up to this?"

Lugs shot me a look, which Mr Etherington must have clocked because he said, "Insolent, rude, ill-mannered, disobedient... You, Ronnie Smith, are all those things, but you have never struck me as the sort to push it this far, not without a reason. So, I ask again, what is that purpose of your...visit?"

"I can't tell you, sir," I said. "Truth be told, I want to, but I can't."

He tilted his head. "A prank?"

"No, sir."

"Then what?"

"I'm sorry, sir, I can't say."

"Then, the police it shall be." He sounded more irritated than cross now.

Lugs stood up. "Please, sir, don't grass him up. I know what we done ain't right, but it's not wrong either, I don't think."

"You don't think breaking into someone's house to steal something, valuable or otherwise, is wrong?"

"Well, yeah, when you say it like that, it's wrong, but things are...complicated, sir," Lugs continued.

Mr Etherington raised an eyebrow. "Complicated?"

"Oh yeah, real complicated," Lugs said. "I don't know how they got so complicated, but they are."

"Life is complicated," Mr Etherington suddenly boomed. Then he wagged his finger at us. "And that's why you need moral integrity. A strong compass to guide you through. That is what I have tried to instil in you, but I see in that I have failed."

"I don't know, sir," I said quietly.

"What's that supposed to mean? You don't know what? Speak up!"

"I don't know if you can instil something like that in someone else. If you can beat it or cane it into them. Don't you think people have to figure it out for themselves?"

"Says the young man with the crowbar."

"It's hard to know what's right and wrong these days." I looked at Lugs. "Good men are sent to battlefields. Fathers and husbands are shot down from the sky and us kids, well, we're just here, left playing in the shrapnel as the world burns around us."

"But you're not playing now, are you?"

"No, sir. I'm not. And you're right. I am insolent and ill-mannered and all those other things you said about me. But in a world where right and wrong are really hard to tell apart sometimes, I guess you just have to do the best you can. And though I can see that it don't much look like it to you, me being here now, is me doing the best I can."

Mr Etherington tilted his head. "I'm sorry, I don't follow."

I took a deep breath. I was going to have to take a chance.

"Mr Etherington, my brother and our friends are in trouble and right now, I think you're the only person who can help them."

CHAPTER 41

Both Lugs and Mr Etherington looked at me for the longest time. Then Mr Etherington said, "What is it you want me to help you with?"

I took a deep breath. "I want you to let me rob you."

I'd never heard Mr Etherington laugh before, but he did then. "You want me to let you do what?"

"I want you to give me something of yours to prove that we've been here and done what we've been told to do."

Mr Etherington leaned back against the wall. "And who is telling you to do such a thing?"

"Johnny Simmons."

"Johnny Simmons." Mr Etherington closed his eyes. "I feared as much."

Lugs looked at me all questioning. But the way I saw it, I had no other option than to tell Mr Etherington the truth. If he called the police on us, I wouldn't be able to help Micky and the others. It was a risk telling him, but if I was right and Mr Etherington hated Johnny Simmons as much as I did, it might be worth it.

"I told you to stay away from that man."

"And we did," I said.

"The current circumstances would suggest otherwise," Mr Etherington said.

"Micky, Arthur, Graham and Harry, they've been working with him, sir. And now they're in trouble. We're trying to get them out of it."

"By robbing me?"

"Johnny told us you wouldn't be here, said you had a strict routine," Lugs said.

"He would know that, and he's right, I'm normally not. Usually at the allotment, but I forgot my trowel. I think you'd better tell me everything. The truth, mind. I shall know if you're lying."

"I don't lie, sir, well try not to anyway," I said.

He nodded – I think he believed me. "Continue."

"Johnny Simmons is working for some big gangster types, and he's got Micky and the others involved in a robbery. They're going to hit a jewellery shop up in town during an air raid. There's something real valuable they're after. They need a bunch of us kids, so we can separate out and run off with the loot, like a decoy. We have to meet again later to hand it back. I thought that if I could be the one to do this handover, and keep Micky and the others out of it, I could tell the police when to show up."

"You're willing to sacrifice yourself for your friends?"

"Hoping the rozzers might go easy on me, if I help bring in

some big criminals. But Johnny has to trust me first, see? That's why I need you to let me rob you."

Mr Etherington stared at me – his expression unreadable. "You don't know when this raid will be?"

"Nope, or where."

"And why not tell the police now?"

"What we going to tell them? They can't bang someone up for something that hasn't happened. And besides, if Johnny works out that we've told, they're going to come down on us hard. We're talking missing fingers."

"Missing fingers," Lugs repeated nodding solemnly.

Mr Etherington looked from Lugs to me. "This is dangerous, what you're proposing to do, you understand that?"

"I think that, sometimes, you have to walk up to danger and face it head on," I said, "like you did, sir, with that bomb."

Mr Etherington pinched the bridge of his nose and closed his eyes like he was thinking things through real hard. I couldn't call it – if he was going to agree or not. He was taking so long to decide, I suspected he'd say no. The tension built up in me something rotten. But then, when he finally opened his eyes, he disappeared out of the room without saying a word. When he returned a moment later, he put something in my hand.

"Here, take him this. He'll know it's mine."

It was a medal for bravery from the Great War. "Sir, no – something else."

"No. It needs to be that. I have nothing else of value."

"But it's for your bravery," I said, trying to hand it back.

"Don't you have a fancy watch or something else instead?"

"I need my watch. That," he said nodding at the medal, "is just metal, no different to the stuff you boys scrabble about for on the ground. A reminder of war."

"A reminder of courage more like," I said.

"Courage needs no reminders. The thing about courage is that you have it in you, or you don't. I'm of the belief that it can be found in most – when the need arises. Take the medal, Ronnie Smith and take your chance to find the courage in you."

I didn't say anything, just nodded, but Lugs said, "Mr Etherington, that was a right good speech that!"

Mr Etherington looked at Lugs like he was most peculiar, then said. "Be careful, Mr Smith."

"I'll try," I said and turned to head out the back door with Lugs.

"I wasn't always so hard."

"Sir?" Lugs and I stopped and turned round. Mr Etherington had a look on his face I'd never seen before. I think it might have been sorrow.

"The punishments. I only did it because I thought that it was best for you. For all of you." He shook his head. "I was too lenient once and I paid the price."

It wasn't an excuse – it was a reason. Seemed Mr Etherington was just another person, struggling with his past. "Guess it's like I said, sir. sometimes it's hard to know what's right and what's wrong. I guess we all are just trying our best to figure it out."

"And sometimes our best isn't enough. Seems I'm still paying the price for my mistakes now."

"What's that mean, sir?" Lugs asked.

Mr Etherington looked over at the photo on the mantlepiece. "Oh, nothing. Now, you'd best be going – deliver your loot."

I made to leave but Mr Etherington said, "Smith, just one more thing."

"Yes, sir?"

"I once said that you weren't very bright."

"You did, sir."

"I was wrong."

I grinned. "My mum says I have my moments."

CHAPTER 42

J ohnny took the medal, held it up so it dangled in front of his face and smiled. "My, my, my, you've got the old goat's George the Fifth." Micky put a cup of tea down in front of him and joined us at the kitchen table.

I hated handing over Mr Etherington's medal to Johnny, that he seemed so pleased made me feel even worse. My whole insides were juddering – a right horrible mix of anger and anxiety.

"You a pupil of his or something?" Lugs asked.

Johnny snatched the medal up in his hand, then stuffed it in his top pocket. "Something like that. What do you think, Micky? Your brother done good, hey?"

"I guess." Micky shrugged, but when he looked at me, he almost seemed disappointed.

"We in then?" I asked.

Johnny looked me and Lugs up and down and nodded. "Yeah, you're in."

"So, what's next?"

He laughed. "Someone's keen."

"You're the one who talks about seizing opportunities."

"Don't you worry, there's something lined up." He looked over at Micky. "Something big."

"Yeah?" I said, trying to sound excited. "What?"

"You'll find out."

"When?"

"Soon." He drained the rest of his tea, slapped his hands on his thighs and stood up. I knew I wouldn't be getting anything more out of him then.

"You off?" Micky asked.

"Yup, I'll be back again when I need you. Take it easy until then."

After Johnny had left, I suggested we go outside for a kick about, but Micky wasn't keen. Said he was busy, even though all he did was sit down on the sofa and pretend to read old comics. Lugs and I had only just started half-heartedly kicking a ball back forth when he burst out through the front door so hard it bounced back off the wall.

"What did you have to go and do that for?" he shouted, pointing at me.

I stopped the ball under my foot. "What do you mean?"

"Join up with Johnny and me? Why did you have to do it, Ron, why?"

I couldn't understand his reaction. Maybe he was worried I was going to muscle in on his relationship with Johnny. Maybe he just didn't like having me around.

"I thought you'd be pleased that I wasn't having a go at you about it any more."

Micky scuffed at the ground with his shoe. "You shouldn't be doing it."

"You are kidding, right? I wouldn't be if it wasn't for you!"

"Didn't ask you to."

He was so infuriating, I had to hold myself back from shaking the stupid out of him. "I don't get you, Mick!"

"This ain't a game! We ain't collecting shrapnel now. You don't know what you're getting yourself into!"

I thought about telling him that I did. That I knew everything, but I couldn't be sure that he wouldn't just run off and tell Johnny.

"The things Johnny does, the people he knows, they're dangerous!" Micky said.

"Mick, do you want out?" Lugs said.

"Why...why would you think that?" Micky said stumbling over his words.

"Dunno. Hunch, I guess. All that talk about dangerous people. You don't make it sound all that lovely."

Micky opened his mouth but closed it without saying anything, but I saw a flash of uncertainty in his eyes.

"Is Lugs right, do you want out?" I asked.

He shook his head. "It's not an option."

"I didn't ask about options. I asked what you wanted. Do you want out? If you do, I could try and speak to Johnny." The sudden hope that he might say yes, made my words come out quickly.

"There is no *out*, Ronnie."

"Look, maybe now that he's got me, he won't need you," I continued, buoyed by a nervous eagerness.

Micky's eye hardened, the uncertainty replaced by resoluteness. "He *does* need me. He's told me as much. Sure, what he's doing has its risks, but the pay-off is worth it. He's doing this for our family. Because he cares."

"Johnny doesn't care about us! He's using you, Micky."

"He does care! He's stuck around, hasn't he? You always think you know best, but you don't!"

"Ron's only looking out for you," Lugs said.

"And maybe I'm trying to look out for him!" Micky snapped. "So just shut up, Lugs! Shut up would you!?"

Lugs stepped back, looking wounded.

"Sorry, it's not you. It's him," Micky said nodding towards me. "And I don't want out, okay?"

"Then neither do I," I said.

"Don't say I didn't try to warn you," Micky said, then stormed back inside. I kicked the ball real hard so it hit the door just as Micky slammed it shut.

"That didn't go brilliantly," Lugs said.

"Can't he work out that I'm trying to help!" I shouted at Lugs.

"He's scared, Ronnie," Lugs said, "can't you tell he's scared?"

That afternoon, I walked Lugs back to his house. Neither of us spoke much. I was too cross. Cross at Johnny. Cross at Micky.

Cross at myself. Cross with the whole world.

"You okay?" Lugs asked.

I sighed. "I guess. You?"

"Oh yeah, fine. Got caught robbing the headmaster's house and joined a gang of East End fascist criminals, I'm simply sparkling, thanks for asking."

"You don't have to do this, you know? Micky's my brother, he's my responsibility."

"Nice try but he's my responsibility too. And so are you, for that matter."

I laughed. "Is that so?"

"Yup. You need me, Ronnie, and I'm not going to let you do this on your own. We're The Shrapnel Boys, remember? We might not be blood, but we're bonded and, in Johnny Simmons, you and I have a common enemy."

"Do you think it's going to work, this plan?" I asked. I'd been playing it over in my head, trying to think of all the ways it could go wrong, but so many of them ended up with me in prison or taking a hiding from Johnny, that I'd had to stop because it was making me feel so sick.

"It's the only one we've got, so it's gonna have to. Now come on, last one back to mine smells like Hitler's bum crack." Lugs darted off down the road and I took up chase. Every time I'd try and overtake, he'd swerve and block my path. We arrived at his gate, puffing and panting, me protesting that he'd had a head start and him telling me that I was the stinker.

When we'd caught our breath, we noticed that his mum

was standing on the front doorstep, like she'd been waiting out for him. Our laughter trailed off. I think we both knew something weren't right straight away by the look of her. Her face was grey, her hands were clasped tightly together and when she said, "Billy, love," her voice wobbled.

We both knew what was coming.

The smile fell from Lugs's face. "It's Dad, isn't it?"

I took a step closer to him, a single thought playing over and over in my head – please, don't let it be his dad, not his dad, not his dad.

"Why don't you come on inside, Billy?" Mrs Missell said, her voice catching in her throat.

Lugs shook his head, then swallowed hard. "No, now. Tell me now. Is he dead?"

"He's missing in action, love."

Lugs nodded. "So, there's a chance he's okay?"

"We just don't know."

"If we don't know, there's a chance," Lugs said, his voice rising in volume.

"Why don't you come inside, Billy."

"Tell me there's a chance!" Lugs shouted. "I need to know there's a chance!"

His mum started weeping and sank down onto the doorstep. "I don't know, Billy. I don't know, I don't know, I don't know."

Lugs looked at me, tears rolling down his cheeks. "There's a chance, isn't there, Ronnie? Please, say there is."

He sounded so desperate – I thought my heart might break for him.

I put my hands on his shoulders and, even though tears were trying to force their way to my own eyes, I knew it wasn't my time to cry – I needed to be strong for Lugs. So I held them back, tried my best to smile and said, "Yeah, Lugs, there's a chance. There's definitely a chance. When my dad's telegram came it said *missing in action, presumed dead*. There's no presumption in yours. So, I'm very much of the presumption he could still be alive."

His eyes searched mine. "Yeah?"

"Yeah," I said, hoping that it was true.

Lugs screwed his eyes shut for a moment and breathed out deeply. When he opened them again, he nodded, and said, "He's going to be okay," like he was trying to tell himself that was the truth. "He *is* going to be okay."

I wanted to agree, to tell him that his dad was a good man, that there was someone up there and they'd be looking out for him. But it was hard to believe in anything any more.

We both looked down as something soft padded over our feet.

"Tiger!" I said, as he wound his way through Lugs's legs, purring.

Lugs sniffed and wiped his nose, a smile flickering on his lips. "He ain't ever done that before!"

Tiger rubbed himself up against Lugs's legs a little longer then walked over towards Mrs Talbot, who was still sitting on the doorstep, then looked back at Lugs as if saying, *I think you ought to come over and see to your mum.* Lugs got the message.

"Mum, it's okay, it's going to be okay," he said, helping her up. "I'm here."

She took his face in her hands and said, "Oh, my dear boy," and pulled him into a hug.

I held my hand up to say goodbye and I headed off back home, hoping to make it in time to give my own mum a hug before she left for work. As I walked, tiredness crept its way into my limbs and up into my head. And I remembered again what Mrs Green had said about the world changing so fast that it was difficult to keep up with it.

CHAPTER 43

The wait for the big job to happen felt like it went on for ever. In reality, it was only three days after I'd agreed to work for Johnny that he turned up one evening and told us it was all systems go. Micky and I were already in the shelter. The air-raid alarm hadn't gone off yet, but Micky and I had decided there was little point in going inside only to have to come back out again. Mum was on lates again, and Mrs Green was still in the hospital with her hip, although Mum said she was due home really soon. Apparently, everyone was keen to get her off the ward. Mum said she'd met less demanding patients.

Johnny seemed stressed when he bowled into the shelter that evening to tell us it was all happening. He sat on the bunk, his legs bouncing up and down like Harry's had that time and looking just as worried. I thought he'd be calmer – that he was used to this sort of thing – but his eyes darted about everywhere and everything about him felt uneasy. Made me feel uneasy too. And sick. I felt sick to my kneecaps about what we were going to do.

"This can't go wrong. Understand? Lot at stake." Johnny lit a cigarette and brought it to his lips, his fingers shaking.

"It's not going to go wrong though, is it?" Micky said. "You said it won't, if we follow the plan." To be honest, he sounded like he was trying to convince himself.

"It won't go wrong if you lot don't mess up," Johnny said and leaned forward, fixing his eyes first on Micky and then on me. "I want you both to listen up and listen up good. We're going up town tonight. You go and get the other boys, then meet me down by the railway arches in an hour. We've got a van to take us."

"Where exactly are we headed?" I asked. "What jewellery shop?"

"Jewellery shop?" Johnny said, and for a moment, I thought he was going to ask me how I knew, but he didn't. Instead, he said, "Oh, yeah, the jeweller's," and took two quick puffs on his cig. "Find out when you get there. You do the job, you each take a bag, and you split, and you scarper, understand?"

"How are we going to know where to scarper to if we don't know where we are?" I said.

"Just get yourselves back home," he said. "You'll know where you are when we're there and you'll figure it out."

Didn't know why he was getting so irritated – it seemed like a reasonable question to me.

"Who's driving us?" Micky asked.

"What's that matter to you?" Johnny snapped and jumped to his feet. There were beads of sweat on his forehead, even though it weren't warm. I couldn't shake the feeling that there was something he wasn't telling us.

"It's just a question," I said. "You alright, Johnny? You seem—"

"I seem what?" he spat.

"I dunno...tense. What's going on?"

"Nothing's going on. I'm fine!" he barked.

Micky and I shot each other a glance.

"I'm fine," Johnny said and forced a smile. "See? As calm as they come."

We both nodded, but calm wasn't the word I'd have chosen.

He ran his hand through his hair and sat back down. "Can't mess it up, that's all."

"We won't mess it up," Micky said. "We'll do exactly what you tell us to do."

"After it's done, we'll meet up early tomorrow morning for the handover. Five o'clock, at those houses you play in. Make sure you're not followed." Johnny took a last long drag then stamped the cigarette out on the floor. "You make the drop-off and then you go, and you say nothing about any of this."

The dens, it was all going to happen at the dens.

"Okay, Johnny," Micky said. "You can trust us to keep our traps shut, can't he, Ronnie?"

"Yeah, course." I felt my cheeks flush, a little cough escaped from my throat, and I wished I had Micky's knack for lying.

"You'd better," Johnny said, eyeing me. "After the handover's done, I'm going to head off for a while."

I nodded, hoping that if everything went to plan, *my plan*, the only place Johnny Simmons would be heading off to would be to do some time at His Majesty's service.

"You're leaving? But why?" Micky said. He sounded disappointed and it hurt to hear it. I knew, in his heart, Micky wanted out, but I also knew he'd tied part of himself to Johnny Simmons and the knots that bound my brother to that man were big and complicated and would take a while to untangle. And I needed Johnny gone for that to start happening.

"To lay low, avoid any heat which may head my way," Johnny said, his eyes darting about. "This is big, what we're doing."

"You mentioned that," I said.

"Don't get smart with me, kid. You have no idea about how big this thing is, and it's best we keep it that way. But if this war plays out as I think it's gonna, then you'll be thanking me later, you'll see. You'll have the right people on side."

"What's that supposed to mean?" I asked. "What right people?"

Johnny didn't answer, I wanted to push further, ask him how he thought the war was going to play out, and what that had to do with a jewellery robbery. Whether this whole job was somehow linked to his fascist Blackshirts, but he checked his watch and said, "You'd better get going."

I went to open the shelter door then stopped. "Wait, when will we get our cut?" I said. Not that I was worried about that, there wasn't going to be a cut if everything went as I hoped, but

304

I thought it might sound more convincing.

"You'll get it when I give it to you. Oh, and another thing, only one of the bags will have the valuables in and whoever gets that bag, you don't look in it, understand?"

"Don't look in it?" I said. "Why not?"

"Because those are the instructions."

"But Johnny—" Micky began.

"No buts. Trust me, it's better for you this way."

"How's it better?" I asked.

"Two words. Plausible deniability."

Micky and I headed off into the darkening evening to fetch the others, leaving Johnny in the shelter. I would get Lugs and Micky would call on Arthur, Graham and Harry. I hoped Harry would be alright and that he wouldn't give the game away. As we walked quickly down the street, I couldn't get the way Johnny had acted out of my head. A straight-up robbery wouldn't have caused him to get so anxious. Maybe it was the people he was working for. Maybe it was more than that. Maybe this something big was bigger than anything I could possibly imagine.

At the end of the road, I turned to Micky and said, "That stuff Johnny said about the war playing out – does Johnny think the Nazi's are going to win?"

"Let's just say, if it's them and not us, Johnny's going to make sure we'll be alright," Micky said.

I stopped in my tracks. "Micky, is Johnny on the side of Germany?"

"No! Course not! He's just hedging his bets, that's all. Planning for all eventualities."

"And how is us robbing a jewellery shop going to help him *hedge his bets*?"

"If you've got money, you've got power," Micky said.

"That came right out of the Johnny Simmons's guide to life."

"He's right though. You don't see those rich folk – the ones who make all the decisions that put people like Dad in the sky and Mr Missell on the battlefield – fighting alongside them. Johnny's got a plan, and he says it's going to help us."

I really started to feel uneasy, but I knew there was no backing out now. "Don't you think he seems worried though?"

"You heard him, there's a lot at stake."

"What even is 'plausible deniability'? Seems odd to me. You don't have a bad feeling about this?"

Micky stopped still, like he was thinking about it. He didn't look at me, just kept his eyes on the road. "Best not to have feelings, I reckon."

I found Lugs out in the road with Tiger. He was sitting on the pavement, looking glum. Tiger was sitting next to him, looking threatening.

I was going to tell him straight away that the job was on, but he looked so sad that what I had to say didn't seem important in that moment.

I sat down beside him. "Any news about your dad?"

He shook his head. "No, not yet. Mum's talking about moving to my aunty Dora's farm down in Kent. Reckons she can leave her job in the factory and work there instead. Thinks it would be safer."

A weight sank down into my stomach. Maybe it was selfish, but I didn't want him to go.

"Told her I'd rather stay." He nudged me lightly. "Who'd be here to keep an eye on you?"

"That's true," I said forcing a smile.

"I dunno, though, it might be better for Mum to be with her sister. She's not handling things all that great."

"Don't you worry about me, I'll be right."

I said that even though I didn't mean it. I wanted him to worry about me. Sometimes, I felt like he was the only person who did. The only one who knew who I was. I wanted to tell him that I needed him more than his mum did. But you don't say those sorts of things, not out loud.

Lugs stroked Tiger, who hissed for a moment and turned away, then went back for a stroke on his own terms. "Look, I dunno if it will happen. Just talk at the moment. But if I do have to go, it don't mean that we're not best mates any more, okay?"

"Okay," I said, trying not to sound too miserable.

"So anyway, what brings you over here at this time?"

The reminder of what we were about to do made my body tense. "I've come to get you. It's happening, Lugs. The big job at the jeweller's – it's tonight. We're meeting at the railway arches in a bit."

"Right," he said, then let out a low whistle. "Right."

It was hard to figure out what he was thinking – neither his face or his voice were giving anything away.

"I won't think wrong of you, if you decide not to come. You know the types of thing Johnny believes and I've got a bad feeling that what he's got planned has got to do with him being a fascist."

"Maybe that means there's even more of a reason for me to come. Besides, I told you before, I'm a shrapnel boy. I said I'd do it, so I'm doing it."

"Sure?"

"I'll tell Mum I'm sitting the air raid out at yours. She won't like it, but I'll tell her that I might not get to see you much if she drags me down to Aunty Dora's. Wait here."

Lugs disappeared into the house and Tiger turned and glared at me with dark, accusing eyes.

"I know, I know," I said. "But I don't see what choice I have."

Tiger tilted his head.

"Don't look at me like that. If this goes right, then we'll have Johnny Simmons out of our lives for good."

Tiger looked at me, then back at the front door of the house as if saying, *And who brought him in to Lugs's life*? I realized then that I'd been wrong, selfish even, to ever get Lugs involved –

to put him in danger. This wasn't Lugs's fight. This was about me and Johnny Simmons.

I got up and left before Lugs made it back outside, hoping he'd see sense and not follow.

CHAPTER 44

The others were already there by the time I'd made it to the railway arches. It was dark now and the air-raid siren had rung out, which meant the streets were mainly deserted. Micky and the others, who were dressed in their firewatchers' helmets, crowded round Johnny. As soon as I saw him, I could tell his mood had changed. He seemed almost electric as he spoke to them. He rubbed his hands together when he saw me and said, "This is it boys, this is it!"

Arthur and Graham grinned, their eyes flashing, but Micky and Harry looked a bit grey round the edges. I caught Harry's eye and tried to give him a reassuring look. He gave me the smallest of nods in return, and I felt a bit more hopeful that he might not panic and mess things up.

Johnny handed me a helmet and Arthur slung his arm over my shoulder as the first of the German bombers rumbled in the distance.

"Look at us, Ronnie. We ain't kids no more, we're big time."

I smiled, but I didn't like the feeling that was growing in me.

Excitement, that's what it was. I was excited to be out there doing something I shouldn't be doing.

"Everyone else is hiding, but not us." Johnny turned round with his arms out wide. "We're living. Seizing opportunities."

We all nodded, and Arthur said, "Yeah, we are, Johnny!"

Johnny checked his watch, then glanced down the road. "Van should be here soon. You all know what you got to do?"

Harry said, "Err..."

But Graham elbowed him and said, "We sure do."

A van turned into the road, its lights off. Johnny looked at each of us in turn then said, "Thought there were six of you? Where's the lad with the ears?"

Harry frowned and said, "We've all got ears."

"I think he means me."

I turned round to see Lugs standing behind me. Tiger was loitering a little behind him. Swear that cat gave me a look of disgust.

"Lugs!" I was surprised to see him there at first but then I realized he would always have come, no matter what I'd tried to do to put him off.

"Glad you've decided to grace us with your presence. That cat isn't coming though," Johnny said and chucked Lugs a helmet. "Put that on."

The driver of the van, a bloke I'd never clapped eyes on before, dressed as an air-raid warden, got out and opened the back door. "The next generation of Blackshirts," he said to Johnny. "Good to see it."

I was right then. We were off to steal jewellery to line the pockets of some fascists.

Lugs swallowed. I couldn't imagine how hard this must be for him. I leaned towards him and whispered. "But we're not. We're shrapnel boys, remember?"

"*The* Shrapnel Boys," Lugs whispered back.

"Everyone in," Johnny said. We piled into the van and sat down on the floor. Johnny slammed the door shut and he and the driver got in the front. The engine started and off we rumbled down the street.

Arthur and Graham started chatting about all the riches we were about to get our hands on and what they'd buy with the cash when they got it.

"You got money, and you got power," Arthur said. "Look at Johnny, no one messes him about. Those people I stayed with down in the countryside, they thought I was nothing – worthless. Not even fit for a bed. But I'll show them. I'll make something of myself."

"Too right. We all will. Johnny keeps saying it's a big job," Graham said. "Reckon we're going to be robbing something real expensive."

"Like what?" Harry said.

"Dunno. Gold, diamonds, emeralds!" Graham said.

"Holy mackerel!" Harry said. "You don't reckon we're robbing the king, do you?"

"What?" Arthur said. "No! Why would you think that!"

"Who else has all that stuff?" Harry said.

"Johnny must know," Graham said.

"And he does live up in town." Harry threw his hands to his head. "The Crown Jewels. I betcha! We're robbing the chuffin' Crown Jewels. We'll end up in the Tower of London if they catch us!"

"We're not robbing the Crown Jewels," Micky said. "Are we?"

"No, we're not," Arthur said. "Too risky."

"You don't know that!" Harry shot back. "I can't hide the king's flaming crown round mine!"

"Harry, calm down," Graham said. "Johnny knows what he's doing. It's just a jewellery shop, that's all."

Everyone quietened down for a bit. But the silence didn't last long, I think it made everyone feel the nervousness that was thrumming around us. It did me, at any rate.

Lugs was sitting close enough to hear me whisper. "You didn't have to come. I thought it would be better for you if I went without—"

"I know what you thought, and I appreciate it, but I had to come."

I don't know if Arthur heard but he said, "You having second thoughts, or something, Missell?"

Lugs smiled broadly. "Who me? Nah. Wouldn't let you boys down."

"It sure is something, isn't it?" Graham said. "We were enemies and now look at us."

In the back of a van going to rob a jewellery shop, I thought, and as soon as I did, I suddenly realized that them being there

313

was all down to me. The rivalry had always been between me and Arthur. The competition between The Wreckers and The Shrapnel Boys, that was down to me too. If we hadn't had that, then they wouldn't be here now.

But they were, we all were, and before I had any more time to think about how we'd ended up in the situation we were in, the van suddenly pulled in and the engine stopped.

CHAPTER 45

Fires split the sky orange and red as the van doors flew open, and we clambered out onto the street. It was like stepping into a painting. My heart was beating so hard I could feel it in my stomach. In the distance, there was a formation of *Junkers* 88s spreading out over the city. The familiar *ack-ack* sound of the anti-aircraft guns started up, and a Hurricane flew directly over us in the direction of the *Junkers*. I stood still, eyes up, willing the Hurricane pilot on.

A slap on the back and a shout of, "Get moving!" from Johnny pulled me back into the now. Bags were thrust into our arms – except Micky was told he'd get his later – and then we were off, running down the street as the van and drove away.

I tried to get my bearings. The dome of St Paul's was to the right – we must be north of the river and central. Whitehall by the looks of it.

We followed Johnny along the bomb-cratered streets, as the sound of bombers groaned in the sky above and explosions boomed out over London. He kept looking behind him, checking we were keeping up.

"Where are we going?" Lugs called out. "Don't see no jewellery shops round here."

Lugs was right. There wasn't a jeweller's, or much in the way of shops at all. What the hell was going on?

"Not much further!" Johnny shouted.

Harry appeared next to me, his face white and his eyes huge.

"Ronnie," he said, sounding desperate. I waited for him to say more, but he didn't.

"It's okay," I said. "Just head home as soon as you can."

We turned a corner down a street, its impressive buildings looming high above us.

Harry came to a stop. "It's Buckingham Palace! We *are* going to rob the king!"

"It isn't Buckingham Palace," I said, stopping next to him.

"I told you! Didn't I tell you!?" Harry said, not listening to me.

"Harry, this ain't Buckingham Palace! These look like... government buildings."

Unease swelled in me. What were we doing outside government buildings?

Harry tilted his head. "You sure it's not the palace? Looks right fancy to me."

Johnny turned round. "Oi, you two. Stop yakking. This way."

We followed him round the side of one of the buildings. He ran down some steps and we all waited at the top while he banged on a door.

"Johnny, what's going on?" Micky asked. "This isn't a jewellery shop."

"You don't say!" he snapped back and banged harder. "Come on, come on, answer!" He sounded agitated – on edge. What had Johnny got us into? My thoughts started to spiral, and my heart pounded harder and harder. Johnny had a man on the inside, helping him to steal something from the government. This really was big.

"I don't like this," Graham said, his head swivelling about. "I think maybe we should go."

Johnny jabbed his finger at him. "If you want to live to see your next birthday you stay there!"

Graham swallowed and shifted from foot to foot, looking like he was doing everything he could to stop himself from bolting.

The door suddenly opened. An arm holding a bag, just like the ones we were carrying, shot out. Some words I couldn't make out were barked from inside as Johnny grabbed the bag and chucked it at Micky.

"Go on, then! The lot of you, run!"

Nobody moved for a moment. We all knew what we were supposed to do, but suddenly nothing seemed real. I felt like I was looking down from the sky, watching things unfold below me.

Micky held up the bag, confusion and panic in his eyes. "This isn't jewels or gold...it's too light."

"Where's the jewels?" Arthur said.

Johnny practically snarled. "You want to talk about this now or do you want to get out of here and talk about it later?"

"You heard, him! Go!" I shouted. I needed them all out of there and out of trouble, and I needed that bag and whatever was in it, so I could trap Johnny later.

"But Johnny—" Arthur began, but he piped down pretty quick when the door to the building began to rattle furiously on its hinges. A different voice called out. Again, I couldn't make out what was said, but whoever it was didn't sound happy. It clearly wasn't one of Johnny's mates. We'd been rumbled, and sheer terror shot through me.

Johnny charged back up the steps and shoved Micky. "Move! Go on! Get!"

"It's got to be six miles back to Deptford, at least!" I said.

"Then I'd get those legs of yours moving!" he said and charged off down the road.

There was a loud thud from the door, followed by a second, a third, then the sound of wood splintering.

"That isn't going to hold much longer," Lugs said.

Micky looked at me, his face pale, the bag trembling in his hands. "Ronnie?"

I grabbed the bag from him, pushed my empty one into his hands and shouted, "Run!"

We took off after Johnny, Micky leading the way, me and Lugs just behind him. I don't think I've ever run so fast, but Micky, he was like lightning.

I turned round to check the others were following. I won't

318

ever forget the looks of pure terror on their faces.

Two men in army uniform suddenly appeared at the top of the steps. They spotted us and took up chase.

"We've got company!" I shouted.

Lugs checked over his shoulder and stumbled when he saw there were a couple of His Majesty's finest after us.

Up ahead, the road split in two. I waved my hand and shouted, "Separate off! Hang a left!!" Lugs led the others down a road that ran parallel to the one we were on, and I raced after Micky.

He was absolutely motoring – he'd almost caught up with Johnny. I checked behind me again. The soldiers were still following, but we'd widened the gap – there must have been over fifty yards of pavement between us. I realized that they weren't going to get us, we were too fast. Something like euphoria swept over me and I actually whooped.

"Keep going, Mick, we can outrun 'em easy!" I shouted, then I watched in horror as an air-raid warden stepped out into the road. It all happened so quickly – I didn't have a chance to shout a warning. Micky ploughed straight into him. They both hit the floor, the warden landing on top.

"What the hell do you think you're doin'?" the warden cried as he tried to stand up.

Micky rolled onto his back and groaned.

Behind me one of the soldiers bellowed, "Hold on to that child!"

Micky tried to scramble away, but the warden grabbed him by the collar.

Micky called out to Johnny for help. He was closer than me, but the coward didn't stop.

Micky squirmed about trying to get free from the warden's grip, shouting, "Johnny! Johnny, please, help me! Don't leave me again."

Johnny looked over his shoulder and yelled, "Ronnie, keep hold of that bag and go!"

For a second, Micky stopped struggling and stared at Johnny, pain and disbelief in his eyes. I'd always known Johnny was a lowlife, but I didn't take any pleasure watching my brother finally understand that too.

"Let go of my brother!!" I yelled and launched myself at the warden. I began tugging at his arms trying to get him to let go. When that didn't work, I grabbed Micky and tried to pull him free. But the warden was having none of it. He was as big as a bear and as strong as one. Down the road, the soldiers had slowed to a jog. They must have thought that we wouldn't be going anywhere any time soon.

"Gerroff of me!" Micky shouted.

"Don't let the little blighter go, he's just robbed a government building!" a soldier shouted.

I grabbed on to the warden's arm and lifted my legs off the ground. I dangled there, hoping that my weight may cause him to let go of Micky, who writhed about and kicked out his legs, but it seemed Micky had managed to get himself caught by the world's strongest man.

"Hold still!" the warden barked. I looked over at the soldiers marching towards us. If they caught us, Micky and I would be the ones thrown in the slammer and Johnny Simmons would get away scot-free.

"I'm right sorry about this, sir," I said, and booted him between the legs. I know, it's not the done thing, but I didn't see I had much choice. He let go of Micky pretty sharpish and dropped to his knees whimpering. With the bag bouncing about on my back, we tore off towards Lugs and the others, who'd appeared at the end of the road, jumping up and down and shouting at us to hurry up.

"Oi! Stop!" the soldiers shouted, but there was no way on God's green earth that we were going to do that.

When we were ten or so yards from Lugs and the others, I yelled, "Go! Go! Go!" and they started off again.

Lugs shouted, "Four on our tail now! Follow me! Stick together." Johnny's decoy plan had been for us to split up so the soldiers wouldn't know who had the loot, but the thought of doing that again suddenly seemed impossible.

"Where the heck are we going?" Harry yelped.

I sped up to take the lead. "Head south, over the bridge!"

I took them down one more road, and then, suddenly, the river was in sight. My legs were aching, my lungs were burning, and we were still miles from home, but something about seeing the Thames gave me hope. Home was on the other side.

We thundered across Westminster Bridge, the sound of bombers filling the air around us. We could see the explosions over the East End, hear the *ack-ack* of the anti-aircraft guns, feel the heat of the fires. Half-way across the bridge, I checked behind me again.

"There's still two on us!" I shouted.

Harry wailed. "I can't keep running!"

"Yes, you can!" I yelled back. "We'll get to Waterloo and lose them there."

"We're younger and fitter!" Arthur said. "Just keep going!"

We got to the other side of the bridge – air wardens and firefighters were out in force. It looked like the Germans had been busy dropping incendiary bombs. There were fires lighting up all over the place. The heat was incredible. We wove through wardens and flames and broken shells and swung a left towards Waterloo.

A couple of coppers came running straight towards us and I thought we were done for, but they jogged straight past, shouting at us to get inside.

I snatched a look over my shoulder as we headed down the Waterloo Road. I was convinced that we must have lost the soldiers in all the chaos. But they were still there. Whatever was in the bag was clearly very important.

"We need to split up and hide," I said. "They can't follow us all."

Arthur said, "Shrapnel boys together, Wreckers together."

"Meet by Waterloo railway arches when you're sure the coast is clear."

"Got it," Arthur said and led Harry and Billy off down a side road.

Micky, Lugs and I carried on a bit further then turned down a narrow passageway between two buildings.

We were halfway along it when we realized.

"It's a dead end!" Lugs said.

We came to a stop, chests heaving, lungs burning. The wall at the end was too high to climb.

Micky kicked at a stone in frustration. "We're trapped!"

"Should we go back?" Lugs asked.

I didn't think that was a good idea. We might run straight into the soldiers.

I pointed to some crates that were stacked haphazardly against a building. They wouldn't provide much cover, but it was the best we had. "Quick, behind there."

We hunkered down, our backs pressed to the wall. I chanced a glance down the alleyway.

"What the heck was that all about? That wasn't no jewellery robbery—" Lugs began but I held up a hand and shushed him. The soldiers were standing at the end of the passage. I could see the fear I was feeling reflected back in Lugs's eyes. We shrank down, trying to make ourselves as small as possible.

I could feel Micky trembling next to me and while I couldn't see the men from where we were cowering, I could feel their presence – sense them coming towards us.

They knew we were there.

We heard the sound of approaching footsteps.

"Are you sure they came down here?"

"Could have sworn they went this way."

The footsteps stopped. "If we don't find them—"

"We'll find them."

"How in God's name has a bunch of kids got their hands on highly classified information? If that information gets into the wrong hands..." He didn't say any more, didn't need to. The anger in his voice was obvious, but so was the concern.

I looked down at the loot bag.

Classified information. I was holding highly classified information. It felt like the ground was shifting underneath me. My mind tripped over itself, as the pieces came together.

If the war goes the way he thinks it's going.

He'll make sure we're alright.

Johnny the fascist

Johnny the traitor

It wasn't money that Johnny wanted – he was going to trade information with the Nazis in exchange for protection.

The feeling of sickness that came over me was so strong and so sudden, I actually heaved. Johnny was a traitor, and he'd made traitors of us too.

The footsteps started towards us again.

Lugs closed his eyes tight, and Micky started shaking even harder.

The man came to a stop right by the crates. He was so close. He was sure to spot us. Micky leaned in to me. I could feel his heartbeat pounding. I grabbed his hand, preparing myself for the shout that would confirm we'd been found.

I held my breath. He'd seen us. I was sure of it. He'd seen us and we were going to get arrested for being traitors and we'd go to prison or worse and Mum would be left on her own. I let go of Micky's hand and grabbed hold of the strap of my bag. He looked at me and shook his head.

"Stay down," I whispered. "I'll tell them it was me."

Lugs shook his head. "Ronnie, no."

But my mind was made up. I'd tell them now. I'd tell them everything. I'd just have to hope they'd believe me when I explained.

I stood up and stepped into the alleyway just as the bomb exploded.

The last thing I remember was the feeling of weightlessness and a brilliant white light.

CHAPTER 46

I heard our Micky's voice first. It sounded distant over the sound of ringing in my ears. "Ronnie! Ronnie! Wake up!"

I'm trying to, I thought, but I wasn't a hundred per cent certain where my body was to go about the business of waking it up. That might sound strange, but my mind felt separate from it, removed. I didn't know what had happened, where I was even. Or that I'd been blown through the air by a blinking great blast and landed about ten feet from where I'd been standing.

"Ronnie! Ronnie!" It sounded like Micky was calling to me from the bottom of a well.

Someone grabbed my shirt and began shaking me. "Wake up, Ronnie! Wake up!"

Lugs – it was Lugs's voice.

Micky again. "Is he...is he..."

For a moment, we were playing back in our Anderson shelter – me on the floor with them standing over me having shot me for being a Nazi.

That's when I remembered what had happened. The soldier. The explosion.

"He's not, is he? Lugs...is he?" Micky said again.

"Dead?" I managed to say. I opened one eye. "Not completely."

"Ronnie!" Lugs said, a smile breaking out all over his face. "You had us right worried there!"

I managed to prop myself up on one elbow. My ribs hurt and the side of my face was stinging something rotten. Micky was standing back a bit, his hand over his mouth. He looked like he might cry. Actually, I think he was crying. "It's alright, Mick," I said. "Still in one piece." I waggled my finger in my left ear and then the right. "Although my ears aren't half ringing."

"You okay to walk?" Lugs said, then he looked upwards as some roof tiles clattered off the building. "It's just – we ought to make a move if we're going to meet the others. You've been out cold for ten minutes."

"The soldiers —"

"Long gone. One of them got caught up in the explosion. Got blasted back there," Lugs gestured down the alley. "His mate helped him up and they staggered off, probably to get medical help." He held out a hand and helped me to my feet. "You sure you're okay?"

"Not going to lie, I feel like I've done ten rounds in a boxing ring."

"Looks like it and all," Lugs said.

I touched my face. It felt puffy and tender and when I brought my fingers away, they were covered in blood. "How bad is it?"

Lugs grimaced. "Let's just say we've seen you looking lovelier. But you were lucky. Now, can we get out of here?"

I winced and took a couple of very wobbly steps forward. It hurt a bit when I breathed in, and I weren't at my most comfortable, but I knew I hadn't done myself any serious damage. I suddenly realized I didn't have the bag on me. I looked around frantically, but Micky held it up. "Don't worry, I got it."

I took it off him, I didn't want him anywhere near it. "Did you hear what they said?"

Lugs nodded – his face grim. "Classified information."

I opened the bag and pulled out a file. On the front were the words, *WAR OFFICE – MOST SECRET*. "And who do you think would most like to get their hands on something from the War Office?"

Micky didn't say anything, just stared at the file.

"The flamin' Nazis, that's who!" Lugs said. "Micky, mate, robbing jewellery is one thing but this, this is something else entirely!"

"He's betraying the whole country to look after himself," I said.

"I didn't know," Micky began, his voice faltering. "I never thought he'd..."

"It's okay," I said. "I know you didn't know – not about this."

"What we going to do?" Lugs asked. "Should we just dump it?"

"No, we need to get it back to the right people, and Johnny needs to pay for what he's done. We stick with the plan," I said.

Micky frowned. "Plan? What plan?"

"You two are going to go home and I'm going to go to the police. Tell them everything. What we've done and the time and location of the handover."

"Ronnie, you can't. These people Johnny works for are proper bad. If it goes wrong, they aren't just going to give you a slap on the wrists, they'll kill you." Micky grabbed the files off me, held it up and waved it about. "I'm not going to let you risk your life over a few sheets of paper."

Lugs leaned in. "Think you know that's more than paper, Mick."

I snatched the file and started reading through it. There was a load of diagrams and writing and numbers. Couldn't make head nor tail of it. "Whatever this is, it has to be important for Johnny to have gone to all this trouble to get it. I need to get it to the police."

"But what if Johnny's right?" Mick said, in a small voice.

I blinked. "Right about what?"

"The Germans winning the war."

"*What?*" Lugs and I said in unison.

"Just look around you." He swung his arms out wide. "They're blowing us to bits! Maybe if we do what Johnny wants and hand over the bag, we will have some kind of protection if the Nazis take over."

"I don't believe what I'm hearing!" I said and by the look on Lugs's face he couldn't either.

"Johnny's not the only one who thinks so. I went with him

– to some talks. Lots of people think the Germans will beat us."

"You went to some *talks*?" I threw my hands in the air. "Well, that's just bleedin' brilliant! He's been brainwashing you, Mick! You can't be suggesting we help the people who killed our dad!"

"Like you cared about him!" Micky said.

"Dad wasn't a good man, I think in the end he was trying to be though, and I didn't want him to *die*! I cared, alright." My voice cracked. It surprised me to feel tears pricking the backs of my eyes. I pushed them away, cleared my throat. "I cared."

"Who put him up in the sky in the first place? I'll tell you, Churchill and all those other self-important types, all sitting safe in their comfortable houses, while we hide away in freezing damp shelters listening to our neighbours being blown up. Johnny reckons we didn't even need to go to war, could have reached an agreement. Your dad would have understood that, Lugs."

Lugs shook his head in disbelief. "No, he ruddy wouldn't! My dad isn't a fascist! He thinks everyone has a worth!"

"Johnny says there's going to be a new world, when the Germans arrive and he's going to be part of it. He knows people, important people, who are going to run this country. He'll make sure we're alright. He'll make sure Mum's alright."

"He ain't going to make sure I'm alright," Lugs said. "I've heard stories, of what the Nazis arc doing to the Jews over in Europe. I know people over here don't like to believe them, but Jewish people are fleeing their homes, and the ones that don't are being forced out, they're losing everything – their jobs, their possessions, their way of life."

"Micky," I said, "you can't really believe what Johnny believes in. He doesn't care about anybody but himself. He's willing to betray a whole country and he's willing to betray you. He left you when you got caught by that warden back there." I paused, the image of Micky calling out to Johnny finding its way to my mind. "You said *again*. When Johnny ran off and left you, you said, *Don't leave me again*. What did you mean by that?"

Micky bit his lip and looked away.

"He left you before?"

I could see tears glistening in Micky's eyes. "It weren't his fault. I messed up – was too loud and someone caught me stealing from them. Johnny couldn't have done anything to help, and he felt bad about taking off, honest he did."

"The time you fell off your bike? Those bruises? Johnny was there and he did nothing to help? Sweet Jesus, Mick, if it's a dad you are looking for, Johnny Simmons isn't up to the role.

"I know you're scared and that might be the reason you're thinking like this. But it's not an excuse. I know it ain't always easy to know right from wrong but, right now, the choice seems pretty flamin' obvious. Johnny isn't ever going to protect you. And even if he can, at what cost? Time to decide what kind of person you are, Micky."

He looked at me, blinking back tears.

"So, what is it? Are you a Blackshirt or are you one of The Shrapnel Boys? Because the way I see it, you can't be both."

CHAPTER 47

Micky looked from me to Lugs, chin wobbling. "I'm one of The Shrapnel Boys." Then tears started to stream from his eyes. "But I'm scared, Ron."

"Of course you are," I said. "I think the whole world's scared. I'm scared. Lugs, are you scared?"

"Blinkin' terrified, Ron."

"Why's it have to be like this?" Micky said. "We didn't ask for no war."

"We don't get to make the decisions as to what goes on. We're just kids, but you do get to make a decision now. What's it to be – my plan, or Johnny's? Who you going to choose, Mick?"

Micky sniffed, then swallowed. "I choose you."

It felt like my whole chest was expanding relief. I grinned. "About chuffin' time."

"Great," Lugs said, looking up at the sky as a *Dornier* flew over. "Now that's sorted, do you think we can get out of here? You've almost been blown up once and I would rather like it not to happen again."

I led the way through the burning streets of Waterloo to the railway arches. When we got there, we didn't see The Wreckers at first. I wouldn't have blamed them if they'd cleared off home, but then we heard a shout of, "Oi, you lot, over here!"

We could just about make out Arthur's voice over the *crump-crump* of the guns. He was with the others, squatting behind some sandbags, down in the shadows of a railway arch.

"Took your time. Where've you been?" Arthur demanded when we reached them. Then he looked at me and said, "What happened to you?"

"Sorry we're late," Lugs said. "Ronnie here only went and got himself blown up."

Graham said, "Look, we've been thinking —"

"I'm fine, thanks for asking," I interrupted.

Graham said, "Relieved. But listen, it's just that we've got a real bad feeling about what's in that bag. Whatever we're involved in, it wasn't robbing a jeweller's."

"Johnny's a traitor and he's got us handling some classified information from the War Office," I said.

Graham's face fell. "You have to be joking! Tell me you're joking."

"I think Johnny's helping the Nazis," I continued.

"That's just smashing, that is!" Arthur let out a yell and kicked a dustbin, the clattering noise drowned out by the sound of another explosion. "I thought we were just robbing rich people! We didn't sign up for this!"

"Don't worry, I'm handling it," I said. "You lot are going to go home and you're going to pretend nothing happened."

"What do you mean *you're handling it*?" Arthur asked.

"I'm going to the police. Get them to set up a sting at the handover."

"Hells bells, Ronnie, bit risky that, isn't it?" Graham said. "If it goes wrong, Johnny will kill you!"

Graham was right, and the thought terrified me. "What choice do I have?"

Arthur looked at me, right incredulous. "You think the police are going to believe the likes of you? No offence, but if you show up talking about stealing from the War Office for East End gangsters, they'll either arrest you or think you're having them on."

I didn't like it, but he had a point.

Arthur nodded at Graham and Harry, and they huddled together. A moment or two later, after some muttering, they pulled apart.

"We're coming with you," Graham said. "Maybe if there's more of us, they might listen."

"We're *all* coming with you," Lugs said.

"No, you lot need to go home and keep your heads down. There's no sense in us all getting in trouble. This is between me and Johnny Simmons," I said.

Micky said, "No, Ronnie, he's played us all. We all have to put it right."

"Your brother's right." Arthur put his arm round my shoulders. "Whoever said there's no honour amongst thieves?"

I knew exactly who'd said that, and it gave me an idea. "Follow me. I know what we need to do."

"You do?" Lugs said.

"We need to go and see Mr Etherington."

"Mr Etherington?" everyone said in unison.

"I'll explain on the way."

CHAPTER 48

It wasn't an easy journey back to Deptford. London was taking a hell of a beating from the Germans. Roads were blocked off due to building collapses and there were fires breaking out all over the place. We had to keep taking cover whenever we heard that familiar, menacing whistle of a nearby bomb.

Our nerves were frayed by the time we reached New Cross. I knew that what Arthur had said about the police was right. A scrappy bunch of kids turning up at the station with a story about stealing from the War Office would probably see us sent off with a flea in the ear or a police record to our names. But Mr Etherington – well they'd trust the word of a war hero and schoolmaster. After all, authority must be respected. I just had to hope he'd agree.

"Not far now," I said as we began to make our way through streets that were more familiar to us.

And it was then, with home almost in sight, that it happened.

Hard rain.

That's what Mrs Green had called shrapnel, and it showered down on us, angry and hot. I hit the ground and covered my head with my hands as the sharp bits of metal scattered over the street. It was over quickly. We all stood up, brushing ourselves off and groaning.

Arthur grinned. "How many points for that lot?"

But his words were lost to me, because lying amongst the broken bits of shrapnel, his helmet beside him, was the motionless body of my brother.

My heart lurched. I pushed the rising panic down. *He's fine. He's fine. He's fine.*

"Micky? Micky, you alright?" I called out, trying to keep my voice even, first expecting that he'd jump up any second, then praying that he would.

He didn't answer and my stomach clenched.

"Micky, get up, would you?" I didn't run over to him. My feet wouldn't move. *He'll get up. He's fine.*

He's fine.

The others had gone quiet.

Lugs, who was the closest to him, kneeled down at Micky's side. His face turned white. "Ronnie, he doesn't look good."

I walked over on legs that didn't feel like mine. It took me a moment to see in the dark, but a pool of blood circled Micky's head, like some kind of horrible halo.

The world and all its noise and motion fell away. In that moment, Micky was all there was.

"Ronnie, *Ronnie*?" Lugs was calling my name. "He's hurt,

he's hurt real bad, Ron," Lugs said looking up at me.

I crouched down next to my brother, panic and terror colliding in me. I couldn't think straight. "What do I do?"

Lugs placed his hands under Micky. "Help me turn him over. Easy does it."

Carefully, I cradled Micky's head as Lugs, Harry and I rolled him onto his back. There was a large gash in the side of his skull, where some shrapnel must have struck him.

"Hold something on that to stop the flow," I said.

"Here," Arthur said, pulling off his jumper and then his shirt. "Use this."

Graham took off down the road shouting, as he disappeared into the darkness. "I'm going to get someone! Someone medical!"

While Lugs pressed Arthur's top to my brother's head, I bent down and looked for the rise and fall of his chest to see if he was still breathing. The night sky flashed orange above us as a bomb exploded somewhere close to the docks.

"He's alive, isn't he?" Harry asked.

"I don't know!" I shouted back, the desperation finding its way to my voice making it come out harsh and angry. "I can't tell. I can't tell!"

Arthur moved me out the way and gently said, "Let me check, Ronnie."

I stood back, dread settling in the depths of my stomach. "Arthur, is he breathing?"

Arthur didn't look up. Harry moved next to me and put his hand on my shoulder.

"Arthur?" I pressed.

"Yes!" he said. "He's breathing, but it's shallow."

I gasped in a lungful of air. He was breathing. The relief was so huge that I didn't know what to do with it. Where to put an emotion of that size.

"We need to get him to a hospital and quick," Arthur said.

At that moment, Graham returned with a couple of wardens, a man and a woman.

"Move out the way," the man said. He took the bloodied shirt from under Lugs's hand and checked over Micky's wound. "It's deep. Shrapnel gets more of us than the blasted bombs do."

"Can you help him? Please, sir? He's my little brother and I don't know what I'd do—" A great sob burst out of me as I watched the warden examine Micky.

"His pulse is weak. He's losing a lot of blood." The warden was speaking more to the woman than to me.

"But he's going to be okay," I said, my voice hitching in my throat.

"This boy needs a hospital," the man said.

"Get him to one then!" I cried.

"The ambulance will be here shortly," the woman said. "We'll do our best by him."

We stood over Micky for several long minutes, waiting for the ambulance to arrive. Lugs kept telling me, over and over, that Micky was going to be okay, but my mind kept screaming, *What if he's not?* I couldn't lose Micky. Not my Micky.

When the ambulance finally pulled up, it was as though

time had suddenly accelerated. Micky was bundled into the back, the doors were slammed shut and then he was gone.

The lady warden said, "They're taking him to Lewisham. You get home and let whoever needs to know what's happened."

"My mum won't be home," I said, wiping my face with my sleeve. "She works at the hospital. Cathy Smith's her name."

She nodded. "I'll find her. Let her know the situation."

"What were you even doing out here anyway?" the man said. He sounded angry. "The streets are no place for children."

I looked at Micky's bag, lying on the floor next to his pool of blood.

"Far as I can see, sir, the whole bleedin' world is no place for children either."

CHAPTER 49

I stood, staring at the pool of Micky's blood. He wasn't a big lad – how could there be so much of it?

Lugs nudged me gently. "Ronnie, what do you want to do?"

My brain couldn't quite catch on to his words.

"Here." Arthur held his hand out. "Give me the bag, we can take it from here. You go see your brother, leave Johnny Simmons to us."

Johnny Simmons. This was all his fault. Fury cut hard and sharp through my despair. I sniffed and rubbed my eyes with the heels of my hands. "I want to make Johnny Simmons pay for everything he's done. Micky should have been at home in the shelter. We should all be at home!"

"You don't want to go to Micky?" Lugs asked.

I looked down the road, where I'd watched the ambulance leave and shook my head. "The only thing I can do for my brother is to make sure Simmons isn't around when he wakes up. Because Micky's going to wake up. I know he is."

Arthur nodded. "Alright then, let's go see that Simmons

gets what he deserves."

We picked our way through the damaged streets. The whole time I kept thinking about Micky's small broken body on the pavement. And about Mum and how she'd feel when she heard what had happened.

Micky had to be okay. He just had to be. I know some folk might think he brought it on himself, but it was Johnny who saw that my brother was hurting. He saw the hole in him where my dad should be, and he filled it up with his hate.

When we reached his house, I stood on the doorstep and took a deep breath, building up the courage to knock.

"What you waiting for?" Arthur asked.

I think I was scared. Not of Etherington, but that he might say no.

The door swung open, and Mr Etherington stepped outside. He looked us all up and down and said, "So the whole rabble's here then?"

"Not quite. Micky's in the hospital. He's not in a good way," I said, then clenched my jaw so I wouldn't lose my composure.

Mr Etherington nodded, his eyes settling on me. "And what happened to you, Smith? You look like you've been caught up in a bomb blast."

"I was, sir. We were—"

He held up his hand, cutting me off before I could finish explaining. "You had better come inside."

We followed him into the sitting room and all squashed onto the sofa. He went upstairs and told us to wait.

Arthur, Harry and Graham were all sitting bolt upright, heads swivelling around, eyes wide. It felt strange to be in his neat and tidy home, when the world was on fire outside. The steady *tick-tock* of the clock on the wall made it feel like the seconds were moving more slowly. Out on the streets of London time seemed to hurtle at a brutal rate where one moment crashed into another.

"Can't believe we're in the headmaster's house!" Harry said just as Mr Etherington returned with a washcloth, a bowl of water and some iodine.

"Nor can I." Mr Etherington placed the items on the floor, then set a chair down in front of me.

"Didn't really think of you living in an actual house," Harry continued.

Mr Etherington pulled his trousers up by the knees and sat down, then dipped the cloth in the water. "I do not think you are here to discuss my living arrangements." He tilted my chin up, tutted, then gently dabbed the cloth onto the swollen parts of my face. "I take it the robbery has occurred."

I didn't answer. I was too stunned at the care that Etherington was taking over fixing up my face.

"You take it correct, sir," Lugs said. "But things haven't quite gone as we expected them—"

"It weren't jewellery," I blurted out.

"It *wasn't* jewellery." Mr Etherington unscrewed the lid on

343

the iodine and tipped some onto the cloth. "This may sting."

"Yeah, sorry, *wasn't* and don't worry, I've had worse." He looked thoughtful for a moment, then pressed the cloth to a cut by my eyebrow.

I tried not to wince. "See, sir, Johnny Simmons was involved in something bigger."

He screwed the lid back on the bottle, placed it on the side. "Bigger?"

I picked up the bag and he beckoned for me to pass it to him.

He closed his eyes for a moment, then said, "So what did my nephew put you up to?"

My jaw dropped. I couldn't quite wrap my brain around what Mr Etherington was saying.

"Your nephew?" Lugs said. "Johnny Simmons is *your* nephew!?"

"I'll be blown!" Harry said.

"I took him in after my sister died." Mr Etherington's eyes drifted over to the photograph on the mantlepiece. "We were close once, but I lost him to men spewing hateful ideas and dark promises and I couldn't do anything to stop it."

Mr Etherington opened the bag and pulled out the paper file inside.

"Think it's top-secret classified documents from the War Office," I said. "Not quite sure what it's about though."

He flicked through the papers, stroking his moustache – his eyebrows meeting in concentration. Finally, he closed the file.

"You were right to come to me with this."

"What is it, sir?" I asked.

"The documents within that file detail a new range and direction-finding system. Something called RADAR. According to this it can detect the presence, direction, distance and speed of enemy aircraft, ships and other objects."

We all fell silent as we tried to make sense of what Mr Etherington had said.

Eventually, Harry let out a low whistle. "So, if the Germans had this, they'd know where our boys were. They'd be able to attack planes and ships and navigate through the night and in fog."

We all turned to Harry. I'll admit – and I feel bad about this – I was surprised he'd figured it out before the rest of us.

"Exactly right, Master Scott." Mr Etherington looked grim-faced and serious. "If the Germans got hold of this, it would be catastrophic for the war effort. It is imperative that this information does not get into the wrong hands, or many lives could be lost."

The enormity of the situation – what we'd done and what might happen if we didn't fix it – hit me like a punch to the gut. "We're supposed to hand it over to Johnny at our dens at five o'clock this morning. I was hoping that you might go to the police, tell them what's happening, so when I show up to meet Johnny, they can arrest him."

"Those houses you play in?" Mr Etherington asked.

"That's the place."

Mr Etherington looked down at the file again. "Forget the handover. I'll take these documents to the authorities now. We should leave it up to them to determine what to do with Johnny."

I jumped up from the settee, the pain in my side throbbing in protest at my sudden movement. "But this might be the only chance to catch him red-handed. If I don't show, he'll know I've double-crossed him. He'll come after us all!"

"You understand how risky what you're suggesting is?"

"Just living at the moment is risky. Mr Etherington, if I'm not at the dens, then Johnny will know something is up, he'll scarper and the police won't ever catch him, or who he's working for."

"He needs to go down for what he's done," Lugs said. "We have to stop him spewing his poison. He's a dangerous man and so are the people he works for."

Mr Etherington thought for a long, long moment. Then he rose from his chair, the file under his arm. "Very well then. I shall keep hold of the documents and I shall see you at your dens, with reinforcements."

"What are you going to tell them – the rozzers?" Arthur said. "About us, I mean. We want to own up. Tell them the part we played."

Mr Etherington tilted his head. "Is that so?"

Harry said, "Guess it's like what you said, sir, about moral integrity. We decided that we want to have it."

"Very well, gentlemen," he said, and I could have sworn old Ethers choked up a bit.

I held out my hand. "Thank you, sir."

Mr Etherington shook it, and he looked like he might say something, but he didn't. Instead, he placed his other hand on top of mine and gave it a gentle squeeze. For a moment, I thought I was going to get a little choked up too.

CHAPTER 50

We arrived at the dens, clutching our empty bags, half an hour early, I think we were all eager to get it over with. There was no sign of Johnny or anyone else for that matter. My body and my mind were tired, but I was twitchy and couldn't stand still. I kept thinking about Micky, my mind flashing back to the image of him lying hurt on the road. Lugs was pacing about too, his jaw set, and his fists balled at his sides. Athur, Harry and Graham stood in a huddle, starting at every rustle of the trees or far-off siren. I'd tried again to tell them I'd go alone, but they weren't having any of it, and at that moment I was so glad to have them with me.

"Do you think Johnny will show?" Arthur asked, kicking at the pavement.

I looked down the road. "He'll show."

And sure enough, bang on five o'clock in the morning, Johnny Simmons, Mr Dimes and another fella I didn't recognize, turned up. The other man was tall and smartly dressed, but not in the way that Mr Dimes was. This guy looked proper posh.

He had a neatly combed moustache and shiny shoes that had no business walking about in the broken streets of Deptford. I looked around for any sign of Mr Etherington, but he was nowhere to be seen. A wave of sickness billowed up from my ankles. What if he didn't come? What if the police didn't believe him?

Johnny swaggered towards us, that smug grin plastered on his face. "You made it then!"

"Some of us did," I replied.

Johnny's eyes scanned me and the others. "Where's Micky?"

"In the hospital," I said. "He's in a bad way."

Johnny looked concerned and I almost thought he might have a working heart after all. But then he said, "You still got the bag though, right?"

"Yeah," I said and held it up.

"Told you, didn't I, Lord Beckett?" Johnny said. "Kids are good for the grunt work. Next generation I'm bringing up for you."

The posh-looking guy bristled. "No names, you imbecile!"

"I'm sorry, Lord..." Johnny stumbled over his words, realizing his mistake. He turned on us and snapped, "You didn't hear nothing, did you?"

"Nah, Johnny, we didn't," I said.

Lord Beckett looked at me and raised an eyebrow, sizing me up, I guess. Then he motioned with his hand. "Bring it to me, boy. Chop-chop!"

I looked around. Still no sign of Mr Etherington.

"Come along then," Lord Beckett said, irritated at being kept waiting. "Hand it over. We haven't got all day."

I hesitated.

"For God's sake." Johnny marched over and pulled the bag out of my hands. "We don't have time to mess about."

He handed it over to Lord Beckett who opened it, shook it about a bit, and then looked at me. "What's the meaning of this? Explain yourself."

I decided to play for time. "What do you mean, sir?"

"The bloody thing's empty!"

"Is it, sir?"

"I know an empty bag when I see one."

"You sure there's nothing hidden in the corners?"

He held it upside down and shook it. "Empty! See? Where are the documents?"

"Answer him!" Johnny gave me a shove and I staggered back. "What you done with it?"

Before I could respond, Lugs said, "Don't you push him!" and gave Johnny a shove back.

It didn't make much of an impact and Johnny, who looked a little surprised to start with, narrowed his eyes and said, "Oh we've got a live one here!" He grabbed Lugs by the collar, threw him to the ground and said, "Don't do that again or you'll be getting a close-up of the underside of my boot."

Lugs looked up at him, his eyes flashing with anger. I could see there was so much he wanted to say, but I willed him to hold it in. At least until Mr Etherington had shown up and

Johnny was in handcuffs. Graham and Harry helped Lugs to his feet, then stood right close to him – all protective.

"So, as I was saying, where's the file?" Johnny snarled.

I tried hard to control the fear that was building inside of me. I shrugged, trying to look confused. "I dunno. Maybe the bags got mixed up when Micky got hit."

"All of you, open your bags," Lord Beckett said, waving his hand in my mates's direction.

Arthur, Graham, Harry and Lugs opened their bags and Lord Beckett walked along the line.

"Empty," he said. "Empty, empty and empty!" When he got to Lugs's bag at the end he ripped it out of his hands and threw it to the ground. "Find out what they've done with it, please, Simmons. Use any necessary means. There's a good chap."

Johnny had his hands round my neck and me pinned up against the wall of the building in less than three seconds. He put his face right up to mine.

"We're not the type of people you want to play games with, Ronnie! Now, I'm going to ask you this once and once only, where are the documents?"

I stared right back at him, wondering if he could feel the hate coming out of me.

"You say something?" I said, struggling to get my words out. "I didn't quite catch that."

He slammed my back against the wall again. I groaned in pain as my injured side slammed against the brickwork.

"Oi, leave him alone!" Lugs shouted.

"Where's the file!" Johnny blared into my face. "Tell me now or I'll end you."

"I ain't saying nothing!" I spat back. I looked around frantically for any sight of Mr Etherington, but he still wasn't there.

Johnny put his arm on my throat and pushed. "Oh, you'll speak alright. You'll speak, or I'll squeeze every last breath out of you. Where's the file?!"

Lugs and the others rushed over and tried to pull him off me. I could hear Lugs screaming at him, but Johnny's arm stayed hard on my throat. I couldn't breathe, my head began to swim, my vision swirled black. I thought of Mum, of Micky, of Dad.

And then I heard someone say, all calm and matter of fact like, "Is this the file you're looking for?"

Mr Etherington. He was standing there with the file in his hand, straight and tall, like the soldier he was.

Johnny stepped back and, gasping, I fell to the ground like a sack of spuds. As I coughed air back into my lungs, relief flooded through me.

"You?" Johnny said. "What are you doing here?"

"Not just me," Mr Etherington replied, and from behind him about twenty policemen appeared. They came charging towards us, spreading out over the bomb-damaged houses, blowing their whistles. I never thought I'd consider a load of policeman a beautiful sight, but to me, right then, they were.

Johnny tried to make a run for it, but Lugs reacted quickly.

He launched himself at Johnny and took him out below the knees. Johnny tried to wrestle him off, but Lugs clung on. Still struggling to breathe, I stumbled and fell as I tried to stagger over to help. But Lugs didn't need it. He brought his fist back, clocked him one, right on the chin, and shouted, "My name's Billy Missell and I'm Jewish, you Blackshirt ba—"

I didn't hear the end because Arthur bellowed, "Get him lads!" and he, Graham and Harry bundled on top of Johnny too.

More officers appeared from the left and the right and chased down Mr Dimes, who was trying to hotfoot it out of there. They caught up with him, but Mr Dimes put up a good fight, swinging punches left, right and centre. It took four men to bundle him into the back of the police van.

Lord Beckett held his hands up when the first copper approached him and climbed into the van of his own accord, already calling for a lawyer and saying that he had been led there unknowingly.

A couple of officers pulled Johnny out from under my friends and slapped some handcuffs on him.

And there, as I lay amongst the rubble and bits of shrapnel, I realized we'd done it. We'd caught them all and it suddenly felt a lot easier to breathe.

"Mr Smith." Mr Etherington held out a hand and helped me up from the ground.

"I'm right pleased to see you, sir." My voice was weak, and my throat was sore.

"Likewise," Mr Etherington said, then he stepped in front of

353

me as Johnny was frogmarched past us towards the van.

"You'll pay for this!" Johnny snarled as they loaded him into the van. "Both of you!"

"Ignore him," Mr Etherington said.

But I didn't want to. I was done being scared. I walked right up to the van. A police officer tried to shoo me away, but I said, "This won't take long." He must have seen the determination in my eyes because he stepped to the side.

Johnny was wedged in the back between Lord Beckett, Mr Dimes and a couple of policemen. He fought against his handcuffs when he saw me, like he really wanted to come at me. But he couldn't, not this time, and he would never be able to again.

"See ya, Johnny," I said. And when he didn't reply, I stood tall and spoke loudly. "I said, *See ya,* Johnny."

Then I slammed the doors of the van shut, patted it twice and said to the policeman, "He's all yours now."

CHAPTER 51

Mum and Mrs Green were sitting by Micky's bedside, each holding one of his hands as he slept. His head was wrapped up in bandages – made my heart hurt to see him.

Mum clasped her hand over her mouth when she saw me.

"Ronnie love, what have you done to yourself?" She touched my face lightly, her fingers trembling.

"Is he going to be okay?" I asked.

She glanced back at Micky. "The doctors are hopeful, and we must be too."

"He's touched with luck, our Micky. The little fella will be fine. He'll be fine," Mrs Green said, then she made a noise which sounded like she was trying to hold back a sob. "Whatever were you doing out there? It's a wonder you weren't both killed."

I told them. I told them everything. Just said it straight out. Matter of fact like. Who Johnny really was and what he'd done. What we'd done. All of it. Spared no detail. How Micky had been hurt and what had happened at the handover. That Mr

Etherington had brought the police. How Johnny was gone for good.

"I should hope so too!" Vera said. "And it's lucky for him he is, or I'd be taken my frying pan to that head of his!" She prattled on for a while, outrage bursting from her lips. I caught the odd words like *dirty rotten scoundrel* and *Tower of London*, but I was too busy watching Mum to really listen.

She was staring straight ahead, not really looking at anything – lost in her own thoughts. She didn't speak for a long time. I guess it was a lot to take in.

Then she took my hand and said, "I'm so sorry, Ronnie."

"You don't have to apologize!" I said.

"But it's all my fault."

"How d'you figure that?"

"I should have known," she said. "I should have seen Johnny for what he was. You tried to tell me. Again and again. He tried to take you from me, and I didn't see it." Her eyes were filled with tears and her voice was cracking with emotion. "You boys are mine and I'm claiming you back, this instant."

"We've never not been yours," I said.

"How could I have missed it?" Mum shook her head, the pain in her face clear and hard to see.

"Don't blame yourself, Cathy!" Vera said. "That rotter had us all fooled!"

"Ronnie saw him for what he was!"

"The truth isn't always easy to see," I said. "Especially when you're the sort to look for the good in people, like you do, Mum."

"There's no good in Johnny Simmons, that's for sure!" Vera said. "To think, I took beef brisket from that turncoat!"

Mum and Vera eventually fell asleep in their chairs, and I decided to head outside for some air. My mind was a storm of thoughts. Vera was right, there was no good in Johnny Simmons. But I wondered if he'd always been that way. Whether his mum dying had left a hole in him too. Maybe somebody had got to Johnny and had changed him, like he done with Micky. Had there been an opportunity missed that could have stopped him from turning into the man he'd become? I thought about Dad too and which version of him was true. The man who could put such fear into me. Or the pilot who gave his life, trying to prove he was sorry. I suppose like life, people aren't simple. The world, it doesn't allow for that. I guess we are all carrying round the scars of what has happened to us and finding ways to stop ourselves getting wounded again.

I walked and walked, and I didn't stop until I found myself on Lugs's road. I hadn't set out to walk there, but I guess sometimes there's something inside you which guides you to where you need to be.

I had my head down, hands stuffed in my pockets, but I looked up when I heard the clattering of bin lids and the sound of screeching. I knew straight away it was an animal.

And there, backed up against a wall, was Tiger, with a much larger tomcat taking swipes at him. Tiger might have been smaller and scrawnier, but I'd had him down for a scrapper – the type who'd give as good as he got. But he wasn't, not then. He was cowering. He looked small and scared, like he was trying to get away, but his movements were slow and laboured.

I ran over, waving my hands about and shouting, "Oi, leave him alone, you big bully!"

The big cat didn't seem to take any notice of me, instead he almost seemed spurred on, and he lunged at Tiger with his claws out. I felt the anger bubbling in me, and I grabbed the cat by the collar and lifted him up. He was heavy and angry, and he dangled there, legs kicking and squirming and straining. I caught a couple of deep scratches on my arms, but I didn't feel them. I was just focused on Tiger.

"Run then, Tiger, you daft mog!" I shouted as I tried to restrain what felt more like a lion than a house cat. But Tiger just lay there, not moving.

"Run! Tiger! Run, for God's sake!" I yelled, cross that he wouldn't help himself.

But then, I realized he was hurt. Badly hurt. Too injured to defend himself.

I grabbed the big cat round the stomach to get a better hold, because even though he seemed like a rotter I didn't want to strangle him. I staggered down the road while he writhed around, hissing and spitting. "Will you behave yourself!" I shouted. "You've no business setting on Tiger like that just because he's smaller than you!"

I climbed up on some sandbags that were resting against a

high garden wall and placed him over the other side. Then, with the job done, I clapped my hands and said, "Stay there, and think about your actions."

When I got back to Tiger, he was lying against the wall, not moving. I bent down next to him, and the world seem to draw in around us. "Alright Tiger," I said quietly. "He's gone now. Got rid of him for you."

I chanced a stroke, I knew he wasn't one for petting, but I thought he might want the comfort of knowing I was there. When my fingers touched his fur, he felt cold and wet. I took my hand away, and saw it were covered in blood. I thought maybe the big cat had done him some serious damage, but then I saw it. Something hard and sharp buried in his flesh.

Hard rain. I pulled the piece of shrapnel out of his neck. He was wounded – that's why he couldn't fight back against the cat. Already vulnerable. And the big cat had sensed that.

"Tiger?" I said. "Oh, Tiger, no. Not you too, Tiger. Not you too."

I didn't know what to do. How to help. I tore a piece of my shirt off and held it against the gash, but it didn't seem to do anything. The cut was just so deep. And Tiger was just so small.

"Tiger, Tiger, don't go," I said as I felt his body slacken. "Lugs needs you. He can't lose you as well."

I placed my hand on him and bent down to listen.

I held my breath, hoping to hear his.

But nothing. I heard nothing.

He was gone.

"I'm sorry, Tiger, I'm so sorry," I said over and over again. "I'm so sorry."

I picked him up, and slowly, I carried him over to the pavement outside Lugs's house and I sat down and placed him in my lap. And for the first time in a long time, I cried. Really cried. Everything I'd been carrying just came out of me, all at once. I cried for Tiger, and I cried for Micky. I cried for Mum, and I cried for Arthur and Billy and Harry. I cried for the men and women who'd lost their lives, and I cried for Mr Missell and for Lugs. I cried for all of them.

And I cried for my dad.

And I cried for me.

I don't know how long Lugs had been watching when he sat down next to me, crying too. His face was blotchy, like he might have been going at it for ages. "He's only a cat," he sniffed.

"I know," I said.

"The best cat there ever was mind you."

"Absolutely."

"Not sure he even liked me though, to be honest."

"Oh, he did, Lugs, he really did. How could anyone not?"

"You make a good point," Lugs said, rubbing at his eyes.

"He might have been a bit fierce and tricky at times, but love isn't always shown in the ways you'd expect," I said, and I gave him a little thump to prove it.

He thumped me back and said, "True."

Sometimes, I wonder how I would have coped without Lugs. Truth be told, I don't think I could have. Vera would have you believe that our Micky is the lucky one. But I'd have to differ on that. I was lucky too – lucky to have a mate like Lugs.

"Come on," I said, "I think the best cat there ever was deserves a proper burial."

Lugs nodded and, gently, I placed Tiger in his arms. I left them, as Lugs was telling Tiger how he was the most talented cat ever and that, even though he couldn't say it, he knew Tiger loved him. I fetched the spade that I knew Mr Missell kept round the side of their house. There wasn't much room in the garden what with it mainly being taken up with the Anderson shelter, but I found a little spot under the window and I dug.

It didn't take long – we only needed a small hole. I leaned the spade against the house and gave Lugs a nod. He carried Tiger over and laid him down in the earth. We took it in turns to shovel the soil back over him, our tears mixing in with the dirt. We didn't have a headstone for him, but that didn't matter.

"Tiger," Lugs said. "You were a good cat – the best – and you didn't deserve this. It's not your fault that death falls from the sky. But times right now, they aren't how they should be. And those who shouldn't, well, they get hurt. And I just want to say that I'm dreadful sorry for that." He bowed his head and said, "I don't know if that's a proper prayer, but Amen."

And I said, "Amen," too.

Then neither of us said anything for quite a while. I guess it felt like it wasn't just Tiger we were laying to rest that day.

I picked up the spade to take it back to where I'd found it.

I think me breaking our stillness allowed Lugs to say what he wanted to say.

"He was a good man, my dad, Ronnie."

"He really was." I put my hand in his. "I think mine tried to be, in the end."

We stood for a moment, over a tiny grave, looking out at a street in Deptford that was damaged but still standing, trying to make sense of things that can't ever be understood.

"You are alright aren't you, Ronnie? Your Micky's going to be okay?"

"I think so. I hope so," I said, and then I felt myself crumple and the tears fell again. "It's just the world keeps changing, Lugs. For you, for me, for everyone. And no one can do anything to stop it. And it's wrong. It's all so wrong."

Lugs put his arm round me. "I know," he said. "I know. But one day, the world, it's going to change for the better."

"You think?"

Lugs nodded, his chin wobbling. "It has to."

"I hope so. I bleedin' hope so," I said.

"But in the meantime, just remember there are some things that won't change."

And he gave me a thump.

CHAPTER 52

Our Micky came out of hospital a few weeks later. It wasn't the celebration I had expected. He barely spoke and stayed in bed even though the doctors said it would be good for him to get some exercise. I guess he was just processing everything – that's what Vera said anyway. Mum said going through what he went through changes a person, but I couldn't accept that so much of him was gone. Micky, my Micky, was still inside him. I'd almost lost him before, to Johnny. I wasn't going to lose him again.

So I'd go in and chat to him, tell him what we'd been up to. At that time, I spent most of my days with Lugs and The Wreckers, playing in the dens. I told Micky about that and how we wouldn't let Harry have a go on the new rope swing, and about the purple rosebay willowherb that had grown in the bombsites. How I thought it made the place look quite nice and that Mrs Green said it showed that life always finds a way.

I'd tell him how, when we weren't swinging from the rafters, we'd sit and tell ourselves the story of that night in Whitehall.

That the more we told it, the more it warped and changed into something else. There were more men chasing us. Johnny and Mr Dimes and Lord Beckett had guns. And somehow, according to Arthur, The Wreckers had helped stop the Germans winning the war by being there to back me up.

I didn't mind listening to their versions of what went on. I kind of liked hearing them talk about it all in a positive way. A better way. Even if it weren't strictly true, it felt easier to look at it like that. An adventure. But I guess that's how everyone tries to talk about the war these days. We remember our stiff upper lips and how we rallied together. We don't much care to talk about the alternative. Of people forging medical certificates, or hiding salmon up their cardigans, or of walking the streets and getting mixed up in trouble.

One man knew our truth and it was down to him that our evenings were spent fire watching. Because we'd help put Johnny and Mr Dimes and Lord Beckett behind bars, Mr Etherington came to an arrangement with the police. He was to keep an eye on us – see we stuck to the right path. He had decided that being fire spotters would be a good way for us to absolve our souls. Seemed fair enough, considering the others had claimed to be doing it anyway. I think it felt good though, to be doing something useful.

And at school, let's just say Mr Etherington relied on his words, rather than the cane, to keep us in line.

But the whole time I'd be speaking to Micky, he would just sit and listen. The longer his silence went on, the more I worried that I'd never get him back.

Until one frosty Saturday morning, when there was a knock at the front door. Mum answered it. I heard her speaking to someone but couldn't work out who. Then she hollered upstairs, "Micky, Ronnie, there's some boys outside and they want you to come to the window."

Micky didn't look like he wanted to move.

I pulled back the blackout curtains and looked out. And I laughed. "Oh, come on, Micky. You've got to see this."

"What is it?"

"You've got legs, haven't you? Get out of bed and take a look for yourself!"

Micky huffed and threw back his covers and came and stood next to me.

"It's quite the sight, don't you think?" I said.

Micky didn't say anything for a moment, but then he started to giggle. And that giggle turned into a laugh. 'Cos outside, was Lugs, Arthur, Graham and Harry. They were positioned around a go-kart which had the initials MS painted on the front, which I didn't spot straight away on account of them giving us a four bare-bummed salute.

"Get yourself down here, Micky Smith!" Arthur shouted. "Before my backside drops off from the cold!"

"There's a go-kart here with your name on!" Lugs shouted.

"My name?" Micky said. "Why?"

Lugs tapped the side of the kart. "We fixed it up for you!"

"We got to thinking, and as much as us The Wreckers hate

to admit it, you won the shrapnel competition for The Shrapnel Boys. Think it's about time you claimed your winnings!" Arthur called up.

"How do you mean?" Micky shouted back.

"We all agreed that piece of shrapnel that caught you on the bonce, well, that was the biggest bit we've ever seen!"

"Worth about a gazillion points!" Harry said.

"Bet it were hot too, weren't it, Micky?" Lugs shouted up.

"I guess," Micky said.

"Two gazillion points then!" Arthur laughed.

"Seems fair," I said, giving Micky a little nudge. "The hot bits are always worth more."

"So, what do you say?" Lugs shouted. "Are you going to give this baby a spin or are you going to let your brother have first go?"

"I'll go first!" I said and gave Micky a wink.

"Not ruddy likely!" Micky said and he shot down the stairs far faster than anyone who'd spent as long as him in bed had the right to.

Mum shouted after him, "Micky Smith, get a coat on. It's winter and you're only wearing pyjamas!"

But our Micky wasn't worried about the cold. At that moment, for the first time in a long time, I don't think he was worried about anything. He was in that kart and off down the shrapnel-scattered road whooping and laughing.

Mrs Green bowled outside demanding to know what the ruckus was about, but her words were quickly replaced by a huge smile when she caught sight of our Micky hurtling off with the wind in his hair.

Mum thrust two coats into my hand and said, "Off you go! Keep an eye out for him, love."

I set off, running down the street with the others and shouted back to her, "Don't worry, Mum, I always do!"

And as he screeched round a corner, laughing like a drain, I thought, *There you are Micky, there you are.*

THE END

(Author's Note – to follow)

Jenny Pearson has been awarded six mugs, one fridge magnet, one wall plaque and numerous cards for her role as **Best Teacher in the World**. When she is not busy being inspirational in the classroom, she would like nothing more than to relax with her two young boys, but she can't as they view her as a human climbing frame. Jenny has been shortlisted for the *Costa Children's Book Award*, the *Waterstones Children's Book Prize* and the *Week Junior Book Award* and was the winner of the *Laugh Out Loud Book Award*.

An unmissable marketing & publicity campaign will launch Jenny Pearson's first historical novel.

For marketing enquiries, contact: marketing@usborne.co.uk
For publicity enquiries, contact: fritha.lindqvist@usborne.co.uk
For export enquiries, contact: English.export@usborne.co.uk

#ShrapnelBoys